AMANDA

AMANDA

ANNA BALMER MEYERS

ISBN: 978-93-89539-99-8

Published: -

LECTOR HOUSE LLP
E-MAIL: lectorpublishing@gmail.com

SHE STILL FELT THE WONDER OF BEING RESCUED FROM THE FIRE

AMANDA
A DAUGHTER OF THE MENNONITES

BY

ANNA BALMER MYERS

ILLUSTRATED BY
HELEN MASON GROSS

To
My Sister

CONTENTS

ILLUSTRATIONS

Page

CHAPTER I

"WHILE THE HEART BEATS YOUNG"

The scorching heat of a midsummer day beat mercilessly upon the earth. Travelers on the dusty roads, toilers in the fields, and others exposed to the rays of the sun, thought yearningly of cooling winds and running streams. They would have looked with envy upon the scene being enacted in one of the small streams of Lancaster County, Pennsylvania. There a little red-haired girl, barefooted, her short gingham skirt tucked up unevenly here and there, was wading in the cool, shallow waters of a creek that was tree-bordered and willow-arched. Her clear, rippling laughter of sheer joy broke through the Sabbatical calm of that quiet spot and echoed up and down the meadow as she splashed about in the brook.

"Ach," she said aloud, "this here's the best fun! Abody wouldn't hardly know it's so powerful hot out to-day. All these trees round the crick makes it cool. I like wadin' and pickin' up the pebbles, some of 'em washed round and smooth like little white soup beans--ach, I got to watch me," she exclaimed, laughing, as she made a quick movement to retain her equilibrium. "The big stones are slippery from bein' in the water. Next I know I'll sit right down in the crick. Then wouldn't Phil be ready to laugh at me! It wonders me now where he is. I wish he'd come once and we'd have some fun."

As if in answer to her wish a boyish whistle rang out, followed by a long-drawn "Oo-oh, Manda, where are you?"

"Here. Wadin' in the crick," she called. "Come on in."

She splashed gleefully about as her brother came into sight and walked with mock dignity through the meadow to the stream. He held his red-crowned head high and sang teasingly, "Manda, Manda, red-headed Manda; tee-legged, toe-legged, bow-legged Manda!"

"Philip Reist," she shouted crossly, "I am not! My legs are straighter'n yours! You dare, you just dare once, to come in the crick and say that and see what you get!"

Although two years her junior he accepted the challenge and repeated the doggerel as he planted his bare feet in the water. She splashed him and he retaliated, but the boy, though smaller, was agile, and in an unguarded moment he caught the girl by the wrists and pushed her so she sat squarely in the shallow waters of the brook.

"Hey, smarty," he exulted impishly as he held her there, "you will get fresh with me, you will, huh?"

"Phil, let me up, leave me go, I'm all wet."

"Now, how did that happen, I wonder. My goodness, what will Mamma say?" he teased.

"Phil," the girl half coaxed, but he read a desire for revenge in her face.

"Jiminy Christmas, don't cry." He puckered up his lips in imitation of a whimpering girl. "Got enough?"

"Phil," the word rang crossly, "you let me be now."

"All right, cry baby." He loosened his hold on her wrists. "But because you're such a fraid cat I'll not give you what I brought for you."

"What is it?" The girl scrambled to her feet, curiosity helping her to forget momentarily the boy's tricks. "What did you bring me?"

"Something that's little and almost round and blue and I got it in a tree. Now if you're not a blockhead mebbe you can guess what it is." He moved his hand about in his pocket.

"Phil, let me see." The words were plain coaxing then.

"Here." And he drew from his pocket a robin's egg.

"Philip Reist! Where did you get that?" The girl's voice was stern and loud.

"Ach, I found the dandiest nest out on one of the cherry trees and I know you like dinky birds and thought I'd get you an egg. There's three more in the nest; I guess that's enough for any robin. Anyhow, they had young ones in that nest early in the summer."

"You bad boy! How dare you rob a bird's nest? God will punish you for that!" Her eyes blazed with wrath at the thoughtless deed of the lad.

"Ach," he answered boldly, "what's the use fussin' 'bout a dinky bird's egg? You make me sick, Manda. Cry about it now! Oh, the poor little birdie lost its egg," he whined in falsetto voice.

"You--you--I guess I won't wait for God to punish you, Philip Reist." With the words she grabbed and sat him in the water. "You need something *right now* to make you remember not to take eggs from nests. And here it is! When you want to do it after this just think of the day I sat you down in the crick. I'm goin' to tell Mom on you, too, that's what I am."

"Yea, tattle-tale, girls are all tattle-tales!"

He struggled to escape but the hold of his sister was vise-like.

"Will you leave nests alone?" she demanded.

"Ah, who wants to steal eggs? I just brought you one 'cause I thought you'd like it."

"Well, I don't. So let the eggs where they belong," she said as she relaxed her clasp and he rose.

"Now look at us," he began, then the funny spectacle of wet clothes sent each laughing.

"Gee," he said, "won't we get Sam Hill from Mom?"

"What's Sam Hill?" she asked. "And where do you learn such awful slang? Abody can hardly understand you half the time. Mom says you should stop it."

"Yea, that reminds me, Manda, what I come for. Mom said you're to come in and get your dresses tried on. And mebbe you'd like to know that Aunt Rebecca's here again. She just come and is helpin' to sew and if she sees our clothes wet--oh, yea!"

"Oh yea," echoed Amanda with the innocent candor of a twelve-year-old. "Aunt Rebecca--is she here again? Ach, if she wasn't so cranky I'd be glad still when she comes, but you know how she acts all the time."

"Um-uh. Uncle Amos says still she's prickly like a chestnut burr. Jiminy crickets, she's worse'n any burr I ever seen!"

"Well," the girl said thoughtfully, "but chestnut burrs are like velvet inside. Mebbe she'd be nice inside if only abody had the dare to find out."

"Ach, come on," urged the boy, impatient at the girl's philosophy. "Mom wants you to fit. Come on, get pins stuck in you and then I'll laugh. Gee, I'm glad I'm not a girl! Fittin' dresses on a day like this--whew! "

"Well," she tossed her red head proudly, "I'm glad I'm one!" A sudden thought came to her--"Come in, Phil, while I fit and then we'll set in the kitchen and count how often Aunt Rebecca says, My goodness."

"Um-uh," he agreed readily, "come on, Manda. That'll be peachy."

The children laughed in anticipation of a good time as they ran through the hot sun of the pasture lot, up the narrow path along the cornfield fence and into the back yard of their home.

The Reist farm with its fine orchards and great fields of grain was manifestly the home of prosperous, industrious farmers. From its big gardens were gathered choice vegetables to be sold in the famous markets of Lancaster, five miles distant. The farmhouse, a big square brick building of old-fashioned design, was located upon a slight elevation and commanded from its wide front porch a panoramic view of a large section of the beautiful Garden Spot of America.

The household consisted of Mrs. Reist, a widow, her two children, her brother Amos Rohrer, who was responsible for the success of the farm, and a hired girl, Millie Hess, who had served the household so long and faithfully that she seemed an integral part of the family.

Mrs. Reist was a sweet-faced, frail little woman, a member of the Mennonite Church. She wore the plain garb adopted by the women of that sect--the tight-fitting waist covered by a pointed shoulder cape, the full skirt and the white cap upon smoothly combed, parted hair. Her red-haired children were so like their father had been, that at times her heart contracted at sight of them. His had been a strong, buoyant spirit and when her hands, like Moses' of old, had required steadying, he had never failed her. At first his death left her helpless and discouraged as she faced the task of rearing without his help the two young children, children about whom they had dreamed great dreams and for whom they had planned wonderful things. But gradually the widowed mother developed new courage, and though frail in body grew brave in spirit and faced cheerfully the rearing of Amanda and Philip.

The children had inherited the father's strength, his happy cheerfulness, his quick-to-anger and quicker-to-repent propensity, but the mother's gentleness also dwelt in them. Laughing, merry, they sang their way through the days, protesting vehemently when things went contrary to their desires, but laughing the next moment in the irresponsible manner of youth the world over. That August day the promise of fun at Aunt Rebecca's expense quite compensated for the unpleasantness of her visit.

Aunt Rebecca Miller was an elder sister to Mrs. Reist, so said the inscription in the big family Bible. But it was difficult to understand how the two women could have been mothered by one person.

Millie, the hired girl, expressed her opinion freely to Amanda one day after a particularly trying time with the old woman. "How that Rebecca Miller can be your mom's sister now beats me. She's more like a wasp than anything I ever seen without wings. It's sting, sting all the time with her; nothin' anybody does or says is just right. She's faultfindin' every time she comes. It wonders me sometimes if she'll like heaven when she gets up there, or if she'll see some things she'd change if she had her way. And mostly all the plain people are so nice that abody's got to like 'em, but she's not like the others, I guess. Most every time she comes she makes me mad. She's too bossy. Why, to-day when I was fryin' doughnuts she bothered me so that I just wished the fat would spritz her good once and she'd go and leave me be."

It will be seen that Millie felt free to voice her opinions at all times in the Reist family. She was a plain-faced, stout little woman of thirty-five, a product of the Pennsylvania Dutch country. Orphaned at an early age she had been buffeted about sorely until the happy day she entered the Reist household. Their kindness to her won her heart and she repaid them by a staunch devotion. The Reist joys, sorrows, perplexities and anxieties were shared by her and she naturally came in for a portion of Aunt Rebecca's faultfinding.

Cross-grained and trying, Rebecca Miller was unlike the majority of the plain, unpretentious people of that rural community. In all her years she had failed to appreciate the futility of fuss, the sin of useless worry, and had never learned the invaluable lesson of minding her own business. "She means well," Mrs. Reist said in conciliatory tones when Uncle Amos or the children resented the interference of the dictatorial relative, but secretly she wondered how Rebecca could be so--so--she never finished the sentence.

"Well, my goodness, here she comes once!" Amanda heard her aunt's rasping voice as they entered the house.

Stifling an "Oh yea" the girl walked into the sitting-room.

"Hello, Aunt Rebecca," she said dutifully, then turned to her mother-- "You want me?"

"My goodness, your dress is all wet in the back!" Aunt Rebecca said shrilly. "What in the world did you do?"

Before she could reply Philip turned about so his wet clothes were on view. "And you too!" cried the visitor. "My goodness, what was you two up to? Such wet blotches like you got!" "We were wadin' in the crick," Amanda said demurely, as her mother smoothed the tousled red hair back from the flushed forehead.

"My goodness! Wadin' in the crick in dog days!" exploded Aunt Rebecca.

"Now for that she'll turn into a doggie, ain't, Mom?" said the boy roguishly.

Aunt Rebecca looked over her steel-rimmed spectacles at the two children who were bubbling over with laughter. "I think," she said sternly, "people don't learn children no manners no more."

"Ach," the mother said soothingly, "you mustn't mind them. They get so full of laughin' even when we don't see what's to laugh at."

"Yes," put in Amanda, "the Bible says it's good to have a merry heart and me and Phil's got one. You like us that way, don't you, Mom?"

"Yes," the mother agreed. "Now you go put on dry things, then I want to fit your dresses. And, Philip, are you wet through?"

"Naw. These thick pants don't get wet through if I rutch in water an hour. Jiminy pats, Mom, girls are delicate, can't stand a little wettin'."

"You just wait, Phil," Amanda called to him as she ran up-stairs, "you're gettin' some good wettin' yet. I ain't done with you."

"Cracky, who's afraid?" he called.

A little later the girl appeared in dry clothes.

"Ach," she said, "I forgot to wash my hands. I better go out to the pump and clean 'em so I don't get my new dresses dirty right aways."

She ran to the pump on the side porch and jerked the handle up and down, while her brother followed and watched her, defiance in his eyes.

"Well," she said suddenly, "if you want it I'll give it to you now." With that she caught him and soused his head in the tin basin that stood in the trough. "One for duckin' me in the crick, and another for stealin' that bird's egg, and a third to learn you some sense." Before he could get his breath she had run into the house and stood before her mother ready for the fitting. "I like this goods, Mom," she told the mother as the new dress was slipped over her head. "I think the brown goes good with my red hair, and the blue gingham is pretty, too. Only don't never buy me no pink nor red."

"I won't. Not unless your hair turns brown."

"My goodness, but you spoil her," came the unsolicited opinion of Aunt Rebecca. "When I was little I wore what my mom bought me, and so did you. We would never thought of sayin', 'Don't get me this or that.'"

"But with red hair it's different. And as long as blue and brown and colors Amanda likes don't cost more than those she don't want I can't see why she shouldn't have what she wants."

"Well, abody wonders what kind o' children plain people expect to raise nowadays with such caterin' to their vanity."

Mrs. Reist bit her lips and refrained from answering. The expression of joy on the face of Amanda as she looked down at her new dress took away the sting of the older woman's words. "I want," the mother said softly, "I want my children to have a happy childhood. It belongs to them. And I want them to remember me for a kind mom."

"Ach, Mom, you *are* a good mom." Amanda leaned over the mother, who was pinning the hem in the new dress, and pressed a kiss on the top of the white-capped head. "When I grow up I want to be like you. And when I'm big and you're old, won't you be the nicest granny!"

Aunt Rebecca suddenly looked sad and meek. Perhaps a partial appreciation of what she missed by being childless came to her. What thrills she might have known if happy children ran to her with shouts of "Granny!" But she did not carry the thread of thought far enough to analyze her own actions and discover that, though childless, she could attract the love of other people's children if she chose. The tender moment was fleet. She looked at Amanda and Philip and saw in them only two children prone to evil, requiring stern disciplining.

"Now don't go far from the house," said Mrs. Reist later, "for your other dress is soon ready to fit. As soon as Aunt Rebecca gets the pleats basted in the skirt."

"I'll soon get them in. But it's foolishness to go to all that bother when gathers would do just as good and go faster."

Amanda turned away and a moment later she and Phil were seated on the long wooden settee in the kitchen. The boy had silently agreed to a temporary truce so that the game of counting might be played. He would pay back his sister some other time. Gee, it was easy to get her goat-- just a little thing like a caterpillar dropped down her neck would make her holler!

"Gee, Manda, I thought of a bully thing!" the boy whispered. "If that old cross-patch Rebecca says 'My goodness' thirty times till four o'clock I'll fetch a tobacco worm and put it in her bonnet. If she don't say it that often you got to put one in. Huh? Manda, ain't that a peachy game to play?"

"All right," agreed the girl. "I'll get paper and pencil to keep count." She slipped into the other room and in a few minutes the two settled themselves on the settee, their ears straining to hear every word spoken by the women in the next room.

"My goodness, this thread breaks easy! They don't make nothin' no more like they used to," came through the open door.

"That's one," said Phil; "make a stroke on the paper. Jiminy Christmas, that's easy! Bet you we get that paper full of strokes!"

"My goodness, that girl's shootin' up! It wouldn't wonder me if you got to leave these dresses down till time for school. Now if I was you I'd make them plenty big and let her grow into 'em. Our mom always done that."

And so the conversation went on until there were twenty lines on the paper. The game was growing exciting and, under the stress of it, the counting on the old settee rose above the discreet whisper it was originally meant to be. "Twenty-one!" cried Amanda. Aunt Rebecca walked to the door.

"What's you two up to?" she asked. "Oh, you got the hymn-book. My goodness, what for you writin' on the hymn-book?" She turned to her sister. "Ain't you goin' to make 'em stop that? A hymn-book ain't to be wrote on!"

"Twenty-two," cried Phil, secure in the knowledge that his mother would not object to their use of the book and safely confident that the aunt could not dream what they were doing.

"What is twenty-two? Look once, Amanda," said the woman, taking the mention of the number to refer to a hymn.

The girl opened the book. "Beulah Land," she read, a sudden compunction seizing her.

"Ach, yes, Beulah Land--I sang that when I was a girl still. My goodness, abody gets old quick." She sighed and returned to her sewing.

"Twenty-three, countin' the last one," prompted Phil. "Mark it down. Gee, it's a cinch."

But Amanda looked sober. "Phil, mebbe it ain't right to make fun of her so and count after how often she says the same thing. She looked kinda teary when she said that about gettin' old quick."

"Ach, go on," said Philip, too young to appreciate the subtle shades of feelings or looks. "You can't back out of it now. Gee, what's bitin' you? It ain't four o'clock yet, and it ain't right, neither, to go back on a promise. Anyhow, if we don't go on and count up to thirty you got to put the worm in her bonnet--you said you would--girls are no good, they get cold feet."

Thus spurred, Amanda resumed the game until the coveted thirty lines were marked on the paper. Then, the goal reached, it was Phil's duty to find a tobacco worm.

Supper at the Reist farmhouse was an ample meal. By that time the hardest portion of the day's labor was completed and the relaxation from physical toil made the meal doubly enjoyable. Millie saw to it that there was always appetizing food set upon the big square table in the kitchen. Two open doors and three screened windows looking out upon green fields and orchards made the kitchen a cool refuge that hot August day.

Uncle Amos, a fat, flushed little man, upon whose shoulders rested the responsibilities of that big farm, sat at the head of the table. His tired figure sagged somewhat, but his tanned face shone from a vigorous scrubbing. Millie sat beside Mrs. Reist, for she was, as she expressed it, "Nobody's dog, to eat alone." She expected to eat with the folks where she hired. However, her presence at the table did not prevent her from waiting on the others. She made frequent trips to the other side of the big kitchen to replenish any of the depleted dishes.

That evening Amanda and Philip were restless.

"What ails you two?" demanded Millie. "Bet you're up to some tricks again, by the gigglin' of you and the rutchin' around you're doin'! I just bet you're up to something," she grumbled, but her eyes twinkled.

"Nothin' ails us," declared Phil. "We just feel like laughin'."

"Ach," said Aunt Rebecca, "this dumb laughin' is all for nothin'. Anyhow, you better not laugh too much, for you got to cry as much as you laugh before you die."

"Then I'll have to cry oceans!" Amanda admitted. "There'll be another Niagara Falls, right here in Lancaster County, I'm thinkin'."

"Ach," said Millie, "that's just another of them old superstitions."

"Yes," Aunt Rebecca said solemnly, "nobody believes them no more. But it's a lot of truth in 'em just the same. I often took notice that as high as the spiders build their webs in August so high will the snow be that winter. Nowadays people don't study the almanac or look for signs. Young ones is by far too smart. The farmers plant their seeds any time now, beans and peas in the Posey Woman sign and then they wonder why they get only flowers 'stead of peas and beans. They take up red beets in the wrong sign and wonder why the beets cook up stringy. The women make sauerkraut in Gallas week and wonder why it's bitter. I could tell them what's the matter! There's more to them old women's signs than most people know. I never yet heard a dog cry at night that I didn't hear of some one I know dyin' soon after. I wouldn't open an umbrella in the house for ten dollars--it's bad luck--yes, you laugh," she said accusingly to Philip. "But you got lots to learn yet. My goodness, when I think of all I learned since I was as old as you! Of all the new things in the world! I guess till you're as old as I am there'll be lots more."

"Sure Mike," said the boy, rather flippantly. "What's all new since you was little?" he asked his aunt.

"Telephone, them talkin' machines, sewin' machines--anyhow, they were mighty scarce then--trolleys----"

"Automobiles?"

"My goodness, yes! Them awful things! They scare the life out abody. I don't go in none and I don't want no automobile hearse to haul me, neither. I'd be afraid it'd run off."

"Great horn spoon, Aunt Rebecca, but that would be a gay ride," the boy said, while Amanda giggled and Uncle Amos winked to Millie, who made a hurried trip to the stove for coffee.

"Ach," came the aunt's rebuke. "You talk too much of that slang stuff. I guess I'll take the next trolley home," she said, unconscious of the merriment she had caused. "I'd like to help with the dishes, but I want to get home before it gets so late for me. Anyhow, Amanda is big enough to help. When I was big as her I cooked and baked and worked like a woman. Why, when I was just a little thing, Mom'd tell me to go in the front room and pick the snipples off the floor and I'd get down and do it. Nobody does that now, neither. They run a sweeper over the carpets and wear 'em out."

"But the floors are full of germs," said Amanda.

"Cherms--what are them?"

"Why, dreadful things! I learned about them at school. They are little, crawly bugs with a lot of legs, and if you eat them or breathe them in you'll get scarlet fever or diphtheria."

"Ach, that's too dumb!" Aunt Rebecca was unimpressed. "I don't believe in no such things." With that emphatic remark she stalked to the sitting-room for her bonnet. She met Phil coming out, his hands in his pockets. He paused in the doorway as Amanda and her mother joined the guest.

Aunt Rebecca lifted the black silk bonnet carefully from the little table and Amanda shifted nervously from one foot to the other. If only Aunt Rebecca wouldn't hold the bonnet so the worm would fall to the floor! Then the woman gave the stiff headgear a dexterous turn and the squirming thing landed on her head.

"My goodness! My goodness!" she cried as something soft brushed her cheek. Intently inquisitive, she stooped and picked from the floor a fat, green, wriggling tobacco worm.

"One of them cherms, I guess, Amanda, ain't?" she said as she looked keenly at the child.

Amanda blushed and was silent. Philip was unable to hide his guilt. "Now, when did tobacco worms learn to live in bonnets?" she asked the boy as she eyed him reproachfully.

Mrs. Reist looked hurt. Her gentle reproof, "Children, I'm ashamed of you!" cut deeper with Amanda than the scolding of Aunt Rebecca--"You're a bad pair! Almost you spoiled me my good bonnet. If I'd squeezed that worm on my cap it would have ruined it! My goodness, you both need a good spankin', that's what. Too bad you ain't got a pop to learn you!"

"It was only for fun, Aunt Rebecca," said Amanda, truly ashamed. But Phil put his hand over his mouth to hide a grin.

"Fun--what for fun is that--to be so disrespectful to an old aunt? And you, Philip, ain't one bit ashamed. Your mom just ought to make you hunt all the worms in the whole tobacco patch. My goodness, look at that clock! Next with this dumb foolin' I'll miss that trolley yet. I must hurry myself now."

"I'm sorry, Aunt Rebecca," Amanda said softly, eager to make peace with the woman, whom she knew to be kind, though a bit severe.

"Ach, I don't hold no spite. But I think it's high time you learn to behave. Such a big girl like you ought to help her brother be good, not learn him tricks. Boys go to the bad soon enough. I'm goin' now," she addressed Mrs. Reist, "and you let me know when you boil apple butter and I'll come and help stir."

"All right, Rebecca. I hope the children will behave and not cut up like to-day. You are always so ready to help us--I can't understand why they did such a thing. I'm ashamed."

"Ach, it's all right, long as my bonnet ain't spoiled. If that had happened then there'd be a different kind o' bird pipin'."

After she left Philip proceeded to do a Comanche Indian dance--in which Amanda joined by being pulled around the room by her dress skirt--in undisguised hilarity over the departure of their grim relative. Boys have little understanding of the older person who suppresses their animal energy and skylarking happiness.

"I ain't had so much fun since Adam was a boy," Philip admitted with pretended seriousness, while the family smiled at his drollness.

CHAPTER II

THE SNITZING PARTY

Apple-butter boiling on the Reist farm occurred frequently during August and September. The choice fruit of the orchard was sold at Lancaster market, but bushels of smaller, imperfect apples lay scattered about the ground, and these were salvaged for the fragrant and luscious apple butter. To Phil and Amanda fell the task of gathering the fruit from the grass, washing them in big wooden tubs near the pump and placing them in bags. Then Uncle Amos hauled the apples to the cider press, where they came forth like liquid amber that dripped into fat brown barrels.

Many pecks of pared fruit were required for the apple-butter boiling. These were pared--the Pennsylvania Dutch say snitzed--the night before the day of boiling.

"Mom," Amanda told her mother as they ate supper one night when many apples were to be pared for the next day's use, "Lyman Mertzheimer seen us pick apples to-day and he said he's comin' over to-night to the snitzin' party--d'you care?"

"No. Let him come."

"So," teased Uncle Amos. "Guess in a few years, Manda, you'll be havin' beaus. This Lyman Mertzheimer, now,--his pop's the richest farmer round here and Lyman's the only child. He'd be a good catch, mebbe."

"Ach," Amanda said in her quick way, "I ain't thinkin' of such things. Anyhow, I don't like Lyman so good. He's all the time braggin' about his pop's money and how much his mom pays for things, and at school he don't play fair at recess. Sometimes, too, he cheats in school when we have a spellin' match Friday afternoons. Then he traps head and thinks he's smart."

Uncle Amos nodded his head. "Chip o' the old block."

"Now, look here," chided Millie, "ain't you ashamed, Amos, to put such notions in a little girl's head, about beaus and such things?"

The man chuckled. "What's born in heads don't need to be put in."

Amanda wondered what he meant, but her mother and Millie laughed.

"Women's women," he added knowingly. "Some wakes up sooner than others, that's all! Millie, when you goin' to get you a man? You're gettin' along now--just about my age, so I know--abody that cooks like you do-- "

"Amos, you just keep quiet! I ain't lookin' for a man. I got a home, and if I want something to growl at me I'll go pull the dog's tail."

That evening the kitchen of the Reist farmhouse was a busy place. Baskets of apples stood on the floor. On the table were huge earthen dishes ready for the pared fruit. Equipped with a paring knife and a tin pie-plate for parings every member of the household drew near the table and began snitzing. There was much merry conversation, some in quaint Pennsylvania Dutch, then again in English tinged with the distinctive accent. There was also much laughter as Uncle Amos vied with Millie for the honor of making the thinnest parings.

"Here comes Lyman. Make place for him," cried Amanda as a boy of fifteen came to the kitchen door.

"You can't come in here unless you work," challenged Uncle Amos.

"I can do that," said the boy, though he seemed none too eager to take the knife and plate Mrs. Reist offered him.

"You dare sit beside me," Amanda offered.

Lyman smiled his appreciation of the honor, but the girl's eyes twinkled as she added, "so I can watch that you make thin peelin's."

"That's it," said Uncle Amos. "Boys, listen! Mostly always when a woman's kind to you there's something back of it."

"Ach, Amos, you're soured," said Millie.

"No, not me," he declared. "I know there's still a few good women in the world. Ach, yea," he sighed deeply and looked the incarnation of misery, "soon I'll have three to boss me, with Amanda here growin' like a weed!"

"Don't you know," Mrs. Reist reminded him, "how Granny used to say that one good boss is better than six poor workers? You don't appreciate us, Amos."

"I give up." Uncle Amos spread his hands in surrender. "I give up. When women start arguin' where's a man comin' in at?"

"I wouldn't give up," spoke out Lyman. "A man ought to have the last word every time."

"Ach, you don't know women," said Uncle Amos, chuckling.

"A man was made to be master," the youth went on, evidently quoting some recent reading. "Woman is the weaker vessel."

"Wait till you try to break one," came Uncle Amos's wise comment.

"I," said Lyman proudly, "I could be master of any woman I marry! And I bet, I dare to bet my pop's farm, that any girl I set out to get I can get, too. I'd just carry her off or something. 'All's fair in love and war.'"

"Them two's the same thing, sonny, but you don't know it yet," laughed Uncle Amos. "It sounds mighty strong and brave to talk like you were a giant or king, or something, and I only hope I'm livin' and here in Crow Hill so I can see how you work that game of carryin' off the girl you like. I'd like to see it, I'd sure like to see it!"

"Oh, Uncle Amos, tell us, did you ever go to see the girls?" asked Amanda eagerly.

"Did I ever go to see the girls? Um-uh, I did!" The man laughed suddenly. "I'll tell you about the first time. But now you just go on with your snitzin'. I can't be breakin' up the party with my yarns. I was just a young fellow workin' at home on the farm. Theje was a nice girl over near Manheim I thought I'd like to know better, and so one night I fixed up to try my luck and go see her. It was in fall and got dark pretty early, and by the time I was done with the farm work and dressed in my best suit and half-way over to her house, it was gettin' dusk. Now I never knew what it was to be afraid till that year my old Aunty Betz came to spend a month with us and began to tell her spook stories. She had a long list of them. One was about a big black dog that used to come in her room every night durin' full moon and put its paws on her bed. But when she tried to touch it there was nothing there, and if she'd get up and light the light it would vanish. She said she always thought he wanted to show her something, take her to where there was some gold buried, but she never could get the dog to do it, for she always lighted the light and that scared him away. Then she said one time they moved into a little house, and once when they had a lot of company she slept on a bed in the garret. She got awake at night and found the covers off the bed. She pulled 'em up and something pulled them off. Then she lighted a candle, but there wasn't a thing there. So she went back to bed and the same thing happened again; down went the covers. She got frightened and ran down the stairs and slept on the floor. But that spook was always a mystery. I used to have shivers chasin' each other up and down my back so fast I didn't know how to sit up hardly when she was tellin' them spook stories. But she had one champion one about a man she knew who was walkin' along the country road at night and something black shot up in front of him, and when he tried to catch it and ran after it, he rolled into a fence, and when he sat up, the spook was gone, but there was a great big hole by the fence-post near him, and in the hole was a box of money. She could explain that ghost; it was the spirit of the person who had buried the money, and he had to help some person find it so that he could have peace in the other world. Well, as I said, I was goin' along the road on the way to see that girl, and it was about dark when I got to the lane of her house. I was a little excited, for it was my first trial at the courtin' business. Aunty Betz's spook stories made me kinda shaky in the dark, so it's no wonder I jumped when something black ran across the road and stood by the fence as I came along. I remembered her story of the man who found the gold, and I thought I'd see whether I could have such luck, so I ran to the black thing and made a grab--and--it was a skunk! Well,"--after the laughter died down--"I didn't get any gold, but I got something! I yelled, and the girl I started to call on heard me and come to the door. I hadn't any better sense than to go up to her. But before I could explain, the skunk's weapon told the tale. 'You clear out of here,' she hollered; 'who wants such a smell in the house!' I cleared out, and when I got home Mom was in bed, but Pop was readin' the paper in the kitchen. I opened the door. 'Clear out of here,' he ordered;' who wants such a smell in the house! Go to the wood-shed and I'll get you soap and water and other clothes.' So I went to the wood-shed, and he came out with a lantern and water and clothes and I began to scrub. After I was dressed we went to the barn-yard and he held the lantern while I dug a deep hole, and the clothes, my best Sunday clothes, went down into the ground and dirt on top. And that settled courtin' for a while with me."

Uncle Amos's story *had* interfered with the snitzing.

"Say," said Millie, "how can abody snitz apples when you make 'em laugh till the tears run down over the face?"

"Oh, come on," cried Amanda, "I just thought of it--let's tell fortunes with the peelin's! Everybody peel an apple with the peelin' all in one piece and then throw it over the right shoulder, and whatever letter it makes on the floor is the initial of the person you're goin' to marry."

"All right. Now, Millie, no cheatin'," teased Uncle Amos. "Don't you go peel yours so it'll fall into a Z, for I know that Zach Miller's been after you this long while already."

"Ach, him? He's as ugly as seven days' rainy weather."

"Ach, shoot it," said Phil, disgust written on his face as he threw a paring over his shoulder; "mine always come out an S. Guess that's the only letter you can make. S for Sadie, Susie--who wants them? That's a rotten way to tell fortunes!"

"Now look at mine, everybody!" cried Amanda as she flung her long apple paring over her shoulder.

"It's an M," shouted Phil. "Mebbe for Martin Landis. Jiminy Christmas, he's a pretty nice fellow. If you can hook him----"

"M stands for Mertzheimer," said Lyman proudly. "I guess it means me, Amanda, so you better begin to mind me now when we play at recess at school and spell on my side in the spelling matches."

"Huh," she retorted ungraciously, "Lyman Mertzheimer, you ain't the only M in Lancaster County!"

"No," he replied arrogantly, "but I guess that poor Mart Landis don't count. He's always tending one of his mom's babies--some nice beau he'd make! If he ever goes courting he'll have to take along one of the little Landis kids, I bet."

Phil laughed, but Amanda flushed in anger. "I think that's just grand of Martin to help his mom like that," she defended. "Anyhow, since she has no big girls to help her."

"He washes dishes. I saw him last week with an apron on," said Lyman, contempt in his voice.

"Wouldn't you do that for your mom if she was poor and had a lot of children and no one to help her?" asked the girl.

"Not me! I wouldn't wash dishes for no one! Men aren't made for that."

"Then *I* don't think much of *you*, Lyman Mertzheimer!" declared Amanda with a vigorous toss of her red head.

"Come, come," Mrs. Reist interrupted, "you mustn't quarrel. Of course Lyman would help his mother if she needed him."

Amanda laughed and friendliness was once more restored.

When the last apple was snitzed Uncle Amos brought some cold cider from the spring-house, Millie fetched a dish of cookies from the cellar, and the snitzing party ended in a feast.

That night Mrs. Reist followed Amanda up the stairs to the child's bedroom. They made a pretty picture as they stood there, the mother with her plain Mennonite garb, her sweet face encircled by a white cap, and the little red-haired child, eager, active, her dark eyes glimpsing dreams as they focused on the distant castles in Spain which were a part of her legitimate heritage of childhood. The room was like a Nutting picture, with its rag carpet, old-fashioned, low cherry bed, covered with a pink and white calico patchwork quilt, its low cherry bureau, its rush-bottom chairs, its big walnut chest covered with a hand-woven coverlet gay with red roses and blue tulips. An old-fashioned room and an old-fashioned mother and daughter--the elder had seen life, knew its glories and its dangers, had tasted its sweetness and drained its cups of sorrow, but the child--in her eyes was still the star-dust of the "trailing clouds of glory."

"Mom," she asked suddenly as her mother unbraided the red hair and brushed it, "do you like Lyman Mertzheimer?"

"Why--yes---" Mrs. Reist hesitated.

"Ach, I don't mean that way, Mom," the child said wisely. "You always say abody must like everybody, but I mean like him for real, like him so you want to be near him. He's good lookin'. At school he's about the best lookin' boy there. The big girls say he's a regular Dunnis, whatever that is. But I think sometimes he ain't so pretty under the looks, the way he acts and all, Mom."

"I know what you mean, Amanda. Your pop used to say still that people are like apples, some can fool you good. Remember some we peeled to-night were specked and showed it on the outside, but some were red and pretty and when you cut in them--"

"They were full of worms or rotten!"

"Yes. It's the hearts of people that makes them beautiful."

"I see, Mom, and I'll mind to remember that. I'm gettin' to know a lot o' things now, Mom, ain't? I like when you tell me things my pop said. I'm glad I was big enough to remember him. I know yet what nice eyes he had, like they was always smilin' at you. I wish he wouldn't died, but I'm glad he's not dead for always. People don't stay dead like peepies or birds, do they?"

"No, they'll live again some day." The mother's voice was low, but a divine trust shone in her eyes. "Life would be nothing if it could end for us like it does for the birds."

"Millie says the souls of people can't die. That it's with people just like it's with the apple trees. In winter they look dead and like all they're good for was to chop down and burn, then in spring they get green and the flowers come on them and they're alive, and we know they're alive. I'm glad people are like that, ain't you?"

"Yes." She gathered the child to her arms and kissed the sensitive, eager little face. Neither Mrs. Reist nor Amanda, as yet, had read Locksley Hall, but the truth expressed there was echoing in their souls:

> "Gone forever! Ever? no--for since our dying race began,
> Ever, ever, and forever was the leading light of man.
> Indian warriors dream of ampler hunting grounds beyond the night;
> Even the black Australian dying hopes he shall return, a white.
> Truth for truth, and good for good! The good, the true, the pure, the just--
> Take the charm 'Forever' from them, and they crumble into dust."

"Ach, Mom," the child asked a few moments later, "do you mind that Christmas and the big doll?" An eager light dwelt in the little girl's eyes as she thought back to the happy time when her big, laughing father had made one in the family circle.

"Yes." The mother smiled a bit sadly. But Amanda prattled on gaily.

"That was the best Christmas ever I had! You mind how we went to market in Lancaster, Pop and you and I, near Christmas, and in a window of a store we saw a great, grand, big doll. She was bigger'n me and had light hair and blue eyes. I wanted her, and I told you and Pop and coaxed for you to buy her. Next week when we went to market and passed the store she was still in the window. Then one day Pop went to Lancaster alone and when he came home I asked if the doll was still there, and he said she wasn't in the window. I cried, and was so disappointed and you said to Pop, 'That's a shame, Philip.' And I thought, too, it was a shame he let somebody else buy that doll when I wanted it so. Then on Christmas morning--what do you think--I came down-stairs and ran for my presents, and there was that same big doll settin' on the table in the room! Millie and you had dressed her in a blue dress. Course she wasn't in the window when I asked Pop, for he had bought her! He laughed, and we all laughed, and we had the best Christmas. I sat on my little rocking-chair and rocked her, and then I'd sit her on the sofa and look at her--I was that proud of her."

"That's five, six years ago, Amanda."

"Yes, I was *little* then. I mind a story about that little rockin'-chair, too, Mom. It's up in the garret now; I'm too big for it. But when I first got it I thought it was wonderful fine. Once Katie Hiestand came here with her mom, and we were playin' with our dolls and not thinkin' of the chair, and then Katie saw it and sat in it. And right aways I wanted to set in it, too, and I made her get off. But you saw it and you told me I must not be selfish, but must be polite and let her set in it. My, I remember lots of things."

"I'm glad, Amanda, if you remember such things, for I want you to grow up into a nice, good woman."

"Like you and Millie, ain't? I'm goin' to. I ain't forgot, neither, that once when I laughed at Katie for saying the Dutch word for calendar and gettin' all her English mixed with Dutch, you told me it's not nice to laugh at people. But I forgot it the other day, Mom, when we laughed at Aunt Rebecca and treated her mean. But she's so cranky and--and---"

"And she helped sew on your dresses," added the mother.

"Now that was ugly for us to act so! Why, ain't it funny, Mom, it sounds so easy to say abody should be kind and yet sometimes it's so hard to do it. When Aunt Rebecca comes next time I'm just goin' to see once if I can't be nice to her."

"Of course you are. She's comin' to-morrow to help with the apple butter. But now you must go to sleep or you can't get up early to see Millie put the cider on. Philip, he's asleep this long while already."

A few minutes later the child was in bed and called a last good-night to the mother, who stood in the hall, a little lighted lamp in her hand. Amanda had an eye for beauty and the picture of her mother pleased her.

"Ach, Mom," she called, "just stand that way a little once, right there."

"Why?"

"Ach, you look wonderful like a picture I saw once, in that gray dress and the lamp in your hand. It's pretty."

"Now, now," chided the mother gently, "you go to sleep now. Good-night."

"Good-night," Amanda called after the retreating figure.

CHAPTER III

BOILING THE APPLE BUTTER

Amanda rose early the next morning. Apple-butter boiling day was always a happy one for her. She liked to watch the fire under the big copper kettle, to help with the ceaseless stirring with a long-handled stirrer. She thrilled at the breathless moment when her mother tested the thick, dark contents of the kettle and announced, "It's done."

At dawn she went up the stairs with Uncle Amos to the big attic and opened and closed doors for him as he carried the heavy copper kettle down to the yard. Then she made the same trip with Millie and helped to carry from the attic heavy stone crocks in which to store the apple butter.

After breakfast she went out to the grassy spot in the rear of the garden where an iron tripod stood and began to gather shavings and paper in readiness for the fire. She watched Millie scour the great copper kettle until its interior shone, then it was lifted on the tripod, the cider poured into it, and the fire started. Logs were fed to the flames until a roaring fire was in blast. Several times Millie skimmed the foam from the cider.

"This is one time when signs don't work," the hired girl confided to the child. "Your Aunt Rebecca says that if you cook apple butter in the up-sign of the almanac it boils over easy, but it's the down-sign to-day, and yet this cider boils up all the time."

"I guess it'll all burn in the bottom," said Amanda, "if it's the down-sign."

"Not if you stir it good when the snitz are in. That's the time the work begins. Here's your mom and Philip."

"Ach, Mom,"--Amanda ran to meet her mother--"this here's awful much fun! I wish we'd boil apple butter every few days."

"Just wait once," said Millie, "till you're a little bigger and want to go off to picnics or somewhere and got to stay home and help to stir apple butter. Then you'll not like it so well. Why, Mrs. Hershey was tellin' me last week how mad her girls get still if the apple butter's got to be boiled in the hind part of the week when they want to be done and dressed and off to visit or to Lancaster instead of gettin' their eyes full of smoke stirrin' apple butter."

Mrs. Reist laughed.

"But," Amanda said with a tender glance at the hired girl, "I guess Hershey's ain't got no Millie like we to help."

"Ach, pack off now with you," Millie said, trying to frown. "I got to stop this spoilin' you. You don't think I'd stand in the hot sun and stir apple butter while you go off on a picnic or so when you're big enough to help good?"

"But that's just what you would do! I know you! Didn't you spend almost your whole Christmas savin' fund on me and Phil last year?"

"Ach, you talk too much! Let me be, now, I got to boil apple butter."

Philip ran for several boxes and old chairs and put them under a spreading cherry tree. "We take turns stirrin'," he explained, "so those that don't stir can take it easy while they wait their turn. Jiminy Christmas, guess we'll have a regular party to-day. All of us are in it, and Aunt Rebecca's comin', and Lyman Mertzheimer, and I guess Martin Landis, and mebbe some of the little Landis ones and the whole Crow Hill will be here. Here comes Millie with the snitz!"

The pared apples were put into the kettle, then the stirring commenced. A long wooden stirrer, with a handle ten feet long, was used, the big handle permitting the stirrer to stand a comfortable distance from the smoke and fire.

The boiling was well under way when Aunt Rebecca arrived.

"My goodness, Philip," she began as soon as she neared the fire, "you just stir half! You must do it all around the bottom of the kettle or the butter'll burn fast till it's done. Here, let me do it once." She took the handle from his hands and began to stir vigorously.

"Good!" cried the boy. "Now we can roast apples. Here, comes Lyman up the road, and Martin Landis and the baby. Now we'll have some fun!" He pointed to the toad, where Martin Landis, a neighbor boy, drew near with his two-year-old brother on his arm.

"But you keep away from the fire," ordered Aunt Rebecca.

The children ran off to the yard to greet the newcomers and soon came back joined by Lyman and Martin and the ubiquitous baby.

"I told you," Lyman said with mocking smiles, "that Martin would have to bring the baby along."

Martin Landis was fifteen, but hard work and much responsibility had added to him wisdom and understanding beyond his years. His frank, serious face could at times assume the look of a man of ripened experience. At Lyman's words it burned scarlet. "Ach, go on," he said quietly; "it'd do you good if you had a few to carry around; mebbe then you wouldn't be such a dude."

That brought the laugh at the expense of the other boy, who turned disdainfully away and walked to Aunt Rebecca with an offer to stir the apple butter.

"No, I'll do it," she said in a determined voice.

"Give me the baby," said Mrs. Reist, "then you children can go play." The little tot ran to her outstretched arms and was soon laughing at her soft whispers about young chickens to feed and ducks to see.

"Now," Amanda cried happily, "since Mom keeps the baby we'll roast corn and apples under the kettle."

In spite of Aunt Rebecca's protest, green corn and ripe apples were soon encased in thick layers of mud and poked upon the glowing bed under the kettle.

"Abody'd think none o' you had breakfast," she said sternly.

"Ach," said Mrs. Reist, "these just taste better because they're wrapped in mud. I used to do that at home when I was little."

"Well, I never did. They'll get burned yet with their foolin' round the fire."

Her prophecy came perilously close to fulfilment later in the day. Amanda, bending near the fire to turn a mud-coated apple, drew too close to the lurking flames. Her gingham dress was ready fuel for the fire. Suddenly a streak of flame leaped up the hem of it. Aunt Rebecca screamed. Lyman cried wildly, "Where's some water?" But before Mrs. Reist could come to the rescue Martin Landis had caught the frightened child and thrown her flat into a dense bed of bean vines near by, smothering the flames.

Then he raised her gently. Much handling of his younger sisters and brothers had made him adept with frightened children.

"Come, Manda," he said soothingly, "you're not hurt. Just your dress is burned a little."

"My hand--it's burned, I guess," she faltered.

Again force of habit swayed Martin. He bent over and kissed the few red marks on her fingers as he often kissed the bumped heads and scratched fingers of the little Landis children.

"Ach--" Amanda's hand fluttered under the kiss.

Then a realization of what he had done came to the boy. "Why," he stammered, "I didn't mean--I guess I oughtn't done that--I wasn't thinking, Manda."

"Ach, Martin, it's all right. You didn't hurt it none." She misunderstood him. "See, it ain't hurt bad at all. But, Martin, you scared me when you threw me in that bean patch! But it put the fire out. You're smart to think of that so quick."

"Oh, yes," Mrs. Reist found her voice, and the color crept back to her cheeks again. "Martin, I can't thank you enough."

"Um," Lyman said sneeringly, "now I suppose Martin's a hero."

"So he is!" said the little girl with decision. "He saved my life, and I ain't forgettin' it neither." Then she sat down by her mother's side and began to play with the baby.

"Well, guess the fun's over," said Lyman. "You went and spoiled it by catching fire." He went off in sulky mood.

"My goodness," exclaimed Aunt Rebecca, "mebbe now you'll keep away from this fire once."

Amanda kept away. The fun of the apple-butter boiling was ended for her.

She sat quietly under the tree while Millie and Aunt Rebecca and Phil took turns at stirring. She watched passively while Millie poured pounds of sugar into the boiling mass. She even missed the customary thrill as some of the odorous contents of the kettle were tested and the verdict came, "It's done!" The thrills of apple-butter boiling were as nothing to her now. She still felt the wonder of being rescued from the fire, rescued by a nice boy with a strong arm and a gentle voice-- what if it was only a boy she had known all her life!--her heart enshrined its first hero that day.

She forgot the terror that had seized her as the flames licked up her dress, the scorching touch on her hand was obliterated from her memory and only the healing gentleness of the kiss remained.

"He kissed my hand," she thought that night as she lay under her patchwork quilt. "It was just like the stories we read about in school about the 'knights of old that were brave and bold.'"

She thought of the picture on the schoolhouse wall. Sir Galahad, the teacher had called it, and read those lovely lines that Amanda remembered and liked-- "My strength is as the strength of ten because my heart is pure."

Martin was like that!

CHAPTER IV

A VISIT TO MARTIN'S MOTHER

When Amanda awoke the next morning her first thought was of the burnt hand and its healing kiss. "Why, Martin--ach, Martin--he kissed my hand," she said softly to herself. "Just like they do in the stories about knights--knights always kiss their ladies' hands. Ach, I know what I'll do! I'll play Martin Landis is my knight and I'm his lady grand. Wish Mom was here, then I'd ask her if she knows anything about what knights do and how the ladies ought to act to them. But she's in Lancaster. Mebbe Millie would know. I'll go ask her once."

Millie was baking pies when the girl sought her for the information.

"Say, Millie!"

"Ach, what?" The hired girl brushed the flour from her bare arms and turned to look at Amanda. "Now I know what you want--you smell the pies and you want a half-moon sample to eat before it's right cold and get your stomach upset and your face all pimply. Ain't?"

"No," began the child, then added diplomatically, "why, yes, I do want that, but that ain't what I come for."

Millie laughed. "Then what? But don't bother me for long. I got lots to do yet. I want to get the pies all done till your mom gets back."

"Why, Millie, I wondered, do you know anything about knights?"

"Not me. I sleep nights."

"Ach, Millie--knights--the kind you read about, the men that wear plumes in their hats."

"Feathers, you mean? Why, the only man I ever heard of wearin' a feather in his hat was Yankee Doodle."

"Ach, Millie, you make me mad! But I guess you don't know. Well, tell me this--if somebody did something for you and you wanted to show you 'preciated it, what would you do?"

"That's an easy one! I'd be nice to them and do things for them or for their people. Now you run and let me be. 'Bout half an hour from now you dare come in for your half-moon pie. Ach, I most forgot! Your mom said you shall take a little crock of the new apple butter down to Mrs. Landis."

"A little crock won't go far with all them children."

"Ach, yes. It'll smear a lot o' bread. I'll pack it in a basket so you can carry it easy. Better put on your sunbonnet so your hair won't burn red."

THE RHUBARB LEAF PARASOL

"Redder, you mean, ain't? But I won't need a bonnet. I'll take my new parasol."

"Parasol," echoed Millie. "Now what---"

But Amanda ran away, laughing, and returned in a few minutes holding a giant rhubarb leaf over her head. "Does the green silk of my parasol look good with my hair?" she asked with an exaggerated air of grandeur.

"Go on, now," Millie said, laughing, "and don't spill that apple butter or you'll get parasol."

With a merry good-bye Amanda set off, the basket upon her arm, one hand grasping the red stem of the rhubarb parasol while the great green leaf flopped up and down upon her head in cool ministration.

Down the sunny road she trudged, spasmodically singing bits of gay songs, then again talking to herself. "This here is a dandy parasol. Cooler'n a real one and lots nicer'n a bonnet or a hat. Only I wish it was bigger, so my arms would be covered, for it's hot out to-day."

When she reached the little red brick country schoolhouse, half-way between her home and the Landis farm, she paused in the shade of a great oak that grew in the school-yard.

"Guess I'll rest the apple butter a while in this shade," she said to herself, "and pick a bouquet for my knight's mom." From the grassy roadside she gathered yellow and gold butter-and-eggs, blue spikes of false dragon's head, and edged them with a lacy ruffle of wild carrot flowers.

"There, that's grand!" she said as she held the bouquet at arm's length and surveyed it carefully. "I'll hold it out, just so, and I'll say to Mrs. Landis, 'Mother of my knight, I salute you!' I know she'll be surprised. Mebbe I might tell her just how brave her Martin is and how I made him a knight. She'll be glad. It must be a satisfaction to have a boy a knight." She smiled in happy anticipation of the wonderful message she was going to bring Mrs. Landis. Then she replaced the rhubarb parasol over her head, picked up the basket, and went down the country road to the Landis farm.

"It's good Landis's don't live far from our place," she thought. "My parasol's wiltin'."

Like the majority of houses in the Crow Hill section of country, the Landis house was set in a frame of green trees and old-fashioned flower gardens. It flaunted in the face of the passer-by an old-time front yard. The wide brick walk that led straight from the gate to the big front porch was edged on both sides with a row of bricks placed corners up. On either side of the walk were bushes, long since placed without the discriminating eye of a landscape gardener but holding in their very randomness a charm unrivaled by any precise planting. Mock-orange bushes and lilacs towered above the low deutzias, while masses of zinnias, petunias, four-o'clocks, and a score of other old-fashioned posies crowded against each other in the long beds that edged the walks and in the smaller round beds that were dotted here and there in the grass. Jaded motorists from the city drove their cars slowly past the glory of the Landis riot of blossoms.

As Amanda neared the place she looked ruefully at her knot of wild flowers. "She's got so many pretty ones," she thought. "But, ach, I guess she'll like these here, too, long as they're a present."

Two of the Landis children ran to greet Amanda as she opened the gate and entered the yard.

"I'll lay my parasol by the gate," she said. "Where's your mom?"

"In the kitchen, cannin' blackberries," said little Henry.

As Amanda rounded the corner of the house, the two children clinging to her arm, Mrs. Landis came to the kitchen door.

"Mother of my knight, I salute you," said Amanda, making as low a bow as the two barnacle children, the bouquet and the basket with its crock of apple butter, would allow.

"What," laughed Mrs. Landis. "Now what was that you said? The children make so much noise I can't hear sometimes. Henry, don't hang so on Amanda's arm, it's too hot."

"I said--why, I said--I have some apple butter for you that Mom sent and I picked a bouquet for you," the child replied, her courage suddenly gone from her.

"Now, ain't that nice! Come right in." The woman held the screen door open for the visitor.

Mrs. Landis, mother of the imaginary knight and of six other children, was a sturdy, well-built woman, genial and good-natured, as stout people are reputed to be. In spite of hard work she retained a look of youthfulness about her which her plain Mennonite dress and white cap accentuated. An artist with an appreciative eye might have said that the face of that mother was like a composite picture of all the Madonnas of the old masters--tender, love-lighted yet far-seeing and reverent.

Amanda had always loved Mrs. Landis and spent many hours in her home, attracted by the baby--there always was one, either in arms or just wobbling about on chubby little legs.

"Now ain't it nice of your mom to send us that new apple butter! And for you to pick the flowers for me! Sattie for both. I say still that the wild flowers beat the ones on the garden beds. And how pretty you fixed them!"

"Mom, Mom," whispered little Henry, "dare I smear me a piece of bread?"

"Yes, if you don't make crumbs."

"Oh, Mom," cried Mary Landis, who came running in from the yard. "What d'you think? Manda left her green parasol out by the front gate and Henry's chewed the handle off of it!"

"Chewed the handle off a parasol--what--how?" said the surprised mother.

Amanda laughed. "But don't you worry about it, Mrs. Landis," she said, "for it was a rhubarb parasol."

"Oh!" A merry laugh followed the announcement about the edible parasol handle and Mrs. Landis went back to spreading thick slices of bread with apple butter while three pairs of eager hands were reaching out to her.

A tiny wail which soon grew in volume sounded from a room in the front of the house.

"The baby's awake," said Amanda. "Dare I fetch him?"

"Yes. Go right in."

Amanda went through two rooms and came to a semi-darkened side room where the smallest Landis was putting forth a loud protest at his fancied neglect.

"Come on, Johnny, don't cry no more. Manda's goin' to take you--see!" She raised the baby, who changed from crying to laughter.

"Ain't he dear!" Amanda said as she brought the baby into the kitchen. "And so bright he is for not quite six months old. I remember how old he is because it was on my mom's last birthday in March that Millie said you had another baby and I remember, too, that Aunt Rebecca was there and she said, 'What, them Landis's got another baby! Poor thing!' I asked Mom why she said that and she thought Aunt Rebecca meant that babies make so much work for you."

"Ach, abody works anyhow, might as well work tendin' babies. Put your cheek against Johnny's face once, Amanda."

Amanda bent her head and touched the soft cheek of the child. "Why," she said, "ain't it soft, now! Ain't babies just too dear and sweet! I guess Aunt Rebecca don't know how nice they are."

"Poor thing," said Mrs. Landis.

"Poor--she ain't poor!" Amanda corrected her. "She owns two farms and got lots of money besides."

"But no children--poor thing," repeated Mrs. Landis.

Amanda looked at her, wondering.

"Amanda," said the white-capped mother as she wiped some blackberry juice from little Henry's fingers, "abody can have lots of money and yet be poor, and others can have hardly any money and yet be rich. It's all in what abody means by rich and what kind of treasures you set store by. I wouldn't change places with your rich Aunt Rebecca for all the farms in Lancaster County."

"Well, I guess not!" Amanda could understand her attitude. "And Mom and Millie say still you got such nice children. But Martin now," she said with assumed seriousness as she saw him step on the porch to enter the kitchen--"your Martin pushed me in a bean patch yesterday and I fell down flat on my face."

"Martin!" his mother began sternly. "What for did you act so?"

"Amanda, don't you tell!" the boy commanded, his face flushing. "Don't you dare tell!"

"I got to now, I started it. Ach, Mrs. Landis, you dare be proud of him! My dress caught fire and none of us had sense but him. He smothered it by throwin' me in the bean patch and he--he's a hero!"

"A hero!" cried little Henry. "Mart's a hero!" while the mother smiled proudly.

"Manda Reist," Martin spoke quickly as he edged to the door. "Amanda Reist, next time--next time I'll--darn it, I'll just let you burn up!" He ran from the room and disappeared round the corner of the house.

"Why"--Amanda's lips trembled--"ain't he mean! I just wanted to be nice to him and he got mad."

"Don't mind him," soothed the mother. "Boys are funny. He's not mad at you, he just don't like too much fuss made over what he done. But all the time he's tickled all over to have you call him a hero."

"Oh--are boys like that? Phil's not. But he ain't a knight. I guess knights like to pretend they're very modest even if they're full of pride." Mrs. Landis was too busy putting blackberries into the jars to catch the import of the child's words. The word knight escaped her hearing.

"Well, I must go now," said the small visitor. "I'll come again."

"All right, do, Amanda."

She put the baby in its coach, took up the empty basket, and after numerous good-byes to the children went down the road to her home. The rhubarb parasol gone, the sun beat upon her uncovered head but she was unmindful of the intense heat. Her brain was wholly occupied with thoughts of Martin Landis and his strange behavior.

"Umph," she decided finally, "men *are* funny things! I'm just findin' it out. And I guess knights are queerer'n others yet! Wonder if Millie kept my half-moon pie or if Phil sneaked it. Abody's just got to watch out for these men folks!"

CHAPTER V

AT AUNT REBECCA'S HOUSE

Several weeks after the eventful apple-butter boiling at the Reist farm, Aunt Rebecca invited the Reist family to spend a Sunday at her home.

"I ain't goin', Mom," Philip announced. "I don't like it there. Dare I stay home with Millie?"

"Mebbe Millie wants to come along," suggested his mother.

"Ach, I guess not this time. Just you go and Phil and I'll stay and tend the house and feed the chickens and look after things."

"Well, I'm goin'!" spoke up Amanda. "Aunt Rebecca's funny and bossy but I like to go to her house, it's so little and cute, everything."

"Cute," scoffed the boy. "Everything's cute to a girl. You dare go, I won't! Last time I was there I picked a few of her honeysuckle flowers and pulled that stem out o' them to get the drop of honey that's in each one, and she caught me and slapped my hand--mind you! Guess next she'll be puttin' up some scare-bees to keep the bees off her flowers. But say, Manda, if she gives you any of them little red and white striped peppermint candies like she does still, sneak me a few."

"Humph! You don't go to see her but you want her candy! I'd be ashamed, Philip Reist!"

"Hush, hush," warned Mrs. Reist. "Next you two'll be fightin', and on a Sunday, too."

The girl laughed. "Ach, Mom, guess we both got the tempers that goes with red hair. But it's Sunday, so I'll be good. I'm glad we're goin' to Aunt Rebecca. That's a nice drive."

Aunt Rebecca lived alone in a cottage at the edge of Landisville, a beautiful little town several miles from the Reist farm at Crow Hill. During her husband's life they lived on one of the big farms of Lancaster County, where she slaved in the manual labor of the great fields. Many were the hours she spent in the hot sun of the tobacco fields, riding the planter in the early spring, later hoeing the rich black soil close to the little young plants, in midsummer finding and killing the big green tobacco worms and topping and suckering the plants so that added value might be given the broad, strong leaves. Then later in the summer she helped the men to thread the harvested stalks on laths and hang them in the long open shed to dry.

Aunt Rebecca had married Jonas Miller, a rich man. All the years of their life together on the farm seemed a visible verification of the old saying, "To him that hath shall be given." A special Providence seemed to hover over their acres of tobacco. Storms and destructive hail appeared to roam in a swath just outside their farm. The Jonas Miller tobacco fields were reputed to be the finest in the whole Garden Spot county, and the Jonas Miller bank account grew correspondingly fast. But the bank account, however quickly it increased, failed to give Jonas Miller and his wife full pleasure, unless, as some say, the mere knowledge of possession of wealth can bring pleasure to miserly hearts. For Jonas Miller was, in the vernacular of the Pennsylvania Dutch, "almighty close." Millie, Reists' hired girl, said," That there Jonas is too stingy to buy long enough pants for himself. I bet he gets boys' size because they're cheaper, for the legs o' them always just come to the top o' his shoes. Whoever lays him out when he's dead once will have to put pockets in his shroud for sure! And he's made poor Becky just like him. It ain't in her family to be so near; why, Mrs. Reist is always givin' somebody something! But mebbe when he dies once and his wife gets the money in her hand she'll let it fly."

However, when Jonas Miller died and left the hoarded money to his wife she did not let it fly. She rented the big farm and moved to the little old-fashioned house in Landisville--a little house whose outward appearance might have easily proclaimed its tenant poor. There she lived alone, with occasional visits and visitors to break the monotony of her existence.

That Sunday morning of the Reist visit, Uncle Amos hitched the horse to the carriage, tied it by the front fence of the farm, then he went up-stairs and donned his Sunday suit of gray cloth. Later he brought out his broad-brimmed Mennonite hat and called to Amanda and her mother, "I'm ready. Come along!"

Mrs. Reist wore a black cashmere shawl pinned over her plain gray lawn dress and a stiff black silk bonnet was tied under her chin. Amanda skipped out to the yard, wearing a white dress with a wide buff sash. A matching ribbon was tied on her red hair.

"Jiminy," whistled Uncle Amos as she ran to him and swung her leghorn hat on its elastic. "Jiminy, you're pretty---"

"Oh, am I, Uncle Amos?" She smiled radiantly. "Am I really pretty?"

"Hold on, here!" He tried to look very sober. "If you ain't growin' up for sure! Lookin' for compliments a'ready, same as all the rest. I was goin' to say that you're pretty fancy dressed for havin' a Mennonite mom."

"Oh, Uncle Amos!" Amanda laughed and tossed her head so the yellow bow danced like a butterfly. "I don't believe you at all! You're too good to be findin' fault like that! Millie says so, too."

"She does, eh? She does? Just what does Millie say about me now?"

"Why, she said yesterday that you're the nicest man and have the biggest heart of any person she knows."

"Um--so! And Millie says that, does she? Um--so! well, well"--a glow of joy spread in his face and stained his neck and ears. Fortunately, for his future peace of mind, the child did not notice the flush. A swallowtail butterfly had flitted among the zinnias and attracted the attention of Amanda so it was diverted from her uncle. But he still smiled as Millie opened the front door and she and Mrs. Reist stepped on the porch.

Millie, in her blue gingham dress and her checked apron, her straight hair drawn back from her plain face, was certainly no vision to cause the heart of the average man to pump faster. But as Amos looked at her he saw suddenly something lovelier than her face. She walked to the gate, smoothing the shawl of Mrs. Reist, patting the buff sash of the little girl.

"Big heart," thought Amos, "it's her got the big heart!"

"Good-bye, safe journey," the hired girl called after them as they started down the road. "Don't worry about us. Me and Phil can manage alone. Good-bye."

The road to Landisville led past green fields of tobacco and corn, large farmhouses where old-fashioned flowers made a vivid picture in the gardens, orchards and woodland tracts, their green shade calling invitingly. Once they crossed a wandering little creek whose shallow waters flowed through lovely meadows where boneset plants were white with bloom and giant eupatorium lifted its rosy heads. A red-headed flicker flew screaming from a field as they passed, and a fussy wren scolded at them from a fence corner.

"She'll have a big job," said Uncle Amos, "if she's goin' to scold every team and automobile that passes here this mornin'. Such a little thing to be so sassy!"

As they came to Landisville and drove into the big churchyard there were already many carriages standing in the shade of the long open shed and numerous automobiles parked in the sunny yard.

A few minutes later they entered the big brick meeting-house and sat down in the calm of the sanctuary. The whispers of newcomers drifted through the open windows, steps sounded on the bare floor of the church, but finally all had entered and quiet fell upon the place.

The simple service of the Mennonite Church is always appealing and helpful. The music of voices, without any accompaniment of musical instrument, the simple prayers and sermons, are all devoid of ostentation or ornamentation. Amanda liked to join in the singing and did so lustily that morning. But during the sermon she often fell to dreaming. The quiet meeting-house where only the calm voice of the preacher was heard invited the building of wonderful castles in Spain. Their golden spires reared high in the blue of heaven... she would be a lady in a trailing, silken gown, Martin would come, a plumed and belted knight, riding on a pure white steed like that in the Sir Galahad picture at school, and he'd repeat to her those beautiful words, "My strength is as the strength of ten because my heart is pure." Was there really any truth in that poem? Could one be strong as ten because the heart was pure? Of course! It had to be true! Martin could be like that. He'd lift her to the saddle on the pure white horse and they'd ride away together to one of those beautiful castles in Spain, high up on the mountains, so high they seemed above the clouds...

Then she came back to earth suddenly. The meeting was over and Aunt Rebecca stood ready to take them to her home.

The country roads were filled with carriages and automobiles; the occupants of the former nodded a cordial how-de-do, though most of them were strangers, but the riders in the motors sped past without a sign of friendliness.

"My goodness," said Aunt Rebecca, "since them automobiles is so common abody don't get many how-de-dos no more as you travel along the country roads. Used to be everybody'd speak to everybody else they'd meet on the road--here, Amos," she laid a restraining hand upon the reins. "Stop once! I see a horseshoe layin' in the road and it's got two nails in it, too. That's powerful good luck! Stop once and let me get it."

Amos chuckled and with a loud "Whoa" brought the horse to a standstill. Aunt Rebecca climbed from the carriage, picked up the trophy of good luck and then took her seat beside her brother again, a smile upon her lined old face.

"That's three horseshoes I have now. I never let one lay. I pick up all I find and take them home and hang them on the old peach tree in the back yard. I know they bring good luck. Mebbe if I hadn't picked up all them three a lot o' trouble would come to me."

"Have it your way," conceded Uncle Amos. "They don't do you no hurt, anyhow. But, Rebecca," he said as they came within sight of her little house, "you ought to get your place painted once."

"Ach, my goodness, what for? When it's me here alone. I think the house looks nice. My flowers are real pretty this year, once. Course, I don't fool with them like you do. I have the kind that don't take much tendin' and come up every year without bein' planted. Calico flowers and larkspur and lady-slippers are my kind. This plantin' and hoein' at flowers is all for nothin'. It's all right to work so at beans and potatoes and things you can eat when they grow, but what good are flowers but to look at! I done my share of hoein' and diggin' and workin' in the ground. I near killed myself when Jonas lived yet, in them tobacco patches. I used to say to him still, we needn't work so hard and slave like that after we had so much money put away, but he was for workin' as long as we could, and so we kept on till he went. He used to say money gets all if you begin to spend it and don't earn more. Jonas was savin'."

"He sure was, that he was," seconded Uncle Amos with a twinkle in his eyes. "Savin' for you and now you're savin' for somebody that'll make it fly when you go, I bet. Some day you'll lay down and die and your money'll be scattered. If you leave me any, Becky," he teased her, "I'll put it all in an automobile."

"What, them wild things! Road-hogs, I heard somebody call 'em, and I think it's a good name. My goodness, abody ain't safe no more since they come on the streets. They go toot, toot, and you got to hop off to one side in the mud or the ditch, it don't matter to them. I hate them things! Only don't never take me to the graveyard in one of them."

"By that time," said Uncle Amos, "they'll have flyin' machine hearses; they'll go faster."

"My goodness, Amos, how you talk! Ain't you ashamed to make fun at your old sister that way! But Mom always said when you was little that you seemed a little simple, so I guess you can't help it."

"Na-ha," exulted Amanda, with impish delight. "That's one on you. Aunt Rebecca ain't so dumb like she lets on sometimes."

"Ach, no," Aunt Rebecca said, laughing. "'A blind pig sometimes finds an acorn, too.'"

Aunt Rebecca's table, though not lavishly laden as are those of most of the Pennsylvania Dutch, was amply filled with good, substantial food. The fried sausage was browned just right, the potatoes and lima beans well-cooked, the cold slaw, with its dash of red peppers, was tasty and the snitz pie--Uncle Amos's favorite--was thick with cinnamon, its crust flaky and brown.

After the dishes were washed Aunt Rebecca said, "Now then, we'll go in the parlor."

"Oh, in the parlor!" exclaimed Amanda. "Why, abody'd think we was company. You don't often take us in the parlor."

"Ach, well, you won't make no dirt and I just thought to-day, once, I'd take you in the parlor to sit a while. It don't get used hardly. Wait till I open the shutters."

She led the way through a little hall to the front room. As she opened the door a musty odor came to the hall.

"It smells close," said Aunt Rebecca, sniffing. "But it'll be all right till I get some screens in." She pulled the tasseled cords of the green shades, opened the slatted shutters, and a flood of summer light entered the room. "Ach," she said impatiently as she hammered at one window, "I can hardly get this one open still, it sticks itself so." But after repeated thumps on the frame she succeeded in raising it and placing an old-fashioned sliding screen.

"Now sit down and take it good," she invited.

Uncle Amos sank into an old-fashioned rocker with high back and curved arms, built throughout for the solid comfort of its occupants. Mrs. Reist chose an old hickory Windsor chair, Aunt Rebecca selected, with a sigh of relief, a fancy reed rocker, given in exchange for a book of trading stamps.

"This here's the best chair in the house and it didn't cost a cent," she announced as she rocked in it.

Amanda roamed around the room. "I ain't been in here for long. I want to look around a little. I like these dishes. I wish we had some like them." She tiptoed before a corner cupboard filled with antiques.

"Ach, yes," her aunt answered, "mebbe it looks funny, ain't, to have a glass cupboard in the parlor, but I had no other room for it, the house is so little. If I didn't think so much of them dishes I'd sold them a'ready. That little glass with the rim round the bottom of it I used to drink out of it at my granny's house when I was little. Them dark shiny dishes like copper were Jonas's mom's. And I like to keep the pewter, too, for abody can't buy it these days."

Amanda looked up. On the top shelf of the cupboard was a silver lustre pitcher, a teapot of rose lustre, a huge willow platter with its quaint blue design, several pewter bowls, a plate with a crude peacock in bright colors--an array of antiques that would have awakened covetousness in the heart of a connoisseur.

A walnut pie-crust tilt top table stood in one corner of the room, a mahogany gateleg occupied the centre, its beauty largely concealed by a cover of yellow and white checked homespun linen, upon which rested a glass oil lamp with a green paper shade, a wide glass dish filled with pictures, an old leather-bound album with heavy brass clasps and hinges. A rag carpet, covered in places with hooked rugs, added a proper note of harmony, while the old walnut chairs melted into the whole like trees in a woodland scene. The whitewashed walls were bare save for a large square mirror with a wide mahogany frame, a picture holder made from a palm leaf fan and a piece of blue velvet briar stitched in yellow, and a cross-stitch canvas sampler framed with a narrow braid of horsehair from the tail of a dead favorite of long ago.

"What's pewter made of, Aunt Rebecca?" asked the child.

"Why, of tin and lead. And it's a pity they don't make it and use lots of it like they used to long ago. For you can use pewter spoons in vinegar and they don't turn black like some of these things that look like silver but ain't. Pewter is good ware and I think sometimes that the people that lived when it was used so much were way ahead of the people to-day. Pewter's the same all through, no thin coatin' of something shiny that can wear off and spoil the spoons or dishes. It's old style now but it's good and pretty."

"Yes, that's so," agreed Amanda. It was surprising to the little girl that the acidulous old aunt could, so unexpectedly, utter beautiful, suggestive thoughts. Oh, Aunt Rebecca's house was a wonderful place. She must see more of the treasures in the parlor.

Finally her activity annoyed Aunt Rebecca. "My goodness," came the command, "you sit down once! Here, look at the album. Mebbe that will keep you quiet for a while."

Amanda sat on a low footstool and took the old album on her knees. She uttered many delighted squeals of surprise and merriment as she turned the thick pages and looked at the pictures of several generations ago. A little girl with ruffled pantalets showing below her full skirt and a fat little boy with full trousers reaching half-way between his knees and his shoetops sent Amanda into a gale of laughter. "Oh, I wish Phil was here. What funny people!"

"Let me see once," asked Aunt Rebecca. "Why, that's Amos and your mom."

Mrs. Reist smiled and Uncle Amos chuckled. "We're peaches there, ain't? I guess if abody thinks back right you see there were as many crazy styles in olden times as there is now."

Tintypes of men and women in peculiar dress of Aunt Rebecca's youth called forth much comment and many questions from the interested Amanda. "Are there no pictures in here of you?" she asked her aunt.

"Yes, I guess so. On the last page or near there. That one," she said as the child found it, a tintype of a young man seated on a vine-covered seat and a comely young woman standing beside him, one hand laid upon his shoulder.

"And is that Uncle Jonas?"

"No--my goodness, no! That's Martin Landis."

"Martin Landis? Not my--not the Martin Landis's pop that lives near us?"

"Yes, that one."

"Why"--Amanda was wide-eyed and curious--"what were you doin' with your hand on his shoulder so and your picture taken with him?"

Aunt Rebecca laughed. "Ach, I had dare to do that for we was promised then, engaged they say now."

"You were goin' to marry Martin Landis's pop once?" The girl could not quite believe it.

"Yes. But he was poor and along came Jonas Miller and he was rich and I took him. But the money never done me no good. Mebbe abody shouldn't say it, since he's dead, but Jonas was stingy. He'd squeeze a dollar till the eagle'd holler. He made me pinch and save till I got so I didn't feel right when I spent money. Now, since he's gone, I don't know how. I act so dumb it makes me mad at myself sometimes. If I go to Lancaster and buy me a whole plate of ice-cream it kinda bothers me. I keep wonderin' what Jonas'd think, for he used to say that half a plate of cream's enough for any woman. But mebbe it was to be that I married Jonas instead of Martin Landis. Martin is a good man but all them children--my goodness! I guess I got it good alone in my little house long side of Mrs. Landis with all her children to take care of."

Amanda remembered the glory on the face of Mrs. Landis as she had said, "Abody can have lots of money and yet be poor and others can have hardly any money and yet be rich. It's all in what abody means by rich and what kind of treasures you set store by. I wouldn't change places with your rich Aunt Rebecca for all the farms in Lancaster County." Poor Aunt Rebecca, she pitied her! Then she remembered the words of the memory gem they had analyzed in school last year, "Where ignorance is bliss 'tis folly to be wise." She could understand it now! So long as Aunt Rebecca didn't see what she missed it was all right. But if she ever woke up and really felt what her life might have been if she had married the poor man she loved--poor Aunt Rebecca! A halo of purest romance hung about the old woman as the child looked up at her.

"My goodness," the woman broke the spell, "it's funny how old pictures make abody think back. That old polonaise dress, now," she went on in reminiscent strain, "had the nicest buttons on. I got some of 'em yet on my charm string."

"Charm string--what's a charm string?"

"Wait once. I'll show you."

The woman left the room. They heard her tramp about up-stairs and soon she returned with a long string of buttons threaded closely together and forming a heavy cable.

"Oh, let me see! Ain't that nice!" exclaimed Amanda. "Where did you ever get so many buttons and all different?"

"We used to beg them. When I was a girl everybody mostly had a charm string. I kept puttin' buttons on mine till I was well up in my twenties, then the string was full and big so I stopped. I used to hang it over the looking glass in the parlor and everybody that came looked at it."

Amanda fingered the charm string interestedly. Antique buttons, iridescent, golden, glimmering, some with carved flowers, others globules of colored glass, many of them with quaint filigree brass mounting over colored background, a few G. A. R. buttons from old uniforms, speckled china ones like portions of bird eggs--all strung together and each one having a history to the little old eccentric woman who had cherished them through many years.

"This one Martin Landis give me for the string and this one is from Jonas' wedding jacket and this pretty blue glass one a girl gave me that's dead this long a'ready."

"Oh"--Amanda's eyes shone. She turned to her mother, "Did you ever have a charm string, Mom?"

"Yes. A pretty one. But I let you play with it when you were a baby and the string got broke and the buttons put in the box or lost."

"Ach, but that spites me. I'd like to see it and have you tell where the buttons come from. I like old things like that, I do."

"Then mebbe you'd like to see my friendship cane," said Aunt Rebecca.

"Oh, yes! What's that?" Amanda rose from her chair, eager to see what a friendship cane could be.

"My goodness, sit down! You get me all hoodled up when you act so jumpy," said the aunt. Then she walked to a corner of the parlor, reached behind the big cupboard and drew out a cane upon which were tied some thirty ribbon bows of various colors.

"And is that a friendship cane?" asked Amanda. "What's it for?"

"Ach, it was just such a style, good for nothin' but for the girls of my day to have a little pleasure with. We got boys and girls to give us pretty ribbons and we exchanged with some and then we tied 'em on the cane. See, they're all old kinds o' ribbons yet. Some are double-faced satin and some with them little scallops at the edge, and they're pretty colors, too. I could tell the name of every person who give me a ribbon for that cane. My goodness, lots o' them boys and girls been dead long a'ready. I guess abody shouldn't hold up such old things so long, it just makes you feel bad still when you rake 'em out and look at 'em. Here now, let me put it away, that's enough lookin' for one day." She spoke brusquely and put the cane into its hiding-place behind the glass cupboard.

As Amanda watched the stern, unlovely face during the critical, faultfinding conversation which followed, she thought to herself, "I just believe that Uncle Amos told the truth when he said that Aunt Rebecca's like a chestnut burr. She's all prickly on the outside but she's got a nice, smooth side to her that abody don't often get the chance to see. Mebbe now, if she'd married Martin Landis's pop she'd be by now just as nice as Mrs. Landis. It wonders me now if she would!"

CHAPTER VI

SCHOOL DAYS

Mrs. Reist's desire for a happy childhood for her children was easily realized, especially in the case of Amanda. She had the happy faculty of finding joy in little things, things commonly called insignificant. She had a way of taking to herself each beauty of nature, each joy note of the birds, the airy loveliness of the clouds, and being thrilled by them.

With Phil and Martin Landis--and the ubiquitous Landis baby--she explored every field, woods and roadside in the Crow Hill section of the county. From association with her Phil and Martin had developed an equal interest in outdoors. The Landis boy often came running into the Reist yard calling for Amanda and exclaiming excitedly, "I found a bird's nest! It's an oriole this time, the dandiest thing way out on the end of a tiny twig. Come on see it!"

Amanda was the moving spirit of that little group of nature students. Phil and Martin might have never known an oriole from a thrush if she had not led them along the path of knowledge. Sometimes some of the intermediate Landis children joined the group. At times Lyman Mertzheimer sauntered along and invited himself, but his interest was feigned and his welcome was not always cordial.

"You Lyman Mertzheimer," Amanda said to him one day, "if you want to go along to see birds' nests you got to keep quiet! You think it's smart to scare them off the nests. That poor thrasher, now, that you scared last week! You had her heart thumpin' so her throat most burst. And her with her nest right down on the ground where we could watch the babies if we kept quiet. You're awful mean!"

"Huh," he answered, "what's a bird! All this fuss about a dinky brown bird that can't do anything but flop its wings and squeal when you go near it. It was fun to see her flop all around the ground."

"Oh, you nasty mean thing, Lyman Mertzheimer"--for a moment Amanda found no words to express her contempt of him--"sometimes I just hate you!"

He went off laughing, flinging back the prediction, "But some day you'll do the reverse, Amanda Reist." He felt secure in the belief that he could win the love of any girl he chose if he exerted himself to do so.

The little country school of Crow Hill was necessarily limited in its curriculum, hence when Amanda expressed a desire to become a teacher it was decided to send her to the Normal School at Millersville. At that time she was sixteen and was grown into an attractive girl.

"I know I'm not beautiful," she told her mother one day after a long, searching survey in the mirror. "My hair is too screaming red, but then it's fluffy and I got a lot of it. Add to red hair a nose that's a little pug and a mouth that's a little too big and I guess the combination won't produce any Cleopatra or any Titian beauty."

"But you forgot the eyes," her mother said tenderly. "They are pretty brown and look--ach, I can't put it in fine words like you could, but I mean this: Your eyes are such honest eyes and always look so happy, like you could see through dark places and find the light and could look on wicked people and see the good in them and be glad about it. You keep that look in your eyes and no pretty girl will be lovelier that you are, Amanda."

"Mother," the girl cried after she had kissed the white-capped woman, "if my eyes shine it's the faith and love you taught me that's shining in them."

During the summer preceding Amanda's departure for school there was pleasant excitement at the Reist farm. Millie was proud of the fact that Amanda was "goin' to Millersville till fall" and lost no oppor-tunity to mention it whenever a friend or neighbor dropped in for a chat.

Aunt Rebecca did not approve of too much education. "Of course," she put it, "you're spendin' your own money for this Millersville goin', but I think you'd do better if you put it to bank and give it to Amanda when she gets married, once. This here rutchin' round to school so long is all for nothin'. I guess she's smart enough to teach country school without goin' to Millersville yet."

However, her protests fell heedlessly on the ears of those most concerned and when the preparation of new clothes began Aunt Rebecca was the first to offer her help. "It's all for nothin', this school learnin', but if she's goin' anyhow I can just as well as not help with the sewin'," she announced and spent a few weeks at the Reist farm, giving valuable aid in the making of Amanda's school outfit.

Those two weeks were long ones to Philip, who had scant patience with the querulous old aunt. But Amanda, since she had glimpsed the girlhood romance of the woman, had a kindlier feeling for her and could smile at the faultfinding or at least run away from it without retort if it became too vexatious.

Crow Hill was only an hour's ride from the school at Millersville, so Amanda spent most of her weekends at home. Each time she had wonderful tales to tell, at least they seemed wonderful to the little group at the Reist farmhouse. Mrs. Reist and Uncle Amos, denied in their youth of more than a very meagre education, took just pride in the girl who was pursuing the road to knowledge. Philip, boy-like, expressed no pride in his sister, but he listened attentively to her stories of how the older students played pranks on the newcomers. Millie was proud of hav-ing *our Amanda* away at school and did not hesitate to express her pride. She felt sure that before the girl's three years' course was completed the name of Amanda Reist would shine above all others on the pages of the Millersville Normal School records.

"Oh, I've learned a few things about human nature," said Amanda on her second visit home. "You know I told you last week how nice the older girls are to the new ones. A crowd of Seniors came into our room the other day and they were lovely! One of them told me she adored red hair and she just knew all the girls were going to love me because I have such a sweet face and I'm so dear--she emphasized every other word! I wondered what ailed her. She didn't know me well enough to talk like that. Before they left she began to talk about the Page Literary Society--'Dear, we're all Pageites, and it's the best, finest society in the school. We do have such good times. You ought to join. All the very nicest girls of the school are in it.' I promised to think it over. Well, soon after they left another bunch of girls came into our room and they were just as sweet to us. By and by one of them said, 'Dear, we're all in the Normal Literary Society. It's the best society in the school; all the very nicest girls belong to it. You should join it.'"

"Ha, electioneering, was they!" said Uncle Amos, laughing. "Well, leave it to the women. When they get the vote once we men got to pony up. But which society did you join?"

"Neither. I'm going to wait a while and while I'm waiting I'm having a glorious time. The Pageites invited me to a fudge party one night, the Normalites took me for a long walk, a Pageite treated me to icecream soda one day and a Normalite gave me some real home-made cake the same afternoon. It's great to be on the fence when both sides are coaxing you to jump their way."

"Well," said Millie, her face glowing with interest and pride in the girl, "if you ain't the funniest! I just bet them girls all want you to come their way. But what kind o' meals do you get?"

"Good, Millie. Of course, though, I haven't any cellar to go to for pie or any cooky crock filled with sand-tarts with shellbarks on the top."

"Don't you worry, Manda. I'll make you sand-tarts and lemon pie and everything you like every time you come home still."

"Millie, you good soul! With that promise to help me I'll work like a Trojan and win some honors at old M.S.N.S. Just watch me!"

Amanda did work. She brought to her studies the same whole-hearted interest and enthusiasm she evinced in her hunts for wild flowers, she applied to them the same dogged determination and untiring efforts she showed in her long search for hidden bird nests, with the inevitable result that her brain, naturally alert and brilliant, grasped with amazing celerity both the easy and the hard lessons of the Normal Training course.

Millie's prediction proved well founded--Amanda Reist stood well in her classes. In botany she was the preeminent figure of the entire school. "Ask Amanda Reist, she'll tell you," became the slogan among the students. "Yellow violets, lady-slippers, wild ginger--she'll tell you where they grow or get a specimen for you."

When the time for graduation drew near Amanda was able to carry home the glad news that she ranked third in her class and was chosen to deliver an oration at the Commencement exercises.

"That I want to hear," declared Millie, "and I'll get a new dress to wear to it, too."

On the June morning when the Commencement exercises of the First Pennsylvania State Normal School took place there were hundreds of happy, eager visitors on the campus at Millersville, and later in the great auditorium, but none was happier than Millie Hess, Reists' hired girl. The new dress, bought in Lancaster and made by Mrs. Reist and Aunt Rebecca, was a white lawn flecked with black. Millie had decided on a plain waist with high neck, the inch wide band at the throat edged with torchon lace, after the style she usually wore, the skirt made full and having above the hem, as Millie put it, "Just a few tucks, then wait a while, then tucks again." But Amanda, happening on the scene as the dress was tried on, protested at the high neck.

"Please, Millie," she coaxed, "do have the neck turned down, oh, just a little! I'd have a nice pleated ruffle of white net around it and a little V in front. You'd look fine that way."

"Me-fine! Go long with you, Amanda Reist! Ain't I got two good eyes and a lookin'-glass? But I guess I would look more like other folks if I had it made like you say. But now I don't want it too low. You dare fix it so it looks right." Displaying the same meek acquiescence in the desire of Amanda she bought a stylish hat instead of the big flat sailor with its taffeta bow she generally chose. The hat was Amanda's selection, a small, modest little thing with pale pink and gray roses misty with a covering of black tulle.

"Me with pink roses on my hat and over forty years old," said Millie wonderingly, but when she tried it on and saw the improvement in her appearance she smiled happily. "It's the prettiest hat I ever had and I'll hold it up and take good care of it so it'll last me years. I'm gettin' fixed up for sure once, only my new shoes don't have no squeak in 'em at all."

"That's out of style," Amanda informed her kindly.

"It is? Why, when I was little I remember hearin' folks tell how when they bought new shoes they always asked for a 'fib's worth of squeak' in 'em."

"And now they pay the shoemaker more than a 'fib' to put a few pegs in the shoes and take the squeak out."

"Well, well, how things get different! But then I'm glad mine don't make no noise if that's the way now."

Commencement day Millie could have held her own with any well-dressed city woman. Her plain face was almost beautiful as she stood ready for the great event of Amanda's life. At the last moment she thought of the big bush of shrubs in the yard--"I must get me a shrub to smell in the Commencement," she decided. So she gathered one of the queer-looking, fragrant brown blossoms, tied it in the corner of her handkerchief and bruised it gently so that the sweet perfume might be exuded. "Um-ah," she breathed in the odor, "now I'm ready for Millersville."

As she stood with Mrs. Reist and Philip on the front porch waiting for Uncle Amos she said to Mrs. Reist, "Ain't Amanda fixed me up fine? Abody'd hardly know me."

Mrs. Reist in her plain gray Mennonite dress and stiff black silk bonnet was, as usual, an attractive figure. Philip, grown to the dignity of long trousers, carried himself with all the poise of seventeen. He was now a student in the Lancaster High School and had he not learned to dress and act like city boys do! Uncle Amos, in his best Sunday suit of gray, his Mennonite hat in his hand, ambled along last as the little group went down the aisle of the Millersville chapel to see Amanda's graduation.

As Amanda marched in, her red hair parted on the side and coiled into a womanly coiffure, wearing a simple white organdie, she was just one of the hundred graduates who marched into the chapel. But later, as she stood alone on the platform and delivered her oration, "The Flowers of the Garden Spot," she held the interested attention of all in that vast audience. She knew her subject and succeeded in waking in the hearts of her hearers a desire to go out in the green fields and quiet woods and find the lovely habitants of the flower world.

After it was all over and she stood, shining-eyed and happy, among her own people in the chapel, Martin Landis joined them. He, too, had left childhood behind. The serious gravity of his new estate was deepened in his face, but the same tenderness that had soothed the numerous Landis babies also still dwelt there. One of the regrets of his heart was the fact that nature had denied him great stature. He had always dreamed of growing into a tall man, powerful in physique, like Lyman Mertzheimer. But nature was obstinate and Martin Landis reached manhood, a strong, sturdy being, but of medium height. His mother tried to assuage his disappointment by asserting that even if his stature was not great as he wished his heart was big enough to make up for it. He tried to live up to her valuation of him, but it was scant comfort as he stood in the presence of physically big men. Life had not dealt generously with him as with Amanda in the matter of education. He wanted a chance to study at some institution higher than the little school at Crow Hill but his father needed him on the farm. The elder man was subject to attacks of rheumatism and at such times the brunt of farm labor fell upon the shoulders of Martin.

Money was scarce in the Landis household, there were so many mouths to feed and it seemed to Martin that he would never have the opportunity to do anything but work in the fields from early spring to late autumn, snatch a few months for study in a business college in Lancaster, then go back again to the ploughing and arduous duties of his father's farm. He thought enviously of Lyman Mertzheimer, whose father had sent him to a well-known preparatory school and then started him in a full course in one of the leading universities of the country. If he had a chance like that! If he could only get away from the farm long enough to earn some money he knew he could work his way through school and fit himself for some position he would like better than farming. Some such thoughts ran through his brain as he went to congratulate Amanda on her graduation day.

"Oh, Martin!" she greeted him cordially. "So you got here, after all. I'm so glad!"

"So am I. I wouldn't have missed that oration for a great deal. I could smell the arbutus--say, it was great, Amanda!"

At that moment Lyman Mertzheimer joined them.

"Congratulations, Amanda," he said in his affected manner. As the good-looking son of a wealthy man he credited himself with the possession of permissible pride. "Congratulations," he repeated, ignoring the smaller man who stood by the side of the girl. "Your oration was beautifully rendered. You were very eloquent, but if you will pardon me, I'd like to remind you of one flower you forgot to mention--a very important flower of the Garden Spot."

"I did?" she said as though it were a negligible matter. "What was the flower I forgot?"

"Amanda Reist," he said, and laughed at his supposed cleverness.

"Oh," she replied, vexed at his words and his bold attitude, "I left that out purposely along with some of the weeds of the Garden Spot I might have mentioned."

"Meaning me?" He lifted his eyebrows in question. "You don't really mean that, Amanda." He spoke in winning voice. "I know you don't mean that so I won't quarrel with you."

"Well, I guess you better not!" spoke up Millie who had listened to all that was said. "You don't have to get our Amanda cross on this here day. She done fine in that speech and we're proud of her and don't want you nor no one else to go spoil it by any fuss."

"I see you have more than one champion, Amanda. I'll have to be very careful how I speak to you." He laughed but a glare of anger shone in his eyes.

A few moments later the little party broke up and Lyman went off alone. A storm raged within him--"A hired girl to speak to me like that--a common hired girl! I'll teach her her place when I marry Amanda. And Amanda was high and mighty to-day. Thought she owned the world because she graduated from Millersville! As though that's anything! She's the kind needs a strong hand, a master hand. And I'll be the master! I like her kind, the women who have spirit and fire. But she needs to be held under, subjected by a stronger spirit. That little runt of a Martin Landis was hanging round her, too. He has no show when I'm in the running. He's poor and has no education. He's just a clodhopper."

Meanwhile the clodhopper had also said good-bye to Amanda. For some reason he did not stop to analyze, the heart of Martin Landis was light as he went home from the Commencement at Millersville. He had always detested Lyman Mertzheimer, for he had felt too often the snubs and taunts of the rich boy. Amanda's rebuff of the arrogant youth pleased Martin.

"I like Amanda," he thought frankly, but he never went beyond that in the analysis of his feelings for the comrade of his childhood and young boyhood. "I like her and I'd hate to see her waste her time on a fellow like Lyman Mertzheimer. I'm glad she squelched him. Perhaps some day he'll find there are still some desirable things that money can't buy."

CHAPTER VII

AMANDA REIST, TEACHER

Amanda had no desire to teach far from her home. "I want to see the whole United States if I live long enough," she declared, "but I want to travel through the distant parts of it, not settle there to live. While I have a home I want to stay near it. So I wish I could get a school in Lancaster County."

Her wish was granted. There was an opening in Crow Hill, in the little rural school in which she had received the rudiments of her education. Amanda applied for the position and was elected.

She brought to that little school several innovations. Her love and knowledge of nature helped her to make the common studies less monotonous and more interesting. A Saturday afternoon nutting party with her pupils afforded a more promising subject for Monday's original composition than the hackneyed suggestions of the grammar book's "Tell all you know about the cultivation of coffee." Later, snow forts in the school-yard impressed the children with the story of Ticonderoga more indelibly than mere reading about it could have done. During her last year at Normal, Amanda had read about a school where geography was taught by the construction of miniature islands, capes, straits, peninsulas, and so forth, in the school-yard. She directed the older children in the formation of such a landscape picture. When a blundering boy slipped and with one bare foot demolished at one stroke the cape, island and bay, there was much merriment and rivalry for the honor of rebuilding. The children were almost unanimous in their affection for the new teacher and approval of her methods of teaching. Most of them ran home with eager tales concerning the wonderful, funny, "nice" ways Miss Reist had of teaching school.

However, Crow Hill is no Eden. Some of the older boys laughed at the "silly ideas" of "that Manda Reist" and disliked the way she taught geography and made the pupils "play in the dirt and build capes and islands and the whole blamed geography business right in the school-yard."

It naturally followed that adverse criticism grew and grew, like Longfellow's pumpkin, and many curious visitors came to Crow Hill school. The patrons, taxpayers, directors were concerned and considered it their duty to drop in and observe how things were being run in that school. They found that the three R's were still taught efficiently, even if they were taught with the aid of chestnuts, autumn leaves and flowers; they were glad to discover that an island, though formed in the school-yard from dirt and water, was still being defined with the old standard definition, "An island is a body of land entirely surrounded by water."

If any other school had graduated Amanda, her position might have been a trifle precarious, but Millersville Normal School was too well known and universally approved in Lancaster County to admit of any questionable suggestions about its recent graduate. Most of the people who came to inspect came without any antagonistic feeling and they left convinced that, although some of Amanda Reist's ways were a little different, the scholars seemed to know their lessons and to progress satisfactorily.

Later in the school year she urged the children to bring dried corn husk to school, she brought brightly colored raffia, and taught them how to make baskets. The children were clamorous for more knowledge of basket making. The fascinating task of forming objects of beauty and usefulness from homely corn husk and a few gay threads of raffia was novel to them. Amanda was willing to help the children along the path of manual dexterity and eager to have them see and love the beautiful. Under her guidance they gathered and pressed weeds and grasses and the airy, elusive milkweed down, caught butterflies, and assembled the whole under glass, thus making beautiful trays and pictures.

On the whole it was a wonderful, happy year for the new teacher of the Crow Hill school. When spring came with all the alluring witchery of the Garden Spot it seemed to her she must make every one of her pupils feel the thrill of the song-sparrow's first note and the matchless loveliness of the anemone.

One day in early April, the last week of school, as she locked the door of the schoolhouse and started down the road to her home an unusual glow of satisfaction beamed on her face.

"Only two more days of school, then the big Spelling Bee to wind it up and then my first year's teaching will be over! I have enjoyed it but I'm like the children--eager for vacation."

She hummed gaily as she went along, this nineteen-year-old school teacher so near the end of her first year's work in the schoolroom. Her eyes roved over the fair panorama of Lancaster County in early spring dress. As she neared the house she saw her Uncle Amos resting under a giant sycamore tree that stood in the front yard.

"Good times," she called to him.

"Hello, Manda," he answered. "You're home early."

"Early--it's half-past four. Have you been asleep and lost track of the time?"

He took a big silver watch from a pocket and whistled as he looked at it. "Whew! It is that late! Time for me to get to work again. Your Aunt Rebecca's here."

"Dear me! And I felt so happy! Now I'll get a call-down about something or other. I'm ashamed of myself, Uncle Amos, but I think Aunt Rebecca gets worse as she grows older."

"'Fraid so," the man agreed soberly. "Well, we can't all be alike. Too bad, now, she don't take after me, eh, Amanda?"

"It surely is! You're the nicest man I know!"

"Hold on now," he said; "next you make me blush. I ain't used to gettin' compliments."

"But I mean it. I don't see how she can be your sister and Mother's! I think the fairies must have mixed babies when she was little. I can see many good qualities in her, but there's no need of her being so contrary and critical. I remember how I used to be half afraid of her when I was little. She tried to make Mother dress me in a plain dress and a Mennonite bonnet, but Mother said she'd dress me like a little girl and if I chose I could wear the plain dress and bonnet when I was old enough to know what it means. Oh, Mother's wonderful! If I had Aunt Rebecca for a mother--but perhaps she'd be different then. Oh, Uncle Amos, do you remember the howl she raised when we had our house wired for electricity?"

"Glory, yes! She was scared to death to come here for a while."

"And Phil wickedly suggested we scare her again! But she was afraid of it. She was sure the house would be struck by lightning the first thunder-storm we'd have. And when we put the bath tub into the house-- whew! Didn't she give us lectures then! She has no use for 'swimmin' tubs' to this day. If folks can't wash clean out of a basin they must be powerful dirty! That's her opinion."

Both laughed at the remembrance of the old woman's words. Then the girl asked, "What did she have to say to you to-day? Did she iron any wrinkles out of you?"

"Oh, I got it a'ready." The man chuckled. "I was plantin' potatoes till my back was near broke and I came in to rest a little and get a drink. She told me it's funny people got to rest so often in these days when they do a little work. She worked in the fields often and she could stand more yet than a lot o' lazy men. I didn't answer her but I came out here and got my rest just the same. She ain't bossin' her brother Amos yet! But now I got to work faster for this doin' nothin' under the tree."

When Amanda entered the kitchen she found her mother and the visitor cutting carpet rags. Old clothes were falling under the snip of the shears into a peach basket, ready to be sewn together, wound into balls and woven into rag carpet by the local carpet weaver on his hand loom.

"Hello," said the girl as she laid a few books on the kitchen table.

"Books again," sniffed Aunt Rebecca. "I wonder now how much money gets spent for books that ain't necessary."

"Oh, lots of it," answered the girl cheerfully.

"Umph, did you buy those?"

"Yes, when I went to Millersville."

"My goodness, what a lot o' money goes for such things these days! There's books about everything, somebody told me. There's even some wrote about the Pennsylvania Dutch and about that there Stiegel glass some folks make such a fuss about. I don't see nothin' in that Stiegel glass to make it so dear. Why, I had a little white glass pitcher, crooked it was, too, and nothin' extra to look at. But along come one of them anteak men, so they call themselves, the men that buy up old things. Anyhow, he offered to give me a dollar for that little pitcher. Ach, I didn't care much for it, though it was Jonas's granny's still. I sold it to that man quick before he'd change his mind and mebbe only give me fifty cents."

"You sold it?" asked Amanda. "And was it this shape?"

She made a swift, crude sketch of the well-known Stiegel pitcher shape.

"My goodness, you drawed one just like it! It looked like that."

"Then, Aunt Rebecca, you gave that man a bargain. That was a real Stiegel pitcher and worth much more than a dollar!"

"My goodness, what did I do now! You mean it was worth *more* than that?" The woman was incredulous.

"You might have gotten five, perhaps ten, dollars for it in the city. You know Stiegel glass was some of the first to be made in this country, made in Manheim, Pennsylvania, way back in 1760, or some such early date as that. It was crude as to shape, almost all the pieces are a little crooked, but it was wonderfully made in some ways, for it has a ring like a bell, and the loveliest fluting, and some of it is in beautiful blue, green and amethyst. Stiegel glass is rare and valuable so if you have any more hold on to it and I'll buy it from you."

"Well, I guess! I wouldn't leave you pay five dollars for a glass pitcher! But I wish I had that one back. It spites me now I sold it. My goodness, abody can't watch out enough so you won't get cheated. Where did you learn so much about that old glass?"

"Oh, I read about it in a *book* last year," came the ready answer.

Aunt Rebecca looked at the girl, but Amanda's face bore so innocent an expression that the woman could not think her guilty of emphasizing the word purposely.

"So," the visitor said, "they did put something worth in a book once! Well, I guess it's time you learn something that'll help you save money. All the books you got to read! And Philip's still goin' to school, too. Why don't he help Amos on the farm instead of runnin' to Lancaster to school?"

"He wants to be a lawyer," said Mrs. Reist. "I think still that as long as he has a good head for learnin' and wants to go to school I should leave him go till he's satisfied. I think his pop would say so if he was livin'. Not everybody takes to farmin' and it is awful hard work. Amos works that hard."

"Poof," said Aunt Rebecca, "I ain't heard tell yet of any man workin' himself to death! It wouldn't hurt Philip to be a farmer. The trouble is it don't sound tony enough for the young ones these days. Lawyer-- what does he want to be a lawyer for? I heard a'ready that they are all liars. You're by far too easy!"

"Oh, Aunt Rebecca," said Amanda, "not all lawyers are liars. Abraham Lincoln was a lawyer."

"Ach, I guess he was no different from others, only he's dead so abody shouldn't talk about him."

Amanda sighed and turned to her mother. "Mother, I'm going up to put on an old dress and when Phil comes we're going over to the woods for arbutus."

"All right."

But the aunt did not consider it all right. "Why don't you help cut carpet rags?" she asked. "That would be more sense than runnin' out after flowers that wither right aways."

"If we find any, Millie is going to take them to market to-morrow and sell them. Some people asked for them last week. It's rather early but we may find some on the sunny side of the woods."

"Oh," the woman was mollified, "if you're goin' to sell 'em that's different. Ain't it funny anybody *buys* flowers? But then some people don't know how to spend their money and will buy anything, just so it's buyin'!"

But Amanda was off to the wide stairs, beyond the sound of the haranguing voice.

"Glory!" she said to herself when she reached her room. "If my red hair didn't bristle! What a life we'd have if Mother were like that! If I ever think I have nothing to be thankful for I'm going to remember that!"

A little while later she went down the stairs, out through the yard and down the country road to meet her brother. She listened for his whistle. In childhood he had begun the habit of whistling a strain from the old song, "Soldier's Farewell" and, like many habits of early years, it had clung to him. So when Amanda heard the plaintive melody, "How can I leave thee, how can I from thee part," she knew that her brother was either arriving or leaving.

As she walked down the road in the April sunshine the old whistle floated to her. She hastened her steps and in a bend in the road came face to face with the boy.

At sight of her he stopped whistling, whipped off his cap and greeted her, "Hello, Sis. I thought that would bring you if you were about. Oh, don't look so tickled over my politeness--I just took off my hat because I'm hot. This walk from the trolley on a day like this warms you up."

His words brought a light push from the girl as she took her place beside him and they walked on.

"That's a mournful whistle for a home-coming," Amanda told him. "Can't you find a more appropriate one?"

"My repertoire is limited, sister--I learned that big word in English class to-day and had to try it out on some one."

"Phil, you're crazy!" was the uncomplimentary answer, but her eyes smiled with pride upon the tall, red-haired boy beside her. "I see it's one of your giddy days so I'll sober you up a bit--Aunt Rebecca's at the house."

"Oh, yea!" He held his side in mock agony.

"Again? What's the row now? Any curtain lectures?"

"Be comforted, Phil. She's going home to-night if you'll drive her to Landisville."

"Won't I though!" he said, with the average High School boy's disregard of pure English. "Surest thing you know, Sis, I'll drive her home or anywhere else. What's she doing?"

"Helping Mother cut carpet rags."

"Well, that's the only redeeming feature about her. She does help Mother. Aunt Rebecca isn't lazy. I'm glad to be able to say one nice thing about her. Apart from that she's generally as Millie says, 'actin' like she ate wasps.' But she can't scare me. All her ranting goes in one ear and out the other."

"Nothing there to stop it, eh, Phil?"

"Amanda! That from you! Now I know how Caesar felt when he saw Brutus with the mob."

"It's a case of 'Cheer up, the worst is yet to come,' I suppose, so you might as well smile."

In this manner they bantered until they reached the Reist farmhouse. There the boy greeted the visitor politely, as his sister had done.

"My goodness," was the aunt's greeting to him, "you got an armful of books, too!"

"Yes. I'm going to be a lawyer, but I have to do a lot of hard studying before I get that far."

"Umph, that's nothin' to brag about. I'd think more of you if you stayed home and helped Amos plant corn and potatoes or tobacco."

"I'd never plant tobacco. Chewing and smoking are filthy habits and I'd never have the stuff grow on any farm I owned."

"But the money, Philip, just think once of the money tobacco brings! But, ach, it's for no use talkin' farm to you. You got nothin' but books in your head. How do you suppose this place is goin' to be run about ten years from now if Amanda teaches and you turn lawyer? Amos is soon too old to work it and you can't depend on hired help. Then what?"

"Search me," said the boy inelegantly. "But I'm not worrying about it. We may not want to live here ten years from now. But, Mother," he veered suddenly, "got any pie left from dinner? I'm hungry. May I forage?"

"Help yourself, Philip. There's a piece of cherry pie and a slice of chocolate cake in the cellar."

"Hurray, Mother! I'm going to see that you get an extra star in your crown some day for feeding the hungry."

"But you spoil him," said Aunt Rebecca as Phil went off to the cellar. "And if that boy ain't always after pie! I mind how he used to eat pie when he was little and you brought him to see us. Not that I grudged him the pie, but I remember how he always took two pieces if he got it. And pie ain't good for him, neither, between meals."

"I guess it won't hurt him," said Mrs. Reist; "the boy's growin' and he has just a lunch at noon, so he gets hungry till he walks in from the trolley. Boys like pie. His father was a great hand for pie."

"Well," said the aunt decisively, "I would never spoiled children if I had any. But I had none."

"Thank goodness!" Amanda breathed to herself as she went out to the porch to wait for her brother.

"Um, that pie was good," was his verdict as he joined her. "But say, Sis, didn't you hear the squirrels chatter in there?"

"Come on." Amanda laughed as she swung the basket to her arm and pulled eagerly at the sleeve of the boy's coat. "Let's go after the flowers and forget all about her."

Along the Crow Hill schoolhouse runs a long spur of wooded hills skirting the country road for a quarter of a mile and stretching away into denser timberland. In those woods were the familiar paths Amanda and Phil loved to traverse in search of flowers. In April, when the first warm, sunshiny days came, the ground under the dead leaves of the overshadowing oaks was carpeted with arbutus. Eager children soon found those near the crude rail fence, but Amanda and Phil followed the narrow trails to the secluded sheltered spots where the May flowers had not been touched that spring.

"No roots, Phil!" warned the girl as they knelt in the brown leaves and pushed away the covering from the fragrant blossoms.

"Sure thing not, Sis! We don't want to exterminate the trailing arbutus in Crow Hill. Say, I passed two kids this morning as I was going to the trolley. They had a bunch of arbutus, roots and all. Believe me, I acted up like Aunt Rebecca for about two minutes. But it's a shame to take the roots. I almost hate to pick the flowers--seems as if they're at home here in the woods--belong here, in a way."

"I know what you're thinking about, Phil; that little verse:

> 'Hast thou named all the birds without a gun?
> Loved the wood-rose and left it on its stalk?
> Oh, be my friend, and teach me to be thine.'

I agree with the first half of the requirement, but the latter half can't always be followed. At any rate, the wild rose is better left on the stem, for it withers when plucked. But with arbutus it's different. Why, Phil, some of the people who come to market and buy our wild flowers would never see any if they could not buy them in the city. Imagine, if you can, yourself living in a big city, far away from Crow Hill, where the Mayflowers grow--Philadelphia or New York, or some such formidable-sounding place. The city might engross your attention so you'd be happy for months. But along comes spring with its call to the woods and meadows. Still the city and its demands grip you like a vise, and you can't run away to where the wild green things are pushing to the light. Suppose you saw a flower-stand and a tiny bunch of arbutus--"

"I'd pay my last dollar for them!" declared Philip. "Guess you're right. According to your reasoning, we're as good as missionaries when we find wild flowers and take or send them to the city market to sell. Aunt Rebecca wouldn't see that. She'd see the money end of it. Poor soul! I'm glad I'm not like her."

"Pharisee," chided his sister.

"Well, do you know, Manda, sometimes I think there's something to be said in favor of the Pharisee."

The girl gave him a quizzical look.

The serious and the light were so strangely mingled in the boy's nature. Amanda caught many glimpses into the recesses of his heart, recesses he knew she would not try to explore deeper than he wished. For the natures of brother and sister were strongly similar--light-hearted and happy, laughing and gay, keen to enjoy life, but reading some part of its mysteries, understanding some of its sorrows and showing at times evidences of searching thought and grave retrospect.

"How many dollars' worth do we have?" the boy asked in imitation of Aunt Rebecca's mercenary way.

"Oh, Phil! You're dreadful! But I bet the flowers will be gone in no time when Millie puts them out."

"I'd wager they'd go faster if you sold them," he replied, looking admiringly at the girl. "You'd be a pretty fair peddler of flowers, Sis."

"Oh, Phil, be sensible."

"I mean it, Amanda. You're not so bad looking. Your hair isn't common red, it's Titian. And it's fluffy. Then your eyes are good and your complexion lacks the freckles you ought to have. Your nose isn't Grecian, but it'll do--we'll call it retroussé, for that sounds nicer than pug. And your mouth--well, it's not exactly a rosebud one, but it doesn't mar the general landscape like some mouths do. Altogether, you're real good-looking, even if you are my sister."

"Philip Reist, you're impertinent! But I suppose you are truthful. That's a doubtful compliment you're giving me, but I'm glad to say your veracity augurs well for your success as a lawyer. If you are always as honest as in that little speech you just delivered, you'll do."

"Oh, I'll make grand old Abe Lincoln look to his laurels."

And so, with comradely teasing, threaded with a more serious vein, an hour passed and the two returned home with their baskets filled with the lovely pink and white, delicately fragrant, trailing arbutus.

They found the supper ready, Uncle Amos washed and combed, and waiting on the back porch for the summons to the meal.

Mrs. Reist peeped into the basket and exclaimed in joy as she breathed in the sweet perfume of the fresh flowers. Millie paused in the act of pouring coffee into big blue cups to "get a sniff of the smell," but Aunt Rebecca was impatient at the momentary delay. "My goodness, but you poke around. I like to get the supper out before it gets cold."

There was no perceptible hurry at her words, but a few minutes later all were seated about the big table in the kitchen with a hearty supper spread before them.

Uncle Amos was of a jovial, teasing disposition, prone to occasional shrewd thrusts at the idiosyncrasies of his acquaintances, but he held sacred things sacred and rendered to reverent things their due reverence. It was his acknowledged privilege to say grace, at the meals served in the Reist home.

That April evening, after he said, "Amen," Philip turned to Amanda and said, "Polly wants some too."

The girl burst into gay laughter. Everybody at the table looked at her in surprise.

"What's funny?" asked Aunt Rebecca.

"I'll tell you," Phil offered. "Last Saturday we were back at Harnly's. They have two parrots on the porch, and all morning we tried to get those birds to talk. They just sat and blinked at us, looked wise, but said not a word. I forgot all about them when we went in to dinner, but we had just sat down and bowed our heads for grace when those birds began to talk. They went at it as though some person had wound them up. 'Polly wants some dinner; Polly wants some, too. Give Polly some too.' Well, it struck me funny. Their voices were so shrill and it was such a surprise after they refused to say a word, that I got to laughing. I gave Amanda a nudge, and she got the giggles."

"It was awful," said Amanda. "If Phil hadn't nudged me I could have weathered through by biting my lips."

"I don't see anything to laugh about when two parrots talk," was Aunt Rebecca's remark. "Anyhow, that was no time to laugh. I guess you'll remember what I tell you, some day when you got to cry for all this laughin' you do now."

"Ach," said the mother, "let 'em laugh. I guess we were that way too once."

"Bully for you, Mother," cried the boy; "you're as young as any of us."

"That's what," chimed in Millie.

"Oh, say, Millie," asked Philip, "did you make that cherry pie I finished up after school to-day?"

"Yes. Was it good?"

"Good? It melted in my mouth. When I marry, Millie, I'm going to borrow you for a while to come teach my wife how to make such pies."

"Listen at him now! Ain't it a wonder he wouldn't think to get a wife that knows how to cook and bake? But, Philip Reist, you needn't think I'll ever leave your mom unless she sends me off."

"Wouldn't you, now, Millie?" asked Uncle Amos.

"Why, be sure, not! I ain't forgettin' how nice she was to me a'ready. I had hard enough to make through before I came here to work. I had a place to live out in Readin' where I was to get big money, but when I got there I found I was to go in the back way always, even on Sunday, and was to eat alone in the kitchen after they eat, and I was to go to my room and not set with the folks at all. I just wouldn't live like that, so I come back to Lancaster County and heard about you people wantin' a girl, and here I am."

Amanda looked at the hired girl. In her calico dress and gingham apron, her hair combed back plain from her homely face, she was certainly not beautiful, and yet the girl who looked at her thought she appeared really attractive as the gratitude of her loyal heart shone on her countenance.

"Millie's a jewel," thought Amanda. "And Mother's another. I hope I shall be like them as I grow older."

After the supper dishes were washed, Aunt Rebecca decided it was time for her to go home.

"Wouldn't you like to go in the automobile this time?" suggested Philip. "It would go so much faster and is easier riding than the carriage."

"Faster! Well, I guess that horse of yourn can get me anywhere I want to go fast enough to suit me. I got no time for all these new-fangled things, like wagons that run without horses, and lights you put on and off with a button. It goes good if you don't get killed yet with that automobile."

"Then I'll hitch up Bill," said the boy as he went out, an amused smile on his face.

Amanda was thoughtful as she bunched the arbutus for the market next day. "I wonder how Uncle Jonas could live with Aunt Rebecca," she questioned. Ah, that was an enlightening test. "Am I an easy, pleasant person to live with?" Making full allowance for differences in temperament and dispositions, there was still, the girl thought, a possible compatibility that could be cultivated so that family life might be harmonious and happy.

"It's that I am going to consider when I get married, if I ever do," she decided that day. "I won't marry a man who would 'jaw' like Aunt Rebecca. I'm fiery-tempered myself, and I'll have to learn to control my anger better. Goodness knows I've had enough striking examples of how scolding sounds! But I won't want to squabble with the man I really care for--Martin Landis, for instance--" Her thoughts went off to her castles in Spain as she gathered the arbutus into little bunches and tied them. "He offered to help me fix my schoolroom for the Spelling Bee on Saturday. He's got a big heart, my Sir Galahad of childhood." She smiled as she thought of her burned hand and his innocent kiss. "Poor Martin--he's working like a man these ten years. I'd like to see him have a chance at education like Lyman Mertzheimer has. I know he'd accomplish something in the world then! At any rate, Martin's a gentleman and Lyman's a--ugh, I hate the very thought of him. I'm glad he's not at home to come to my Spelling Bee."

CHAPTER VIII

THE SPELLING BEE

The old-fashioned Spelling Bee has never wholly died out in Lancaster County, Pennsylvania. Each year readers of certain small-town papers will find numerous news-titles headed something like this: "The Bees Will Buzz," and under them an urgent invitation to attend a Spelling Bee at a certain rural schoolhouse. "A Good Time Promised"--"Classes for All"--"Come One, Come All"--the advertisements never fail. Many persons walk or ride to the little schoolhouse. The narrow seats, the benches along the wall, and all extra chairs that can be brought to the place are taken long before the hour set for the bees to buzz. The munificent charge is generally fifteen cents, and where in this whole United States of America can so much real enjoyment be secured for fifteen cents as is given at an old-fashioned Spelling Bee?

That April evening of Amanda's Bee the Crow Hill schoolhouse was filled at an early hour. The scholars, splendid in their Sunday clothes, occupied front seats. Parents, friends and interested visitors from near-by towns crowded into the room.

Amanda, dressed in white, came upon the platform and announced that the scholars had prepared a simple program which would be interspersed through the spelling classes.

Vehement clapping of hands greeted her words and then the audience became silent as the littlest scholar of the school rose and delivered the address of welcome. There followed music and more recitations, all amateurish, but they brought feelings of pride to many mothers and fathers who listened, smiling, to "Our John" or "Our Mary" do his or her best.

But the real excitement began with the spelling classes. The first was open to all children under fourteen. At the invitation, boys and girls walked bravely to the front and joined the line till it reached from one side of the room to the opposite. A teacher from a neighboring town gave out the words. The weeding-out process soon began. Some fell down on simple words, others handled difficult ones with ease and spelled glibly through some which many of the older people present had forgotten existed. Soon the class narrowed down to two. Back and forth, back and forth the words rolled until the teacher pronounced one of the old standby catch-words. One of the contestants shook his head, puzzled, and surrendered.

There was more music, several recitations by the children, a spelling class for older people, more music, then a General Information class, whose participants were asked such questions as, "Who is State Superintendent of Schools?" "How many legs has a fly?" "How many teeth has a cow?" "Which color is at the top of the rainbow arch?" The amazed, puzzled expressions on the faces of the questioned afforded much merriment for the others. It was frequently necessary to wait a moment until the laughter was suppressed before other questions could be asked.

A geographical class was equally interesting. "How many counties has Pennsylvania?" sent five persons to their seats before it was answered correctly. Others succeeded in locating such queer names as Popocatepetl, Martinique, Ashtabula, Rhodesia, Orkney, Comanche.

A little later the last spelling class was held. It was open to everybody. The line was already stretched across the schoolroom when Lyman Mertzheimer, home for a few days of vacation, entered the schoolhouse.

"Oh, dear," thought Amanda, "what does he want here? I'd rather do without his fifteen cents! He expects to make a show and win the prize from every one else."

Lyman, indeed, swaggered down the room and entered the line, bearing the old air of superiority. "I'll show them how to spell," he thought as he took his place. Spelling had been his strong forte in the old days of school, and it was soon evident that he retained his former ability. The letters of the most confusing words fell from his lips as though the very pages of the spelling-book were engraved upon his brain. He held his place until the contest had ruled out all but two beside himself. Then he looked smilingly at Amanda and reared his head in new dignity and determination.

"Stelliform, the shape of a star," submitted the teacher. The word fell to Lyman. He was visibly hesitant. Was it stelli or stella?

Bringing his knowledge of Latin into service, he was inclined to think it was stella. He began, "S-t-e-l-l--"

He looked uncertainly at one of his friends who was seated in the front seat. He, also, was a champion speller.

"Oh, if Joe would only help me!" thought the speller.

As if telepathy were possible, Joe raised the forefinger of his left hand to his eye, looked at Lyman with a meaning glance that told him what he craved to know.

"Iform," finished Lyman in sure tones.

"Correct."

"That was clever of Joe," thought the cheat as the teacher gave out a word to one of the three contestants. "I just caught his sign in time. Nobody noticed it."

But he reckoned without the observant teacher of Crow Hill school. Amanda, seated in the front of the room and placed so she half faced the audience and with one little turn of her head could view the spellers, had seen the cheating process and understood its significance. The same trick had been attempted by some of her pupils several times during the monthly spelling tests she held for the training of her classes.

"The cheat! The big cheat!" she thought, her face flushing with anger. "How I hope he falls down on the next word he gets!"

However, the punishment he deserved was not meted out to him. Lyman Mertzheimer outspelled his opponents and stood alone on the platform, a smiling victor.

"The cheat! The contemptible cheat!" hammered in Amanda's brain.

After the distribution of prizes, cheap reprint editions of well-known books, an auctioneer stepped on the platform and drew from a corner a bushel basket of packages of various sizes and shapes.

"Oyez, Oyez," he called in true auctioneer style, "we have here a bushel of good things, all to be sold, sight unseen, to the highest bidder. I understand each package contains something good to eat, packed and contributed by the pupils of this school. The proceeds of the sale are to be used to purchase good books for the school library for the pupils to read. So, folks, bid lively and don't be afraid to run a little risk. You'll get more fun from the package you buy than you've had for a long time, I'll warrant."

With much talk and gesticulation the spirited bidding was kept up until every package was sold. Shouts of joy came from the. country boys when one opened a box filled with ten candy suckers and distributed them among the crowd. Other bidders won candy, cake, sandwiches, and loud was the laughter when a shoe-box was sold for a dollar, opened and found to contain a dozen raw sweet potatoes.

After the fun of the auction had died down all rose and sang "The Star-Spangled Banner," and the Spelling Bee was over.

The audience soon began to leave. Laughing girls and boys started down the dark country roads. Carriages and automobiles carried many away until a mere handful of people were left in the little schoolhouse.

Lyman Mertzheimer lingered. He approached Amanda, exchanged greetings with her and asked, "May I walk home with you? I have something to tell you."

"Oh, I suppose so," she replied, not very graciously. The dishonest method of gaining a prize still rankled in her. Lyman walked about the room impatiently, looking idly at the drawings and other work of the children displayed above the blackboards.

A moment later Martin Landis came up to Amanda. He had been setting chairs in their places, gathering singing-books and putting the room in order.

"Well, Manda," he said, "it was a grand success! Everything went off fine, lots of fun for all. And I heard Hershey, the director, tell his wife that you certainly know how to conduct a Spelling Bee."

"Oh, did he say that?" The news pleased her. "But I'm glad it's over."

"I guess you are. There, we're all fixed up now. I'll send one of the boys over next week with the team to take back the borrowed chairs. I'll walk home with you, Manda. What's Lyman Mertzheimer hanging around for? Soon as those people by the door leave, we can lock up and go."

"Why--Martin--thank you--but Lyman asked to walk home with me."

"Oh! All right," came the calm reply. "I'll see you again. Good-night, Amanda."

"Good-night, Martin."

She looked after him as he walked away, the plumed knight of her castles in Spain. She had knighted him that day long ago when he had put out the fire and kissed her hand, and during the interval of years that childish affection had grown in her heart. In her thoughts he was still "My Martin." But the object of that long-abiding affection showed all too plainly that he was not cognizant of what was in the heart of his childhood's friend. To him she was still "Just Amanda," good comrade, sincere friend.

Fortunately love and hope are inseparable. Amanda thought frequently of the verse, "God above is great to grant as mighty to make, and creates the love to reward the love." It was not always so, she knew, but she hoped it would be so for her. Martin Landis, unselfish, devoted to his people, honest as a dollar, true as steel--dear Martin, how she wanted to walk home with him that night of the Spelling Bee instead of going with Lyman Mertzheimer!

The voice of the latter roused her from her revery. "I say, Amanda, are we going to stay here all night? Why in thunder can't those fools go home so you can lock the door and go! And I say, Amanda, don't you think Martin Landis is letting himself grow shabby and seedy? He's certainly settling into a regular clodhopper. He shuffled along like a hecker to-night. I don't believe he ever has his clothes pressed."

"Martin's tired to-night," she defended, her eyes flashing fire. "He worked in the fields all day, helping his father. Then he and one of his brothers took their team and went after some chairs I wanted to borrow for the Spelling Bee. They arranged the room for me, too."

"Oh, I see. Poor fellow! It must be the very devil to be poor!"

The words angered the girl. "Well," she flared out, "if you want to talk about Martin Landis, you go home. I'll get home without you."

"Now, Amanda," he pleaded sweetly, "don't get huffy, please! I want you in a good humor. I have something great to tell you. Can't you take a bit of joshing? Of course, it's fine in you to defend your old friends. But I didn't really mean to say anything mean about Martin. You do get hot so easily."

"It must be my red-hair-temper," she said, laughing. "I do fly off the handle, as Phil says, far too soon."

"Shall we go now?" Lyman asked as the last lingering visitors left the room.

The lights were put out, the schoolhouse door locked, and Amanda and Lyman started off on the dark country road. Peals of merry laughter floated back to them occasionally from a gay crowd of young people who were also going home from the Spelling Bee. But there were none near enough to hear what most wonderful thing Lyman had to say to Amanda.

"Amanda," he lost no time in broaching the subject, "I said I have something to tell you. I meant, to ask you."

"Yes? What is it?"

"Will you marry me?"

Before the astonished girl could answer, he put his arms about her and drew her near, as though there could be no possibility of an unfavorable reply.

She flung away from him, indignant. "Lyman," she said, with hot anger in her voice, "you better wait once till I say yes before you try that!"

"Why, Amanda! Now, sweetheart, none of that temper! You can't get cross when I ask you anything like that! I want to marry you. I've always wanted it. I picked you for my sweetheart when we were both children. I've always thought you're the dandiest girl I could find. Ever since we were kids I've planned of the time when we were old enough to marry. I just thought to-night, when I saw several fellows looking at you as though they'd like to have you, I better get busy and ask you before some other chap turns your head. I'll be good to you and treat you right, Amanda. Of course, I'm in college yet, but I'll soon be through, and then I expect to get a good position, probably in some big city. We'll get out of this slow country section and live where there's some life and excitement. You know I'll be rich some day, and then you'll have everything you want. Come on, honey, tell me, are we engaged?"

"Well, I should say not!" the girl returned with cruel frankness. "You talk as though I were a piece of furniture you could just walk into a store and select and buy and then own! You've been taking immeasurably much for granted if you have been thinking all those things you just spoke about."

"But what don't you like about me?" The young man was unable to grasp the fact that his loyal love could be unrequited. "I'm decent."

"Well, that's very important, but there's more than that necessary when two persons think of marrying. You asked me,--I'll tell you--I never cared for you. I don't like your principles, your way of sneering at poor people, your laxity in many things--"

"For instance?" he asked.

"For instance: the way you spelled stelliform to-night and won a prize for it."

"Oh, that!" He laughed as though discovered in a huge joke. "Did you see that? Why, that was nothing. It was only a cheap book I got for the prize. I'll give the book back to you if that will square me in your eyes."

"But don't you see, can't you see, it wasn't the cheap book that mattered? It's the thought that you'd be dishonest, a cheat."

"Well," he snatched at the least straw, "here's your chance to reform me. If you marry me I'll be a different person. I'd do anything for you. You know love is a great miracle worker. Won't you give me a chance to show you how nearly I can live up to your standards and ideals?"

Amanda, moved by woman's quick compassion, spurred by sympathy, and feeling the exaltation such an appeal always carries, felt her heart soften toward the man beside her. But her innate wisdom and her own strong hold on her emotions prevented her from doing any rash or foolish thing. Her voice was gentle as she answered, but there was a finality in it that the man should have noted.

"I'm sorry, Lyman, but I can't do as you say. We can't will whom we will love. I know you and I would never be happy together."

"But perhaps it will come to you." He was no easy loser. "I'll just keep on hoping that some day you'll care for me."

"Don't do that. I'm positive, sure, that I'll never love you. You and I were never made for each other."

But he refused to accept her answer as final. "Who knows, Amanda," he said lightly, yet with all the feeling he was capable of at that time, "perhaps you'll love and marry Lyman Mertzheimer yet! Stranger things than that have happened. I'm sorry about that word. It seemed just like a good joke to catch on to the right spelling that way and beat the others in the match. You are too strict, Amanda, too closely bound by the Lancaster County ideas of right and wrong. They are too narrow for these days."

"Oh, no!" she said quickly. "Dishonesty is never right!"

"Well," he laughed, "have it your way! See how docile I have become already! You'll reform me yet, I bet!"

At the door of her home he bade her good-night and went off whistling, feeling only a slight unhappiness at her refusal to marry him. It was, he felt, but a temporary rebuff. She would capitulate some day. His consummate egotism buoyed his spirits and he went down the road dreaming of the day he'd marry Amanda Reist and of the wonderful gowns and jewels he would lavish upon her.

CHAPTER IX

AT THE MARKET

The words of Lyman Mertzheimer lingered with Amanda for many days. He had seemed so confident, so arrogantly sure, of her ultimate surrender to his desire to marry her. Soon after the Spelling Bee he returned to his college and the girl sighed in relief that his presence was not annoying her. But she reckoned without the efficient United States mail service. The rejected lover wrote lengthy, friendly letters which she answered at long intervals by short, impersonal little notes.

"Oh, yea," she said to herself one day, "why does it have to be Lyman Mertzheimer that falls in love with me? But he might as well fall out as soon as he can. I'll never marry him. I read somewhere that one girl said, 'I'd rather love what I cannot have, than have what I cannot love,' and that's just the way I feel about it. I won't marry Lyman Mertzheimer if I have to die Amanda Reist!"

As soon as her school term was ended Amanda entered into the work of the farm. She helped Millie as much as possible in a determined effort to forget all about the man who wanted her and whom she did not want, and, more than that, to think less about her knight, her Sir Galahad, who evidently had no time to waste on girls.

Millie appreciated Amanda's help. "There's one thing sure," she said proudly to Mrs. Reist, "our Amanda ain't lazy. It seems to abody she's workin' more'n ever this here spring. I guess mebbe she thinks she better get all the ins and outs o' housework so as she can do it right till she gets married once."

"Ach, I guess Amanda ain't thinkin' of marryin' yet," said the mother.

"You fool yourself," was Millie's wise answer. "Is there ever a woman born that don't think 'bout it? Women ain't made that way. There ain't one so ugly nor poor, nor dumb, that don't hanker about it sometimes, even if she knows it ain't for her."

Here the entrance of Amanda cut short the discussion.

"Millie," asked the girl, "shall I go to market with you this week?"

"Why, yes. I'd be glad for you. Of course, you always help get things ready here and your Uncle Amos drives me in and helps to get the baskets emptied and the things on the counters, but I could use you in sellin'."

"Then I'll come. This lovely spring weather makes me want to go. I like to see the people come in to buy flowers and early vegetables. It's like reading a page out of a romance to see the expressions on the faces of the city people as they buy the products of the country."

"Ach, I don't know what you mean. I guess you got too much fine learnin' for me. But all I can see in market is people runnin' up one aisle and down the other to see where the onions or radishes is the cheapest."

Amanda laughed. "That's part of the romance. It proves they are human."

The following Saturday Amanda accompanied Millie to the Lancaster market to help dispose of the assortment of farm products the Reist stall always carried.

Going to market in Lancaster is an interesting experience. In addition to the famous street markets, where farmers display their produce along the busy central streets of the city, there are indoor markets where crowds move up and down and buy butter, eggs and vegetables, and such Pennsylvania Dutch specialties as mince meat, cup cheese, sauerkraut, pannhaus, apple butter, fresh sausage and smear cheese. While lovers of flowers choose from the many old-fashioned varieties--straw flowers, zinnias, dahlias.

The Reist stall was one of the prominent stalls of the market. Twice every week Millie "tended market" there. On the day before market several members of the Reist household were kept busy preparing all the produce, and the next day before dawn Uncle Amos hitched the horse to the big covered wagon and he and Millie, sometimes Amanda and Philip, drove over the dark country roads to the city.

Amanda enjoyed the work. She arranged the glistening domes of cup cheese, placed the fresh eggs in small baskets, uncovered one of the bags of dried corn untied the cloth cover from a gray earthen crock of apple butter, and then stood and looked about the market house. She felt the human interest it never failed to waken in her. Behind many stalls stood women in the quaint garb of the Church of the Brethren or Mennonite. But quaintest of all were the Amish.

The Amish are the plainest and quaintest of the plain sects that flourish in Lancaster County. Unlike their kindred sects, who wear plain garb, they are partial to gay colors in dress. So it is no unusual sight to see Amish women wearing dresses of such colors as forest green, royal purple, king's blue or garnet. But the gay dress is always plainly made, after the model of their sect, generally partially subdued by a great black apron, a black pointed cape over the shoulders and a big black bonnet which almost hides the face of its wearer and necessitates a full-face gaze to disclose the identity of the woman. The strings of the thick white lawn cap are invariably tied in a flat bow that lies low on the chest.

The Amish men are equally interesting in appearance. They wear broad-brimmed hats with low crowns. Their clothes are so extremely plain that buttons, universally deemed indispensable, are taboo and their place is filled by the inconspicuous hook-and-eye, which style has brought upon them the sobriquet, "Hook-and-eye people."

However, interesting as the men and women of the Amish faith are in their dress, they are eclipsed in that aspect by the Amish children. These are invariably dressed as exact replicas of their parents. Little boys, mere children of three and four years, wear long trousers, tight jackets, blocked hair and broad-brimmed, low-crowned hats. Little girls of tender years wear brightly colored woolen dresses, one-piece aprons of black sateen or colored chambray, and the picturesque big stiff bonnets of the faith.

A stranger in Lancaster County seeing an Amish family group might easily wonder if he had not been magically transported to some secluded spot of Europe, far from the beaten paths of modernity. But in the cosmopolitan population of Lancaster the Amish awakes a mere moment's interest to the majority of observers. If a bit of envy steals into the heart of the little Amish girl who stands at the Square and sees a child in white organdie and pink sash tripping along with her feet in silk socks and white slippers, of what avail is it? The hold of family customs is strong among them and the world and its allurements and vanities are things to be left stringently alone.

To Amanda Reist, the Amish children made strong appeal. Their presence was one of the reasons she enjoyed tending market. Many stories she wove in her imagination about the little lads in their long trousers and the tiny girls in their big bonnets.

But when the marketing was in full swing Amanda had scant time for any weaving of imaginary stories. Purchasers stopped at the stall and in a short time the produce was sold, with the exception of cheese and eggs which had been ordered the previous week.

"Ach," complained Millie, "now if these people would fetch this cheese and the eggs we'd be done and could go home. Our baskets are all empty but them. But it seems like some of these here city folks can't get to market till eight o'clock. They have to sleep till seven."

She was interrupted by the approach of a young girl, fashionably dressed.

"Why," exclaimed Amanda, "here comes Isabel Souders, one of the Millersville girls."

Isabel Souders was a girl of the butterfly type, made for sunshine, beauty, but not intended, apparently, for much practical use. Like the butterfly, her excuse for being was her beauty. Pretty, with dark hair, Amanda sometimes had envied her during days at the Normal School. Well dressed, petted and spoiled by well-to-do parents who catered to her whims, she seemed, nevertheless, an attractive girl in manner as well as in appearance. At school something like friendship had sprung up between Amanda and the city girl, no doubt each attracted to the other by the very directness of their opposite personalities and tastes.

Isabel Souders was a year younger than Amanda. She lacked all of the latter's ambition. Music and Art and having a good time were the things that engrossed her attention. At Millersville she had devoted her time to the pursuit of the three. Professors and hall teachers knew that the moving spirit of many harmless pranks was Isabel, but she had a way of glossing things, shedding blame without causing innocent ones to suffer, that somehow endeared her to students and teachers alike.

That market day she came laughing down the market aisle to greet Amanda.

"Hello, Amanda! What do you think of me, here at this early hour of the day? Pin a medal on me! But it was so glorious a day I felt like doing something out of the ordinary. I promised one of the Lancaster girls who is at school now that I'd ask you about the pink moccasins. Are they out yet?"

"Just out. Why?"

"This girl wants one for her collection. I remembered you had a perfect one in your lot of flowers at school and I said I'd see you about them."

"They'll be at their best next Saturday."

"Next Saturday--dear, Helen's going home over the week-end. Oh, could I come out and get one for her?"

"Yes. I'll be glad to take you where they grow. I have a special haunt. If no botanizers or flower hunters find my spot, we'll get a beauty for your friend."

"You're the same old darling, Amanda," said the girl sweetly. "Then I'll be out to your house Saturday afternoon. How do I get there?"

"Take the car to Oyster Point, then walk till you find a mail-box with our name on it, and there I'll be found."

"Thank you, Amanda, you are a dear! I'll be there for the pink moccasin. Won't it be romantic to hunt for such lovely things as they are? You're perfectly sweet to bother about it and offer to take me."

"Oh, I don't mind doing that. I'll enjoy it. Finding the wild pink lady-slipper is a real joy."

Unselfish Amanda, she could not dream of what would come out of that little hunt for the pink moccasin!

CHAPTER X

PINK MOCCASINS

The pink moccasin, the largest of our native orchids, is easily the queen of the rare woodland spot in which it grows. Its flower of bright rose pink, veined with red, is held with the stalwart erectness of an Indian, whose love of solitude and quiet woods it shares.

To Amanda it was one of the loveliest flowers of the woods. She always counted the days as the time drew near when the moccasins bloomed.

When Isabel Souders arrived at the Reist farmhouse she found Amanda ready with basket and trowel for the lady-slipper hunt. Amanda had put on a simple white dress and green-and-white sun hat. She looked with bewilderment at the city girl's attire, but said nothing just then. They stopped long enough for Isabel to meet the mistress of the home and then they went down the road to the Crow Hill schoolhouse.

Suddenly Isabel stood still and panted. "Oh--Manda--you *can* run! Have compassion on me. My hair will be all tumbled after such mad walking, and my organdie torn."

"Hair!" echoed the country girl with a laugh. "Who thinks about hair on a moccasin hunt? You should not go flower hunting in city clothes. With your pink and white dress and lovely Dresden sash, silk stockings and low shoes, you look more fit for a dance than a ramble after deep woods flowers, such as moccasins. But we might as well go on now."

She led the way across the school-yard, climbed nimbly over the rail fence and laughed at Isabel's clumsy imitation of her. Pink azaleas grew in great bushes of bloom throughout the woods. Isabel would have stopped to pick some but Amanda said, "That withers easily. Better pick them when we come back."

They followed a narrow path, so narrow that later the summer luxuriant growth of underbrush would almost obliterate it. But Amanda knew the way to her spot. Deeper into the woods they delved, past bowers of pink azalea and closely growing branches of trees whose tender green foliage was breaking into summer growth. The bright May sunshine dripped through the green and dappled the ground in little discs of gold.

Suddenly the path led up-hill in a steep grade. Amanda stopped and leaned against a slender sapling.

"Stand here and look up," she invited.

Isabel obeyed, her gaze traveling searchingly along the steep trail.

"Oh, the beauties!" she cried as she discovered the pink flowers. "The beauties! Oh, there are more of them! And still more! Oh, Amanda!"

Before them was Amanda's haunt of the pink moccasin. From the low underbrush of spring growth rose several dozen gorgeously beautiful pink lady-slippers, each alone on a thick stem with two broad leaves spreading their green beauty near the base. What miracle had brought the rare shy plants so near the dusty road where rattling wagons and gliding automobiles sped on their busy way?

"May I pick them?" asked the city girl.

"Yes, but only one root. I'll dig that up with the trowel. That's for your friend's botany specimen. The rest we'll pull up gently and we'll get flower, stem and leaves and leave the roots in the ground for other years. I never pick all of the flowers. I leave some here in the woods --it seems they belong here and I can't bring myself to walk off with every last one of them in my arms and leave the hill desolate."

"You *are* a queer girl!" was the frank statement of the city girl. "But you're a dear, just the same."

They picked a number of the largest flowers.

"That's enough," Amanda declared.

Isabel laughed. "I'd take every one if it were my haunt."

"And then other people might come here after some and find the place robbed of all its blooms."

"Oh," said the other girl easily, "I look out for Isabel. Now, please, may I pick some of that pretty wild azalea?" she asked teasingly as they came down the hill.

"Help yourself. That isn't rare. You couldn't take all of that if you tried."

So Isabel gathered branches of the pink bloom until her arms were filled with it and the six moccasins in her hand almost overshadowed.

As the two girls reached the edge of the woods and climbed over the fence into the school-yard Martin Landis came walking down the road.

"Hello," he called gaily. "Been robbing the woods, Amanda?"

"Aren't they lovely?" she asked. Then when he drew near she introduced him to the girl beside her.

Martin Landis was not a blind man. A pretty girl, dark-eyed and dusky-haired, her arms full of pink azaleas, her lips parted in a smile above the flowers, and that smile given to him--it was too pretty a picture to fail in making an impression upon him.

Amanda saw the look of keen interest in the eyes of the girl and her heart felt heavy. What fortune had brought the two together? Had the Fates designed the meeting of Isabel and Martin? "Oh, now I've done it!" thought Amanda. "Isabel wants what she wants and generally gets it. Pray heaven, she won't want 'My Martin!'"

Similar thoughts disturbed her as they stepped on the sunny road once more and stood there talking. With a gay laugh Isabel took the finest pink moccasin from her bunch and handed it to Martin. "Here, I'll be generous," she said in friendly tones.

"Thank you, Miss Souders." The reply was accompanied with a smile of pleasure.

A low laugh rippled from the girl's red lips. Amanda's ears tingled so she did not understand the exchange of light talk. The fear and jealousy in her heart dulled her senses to all save them, but she laughed, said good-bye, and hid her feelings as she and Isabel went down the road to the Reist farmhouse.

"Amanda," the other girl said effusively, "what a fine young man! Is he your beau?"

"No. Certainly not! I have no beau. I've known Martin Landis ever since I was born, almost. He lives down the road a piece. He's a nice chap."

"Splendid! Fine! Such eyes, such wonderfully expressive gray eyes I have never seen. And he has such a strong face. Of course, his clothes are a bit shabby. He'd be great if he fixed up."

"Yes," Amanda agreed mechanically. She was ill-pleased with the dissection of her knight.

Mrs. Reist, with true rural, Pennsylvania Dutch hospitality, invited Isabel to have supper with them, an invitation readily accepted. At the close of the meal Isabel said suddenly to Mrs. Reist, "How would you like to have me board with you for a few weeks--a month, probably?"

"Why, I don't know. All right, I guess, if Millie, here, don't think it makes too much work. Poor Millie's got the worst of all the work to do. I ain't so strong, and there's much always to do. Of course, Amanda helps, but none of us do as much as Millie."

"But me, don't I get paid for it, and paid good?" asked the hired girl, sending a loving glance at Mrs. Reist. "Far as I go it's all right to have Isabel come for a while. Mebbe she can help, too, sometimes with the work."

"I wouldn't be much help, I'm afraid. I never peeled a potato in my life."

Millie looked at the girl with slightly concealed disfavor. "Why, that's a funny way, now, to bring up a girl! I guess it's time you learn such things once! You dare come, and I'll show you how to do a little work. But why do you want to board when your folks live just in Lancaster?"

"Father and Mother are going to the Elks' Convention and to California. They expect to be gone about a month. I was going to stay in Lancaster with my aunt, but I just thought how much nicer it would be to spend that time in the country."

"Well, I guess, too!" Millie was quick to understand how one would naturally prefer the country to the city.

So it was settled that Isabel Souders was to spend June at the Reist farmhouse.

Everybody concerned appeared well pleased with the arrangement. But Amanda's heart hurt. "Why did I take her for those moccasins?" she thought drearily after Isabel had gone back to the city with her precious flowers. "I know Martin will fall in love with her and she with him. Oh, I'm a mean, detestable thing! But I wish she'd go to the coast with her parents!"

CHAPTER XI

THE BOARDER

The big automobile that brought Isabel Souders to the Reist farmhouse one day early in June brought with her a trunk, a suitcase, a bag, an umbrella and a green parasol.

Aunt Rebecca was visiting there that day and she followed Amanda to the front door to receive the boarder.

"My goodness," came the exclamation as the luggage was carried in, "is that girl comin' here for good, with all *that* baggage? And what did you let her come here for on a Friday? That's powerful bad luck!"

"For me," thought Amanda as she went to meet Isabel.

"See," the newcomer pointed to her trunk, "I brought some of my pretties along. I'll have to make hay while the sun shines. I'll have to make the most of this opportunity to win the heart of some country youth. Amanda, dear, wouldn't I be a charming farmer's wife? Can you visualize me milking cows, for instance?"

"No," answered Amanda, "I'd say that you were cut out for a different role." There was a deeper meaning in the country girl's words than the flighty city girl could read.

"Just the same," went on the newcomer, "I'm going to have one wonderful time in the country. You are such a dear to want me here and to take me into the family. I want to do just all the exciting things one reads about as belonging to life in the country. I am eager to climb trees and chase chickens and be a regular country girl for a month."

"Then I hope you brought some old clothes," was the practical reply.

"Not old, but plain little dresses for hard wear. I knew I'd need them."

Later, as Amanda watched the city girl unpack, she smiled ruefully at the plain little dresses for hard wear. Her observant eye told her that the little dresses of gingham and linen must have cost more than her own "best dresses." It was a very lavish wardrobe Isabel had selected for her month on the farm. Silk stockings and crepe de chine underwear were matched in fineness by the crepe blouses, silk dresses, airy organdies, a suit of exquisite tailoring and three hats for as many different costumes. The whole outfit would have been adequate and appropriate for parades on the Atlantic City boardwalk or a saunter down Peacock Alley of a great hotel, but it was entirely too elaborate for a Lancaster County farmhouse.

Millie, running in to offer her services in unpacking, stood speechless at the display of clothes. "Why," she almost stammered, "what in the world do you want with all them fancy things here? Them's party clothes, ain't?"

"No." Isabel shook her head. "Some are to wear in the evening and the plainer ones are afternoon dresses, and the linen and gingham ones are for morning wear."

"Well, I be! What don't they study for society folks! A different dress for every time of the day! What would you think if you had to dress like I do, with my calico dress on all day, only when I wear my lawn for cool or in winter a woolen one for warm?"

Millie went off, puzzled at the ways of society.

"Is she just a servant?" asked Isabel when they heard her heavy tread down the stairs.

"She isn't *just* anything! She's a jewel! Mother couldn't do without Millie. We've had her almost twenty years. We can leave everything to her and know it will be taken care of. Why, Millie's as much a part of the family as though she really belonged to it. When Phil and I were little she was always baking us cookies in the shape of men or birds, and they always had big raisin eyes. Millie's a treasure and we all think of her as being one of the family."

"Mother says that's just the reason she won't hire any Pennsylvania Dutch girls; they always expect to be treated as one of the family. We have colored servants. You can teach them their place."

"I see. I suppose so," agreed Amanda, while she mentally appraised the girl before her and thought, "Isabel Souders, a little more democracy wouldn't be amiss for you."

Although the boarder who came to the Reist farmhouse was unlike any of the members of the family, she soon won her way into their affections. Her sweet tenderness, her apparent childlike innocence, appealed to the simple, unsuspicious country folk. Shaping her actions in accordance with the old Irish saying, "It's better to have the dogs of the street for you than against you," Isabel made friends with Millie and went so far as to pare potatoes for her at busy times. Philip and Uncle Amos were non-committal beyond a mere, "Oh, I guess she's all right. Good company, and nice to have around."

The first Sunday of the boarder's stay in the country she invited herself to accompany the family to Mennonite church. Amanda appeared in a simple white linen dress and a semi-tailored black hat, but when Isabel tripped down the stairs the daughter of the house was quite eclipsed. Isabel's dark hair was puffed out becomingly about cheeks that had added pink applied to them. In an airy orchid organdie dress and hat to match, white silk stockings and white buckskin pumps, she looked ready for a garden party. According to all the ways of human nature more than one little Mennonite maid in that meeting-house must have cast sidelong glances at the beautiful vision, and older members of the plain sect must have thought the old refrain, "Vanity, vanity, all is vanity!"

Aunt Rebecca was at church that morning and came to the Reist home for dinner. She sought out Millie in the kitchen and gave her unsolicited, frank opinion--"My goodness, I don't think much of that there Isabel from Lancaster! She's too much stuck up. Such a get-up for a Sunday and church like she has on to-day! She looks like a regular peacock. It'll go good if she don't spoil our Amanda yet till she goes home."

"Ach, I guess not. She's a little fancier than I like to see girls, but then she's a nice girl and can't do Amanda no hurt."

"She means herself too big, that's what! And them folks ain't the right kind for Amanda to know. It might spite you all yet for takin' her in to board. Next thing she'll be playin' round with some of the country boys here, and mebbe take one that Amanda would liked to get. There's no trustin' such gay dressers. I found that out long a'ready."

"Ach," said Millie, "I guess Amanda don't like none of the boys round here in Crow Hill."

"How do you know? Guess Amanda ain't no different from the rest of us in petticoats. You just wait once and see how long it goes till the boys commence to hang round this fancy Isabel."

Millie hadn't long to wait. Through Mrs. Landis, who had been to Mennonite church and noticed a stranger with the Reist family, Martin Landis soon knew of the boarder. That same evening he dressed in his best clothes. He had not forgotten the dark eyes of Isabel smiling to him over the pink azaleas.

"Where you goin', Mart?" asked his mother. "Over to Landisville to church?"

"No--just out for a little while."

"Take me with," coaxed the littlest Landis, now five years old and the ninth in line.

"Ach, go on!" spoke up an older Landis boy, "what d'you think Mart wants with you? He's goin' to see his girl. Na, ah!" he cried gleefully and clapped his hands, "I guessed it! Look at him blushin', Mom!"

Martin made a grab for the boy and shook him. "You've got too much romantic nonsense in your head," he told the teasing brother. "Next thing you know you'll be a poet!" He released the squirming boy and rubbed a finger round the top of his collar as he turned to his mother.

"I'm just going down to Reists' a while. I met Miss Souders a few weeks ago and thought it would be all right for me to call. The country must seem quiet to her after living in the city."

"Of course it's all right, Martin," agreed his mother. "Just you go ahead."

But after he left, Mrs. Landis sat a long while on the porch, thinking about her eldest boy, her first-born. "He's goin' to see that doll right as soon as she comes near, and yet Amanda he don't go to see when she's alone, not unless he wants her to go for a walk or something like that. If only he'd take to Amanda! She's the nicest girl in Lancaster County, I bet! But he looks right by her. This pretty girl, in her fancy clothes and with her flippy ways--I know she's flippy, I watched her in church--she takes his eye, and if she matches her dress she'll go to his head like hard cider. Ach, sometimes abody feels like puttin' blinders on your boys till you get 'em past some women."

A little later the troubled mother walked back to the side porch, where her husband was enjoying the June twilight while he kept an eye on four of the younger members of the family as they were quietly engaged in their Sabbath recreation of piecing together picture puzzles.

"Martin," she said as she sat beside the man, "I've been thinkin' about our Mart."

"Yes? What?"

"Why, I feel we ain't doin' just right by him. You know he don't like farmin' at all. He's anxious to get more schoolin' but he ain't complainin'. He wants to fit himself so he can get in some office or bank in the city and yet here he works on the farm helpin' us like he really liked to do that kind of work. Now he's of age, and since Walter and Joe are big enough to help you good and we're gettin' on our feet a little since the nine babies are out of the dirt, as they say still, why don't we give Martin a chance once?"

"Well, why not? I'm agreed, Ma. He's been workin' double, and when I'm laid up with that old rheumatism he runs things good as I could. We got the mortgage paid off now. How'd it be if we let him have the tobacco money? I was thinkin' of puttin' in the electric lights and fixin' things up a little with it, but if you'd rather give it to Mart--"

"I would. Much rather! I used oil lamps this long and I guess I can manage with them a while yet."

"All right, but as soon as we can we'll get others. Mart's young and ought to have his chance, like you say. I don't know what for he'd rather sit over a lot o' books in some hot little office or stand in a stuffy bank and count other people's money when he could work on a farm and be out in the open air, but then we ain't all alike and I guess it's a good thing we ain't. We'll tell him he dare have time for goin' to Lancaster to school if he wants. Mebbe he'll be a lawyer or president some day, ain't, Ma?"

"Ach, Martin, I don't think that would be so much. I'd rather have my children just plain, common people like we are. Mart's gone up to Reists' this evening."

"So? To see Amanda, I guess."

"Her or that boarder from Lancaster."

"That ruffly girl we saw this morning?"

"Yes."

"Ach, don't you worry, Ma. Our Mart won't run after that kind of a girl! Anyhow, not for long."

At that moment the object of their discussion was approaching the Reist farmhouse. The entire household, Millie included, sat on the big front porch as the caller came down the road.

"Look," said Philip, and began to sing softly. "Here comes a beau a-courting, a-courting---"

"Phil!" chided Millie and Amanda in one breath.

"Don't worry, Sis," said the irrepressible youth, "we'll gradually efface ourselves, one by one--we're very thoughtful. I'll flip a penny to see whether Isabel stays or you. Heads you win, tails she does."

"Phil!"

The vehement protest from his sister did not deter the boy from tossing the coin, which promptly rolled off the porch and fell into a bed of geraniums.

"See," he continued, "even the Fates are uncertain which one of you will win. I suppose the battle's to the strongest this time. Oh, hello, Martin," he said graciously as the caller turned in at the gate, "Nice day, ain't it?"

"What ails the boy?" asked Martin, laughing as he raised his hat and joined the group on the porch.

"Martin," said Amanda after he had greeted Isabel and took his place on a chair near her, "you'd do me an everlasting favor if you'd turn that brother of mine up on your knees and spank him."

"Now that I'd like to see!" spoke up Millie.

"You would, Millie? You'd like to see me get that? After all the coal I've carried out of the cellar for you, and the other ways I've helped make your burden lighter--you'd sit and see me humiliated! Ingratitude! Even Millie turns against me. I'm going away from this crowd where I'm not appreciated."

"Oh, you needn't affect such an air of martyrdom," his sister told him. "I know you have a book half read; you want to get back to that."

"Say," said Uncle Amos, "these women, if they don't beat all! They ferret all the weak spots out a man. I say it ain't right."

Later in the evening the older members of the household left the porch and the trio of eternal trouble--two girls and a man--were left alone. It was then the city girl exerted her most alluring wiles to be entertaining. The man had eyes and ears for her only. As Mrs. Landis once said, he looked past Amanda and did not see her. She sat in the shadow and bit her lip as her plumed knight paid court before the beauty and charm of another. The heart of the simple country girl ached. But Isabel smiled, flattered and charmed and did it so adeptly that instead of being obnoxious to the country boy it thrilled and held him like the voice of a Circe. They never noticed Amanda's silence. She could lean back in her chair and dream. She remembered the story of Ulysses and his wax-filled ears that saved him from the sirens; the tale of Orpheus, who drowned their alluring voices by playing on his instrument a music sweeter than theirs--ah, that was her only hope! That somewhere, deep in the heart of the man she loved was a music surpassing in sweetness the music of the shallow girl's voice which now seemed to sway him to her will. "If he is a man worth loving," she thought, "he'll see through the surface glamour of a girl like that." It was scant consolation, for she knew that only too frequently do noble men give their lives into the precarious keeping of frivolous, butterfly women.

"Why so pensive?" the voice of Isabel pierced her revery.

"Me--oh, I haven't had a chance to get a word in edgewise."

"I was telling Mr. Landis he should go on with his studies. A correspondence course would be splendid for him if he can't get away from the farm for regular college work."

"I'm going to write about that course right away," Martin said. "I'm glad I had this talk with you, Miss Souders. I'll do as you suggest-- study nights for a time and then try to get into a bank in Lancaster. It is so kind of you to offer to see your father about a position. I'd feel in my element if I ever held a position in a real bank. I'll be indebted to you for life."

"Oh," she disclaimed any credit, "your own merits would cause you to make good in the position. I am sure Father will be glad to help you. He has helped several young men to find places. All he asks in return is that they make good. I know you'd do that."

When Martin Landis said good-night his earnest, "May I come again-- soon?" was addressed to Isabel. She magnanimously put an arm about Amanda before she replied, "Certainly. We'll be glad to have you."

"Oh," thought Amanda, "I'll be hating her pretty soon and then how will I ever endure having her around for a whole month! I'm a mean, jealous cat! Let Martin Landis choose whom he wants--I should worry!"

She said good-night with a stoical attempt at indifference, thereby laying the first block of the hard, high barricade she meant to build about her heart. She would be no child to cry for the moon, the unattainable. If her heart bled what need to make a public exhibition of it! From that hour on the front porch she turned her back on her gay, merry, laughing girlhood and began the journey in the realm of womanhood, where smiles hide sorrows and the true feelings of the heart are often masked.

The determination to meet events with dignity and poise came to her aid innumerable times during the days that followed. When Martin came to the Reist farmhouse with the news that his father was going to give him money for a course in a Business School in Lancaster it was to Isabel he told the tidings and from her he received the loudest handclaps.

The city girl, rosy and pretty in her morning dresses, ensconced herself each day on the big couch hammock of the front porch to wave to Martin Landis as he passed on his way to the trolley that took him to his studies in the city. Sometimes she ran to the gate and tossed him a rose for his buttonhole. Later in the day she was at her post again, ready to ask pleasantly as he passed, "Well, how did school go to-day?" Such seemingly spontaneous interest spurred the young man to greater things ahead.

Many evenings Martin sat on the Reist porch and he and Isabel laughed and chatted and sometimes half-absent-mindedly referred a question to Amanda. Frequently that young lady felt herself to be a fifth wheel and sought some diversion. Excuses were easy to find; the most palpable one was accepted with calm credulity by the infatuated young people.

One day, when three weeks of the boarder's stay were gone, Lyman Mertzheimer came home from college, bringing with him a green roadster, the gift of his wealthy, indulgent father.

He drew up to the Reist house and tooted his horn until Amanda ran into the yard to discover what the noise meant.

"Good-morning, Lady Fair!" he called, laughing at her expression of surprise. "I thought I could make you come! Bump of curiosity is still working, I see. Wait, I'm coming in," he called after her as she turned indignantly and moved toward the house.

"Please!" He called again as she halted, ashamed to be so lacking in cordiality. "I want to see you. That's a cold, cruel way to greet a fellow who's just come home from college and rushes over to see you first thing."

He entered the yard and Amanda bade him, "Come up. Sit down," as she took a chair on the porch. "So you're back for the summer, Lyman."

"Yes. Aren't you delighted?" He smiled at her teasingly. "I'm back to the 'sauerkraut patch' again. Glory, I wish Dad would sell out and move to some decent place."

"Um," she grunted, refraining from speech.

"Yes. I loathe this Dutch, poky old place. The only reason I'm glad to ever see it again is because you live here. That's the only excuse I have to be glad to see Lancaster County. And that reminds me, Amanda, have you forgotten what I told you at the Spelling Bee? Do you still feel you don't want to tackle the job of reforming me? Come, now," he pleaded, "give a fellow a bit of hope to go on."

"I told you no, Lyman. I don't change my mind so easily."

"Oh, you naughty girl!" came Isabel's sweet voice as she drifted to the porch. "I looked all over the house for you, Amanda, and here I find you entertaining a charming young man."

Isabel was lovely as usual. Amanda introduced Lyman to her and as the honeyed words fell from the lips of the city girl the country girl stood contemplating the pair before her. "That's the first time," she thought, "I was glad to hear that voice. I do wish those two would be attracted to each other. They match in many ways."

Lyman Mertzheimer was not seriously attracted to Isabel, but he was at times a keen strategist and the moment he saw the city girl an idea lodged in his brain.

Here was a pretty girl who could, no doubt, easily be made to accept attentions from him. By Jove, he'd make Amanda jealous! He'd play with Isabel, shower attentions upon her until Amanda would see what she missed by snubbing a Mertzheimer!

The following week was a busy one for Isabel. Lyman danced attendance every day. He developed a sudden affection for Lancaster County and took Isabel over the lovely roads of that Garden Spot. They visited the Cloister at Ephrata, the museum of antiques at Manheim, the beautiful Springs Park at Lititz, the interesting, old-fashioned towns scattered along the road. Over state highways they sped along in his green roadster, generally going like Jehu, furiously. The girl enjoyed the riding more than the society of the man. He was exulting in the thought that he must be peeving Amanda.

Nevertheless, at the end of Isabel's visit, Lyman was obliged to acknowledge to himself, "All my fooling round with the other girl never phased Amanda! Kick me for a fool! I'll have to think up some other way to make her take notice of me."

Martin Landis came in for the small portion those days. How could he really enjoy his evenings at the Reist house when Lyman Mertzheimer sat there like an evil presence with his smirking smile and his watchful eyes ever open! Some of the zest went out of Martin's actions. His exuberance decreased. It was a relief to him when the boarder's parents returned from their trip and the girl went home. He had her invitation to call at her home in Lancaster. Surely, there Lyman would not sit like the black raven of Poe's poem! Isabel would not forget him even when she was once more in the city! Martin Landis was beginning to think the world a fine old place, after all. He was going to school, had prospects of securing a position after his own desires, thanks to Isabel Souders, he had the friendship of a talented, charming city girl--what added bliss the future held for him he did not often dream about. The present held enough joy for him.

CHAPTER XII

UNHAPPY DAYS

That September Amanda went back to her second year of teaching at Crow Hill. She went bearing a heavy heart. It was hard to concentrate her full attention on reading, spelling and arithmetic. She needed constantly to summon all her will power to keep from dreaming and holding together her tottering castles in Spain.

From the little Landis children, pupils in her school, she heard unsolicited bits of gossip about Martin--"Our Mart, he's got a girl in Lancaster."

"Oh, you mustn't talk like that!" Amanda interrupted, feeling conscience stricken.

"Ach, that don't matter," came the frank reply; "it ain't no secret. Pop and Mom tease him about it lots of times. He gets all dressed up still evenings and takes the trolley to Lancaster to see his girl."

"Perhaps he goes in on business."

"Business--you bet not! Not every week and sometimes twice a week would he go on business. He's got a girl and I heard Mom tell Pop in Dutch that she thinks it's that there Isabel that boarded at your house last summer once. Mom said she wished she could meet her, then she'd feel better satisfied. We don't want just anybody to get our Mart. But I guess anybody he'd pick out would be all right, don't you, Aman--I mean, Miss Reist?"

"Yes, I guess so--of course she would," Amanda agreed.

One winter day Martin himself mentioned the name of Isabel to Amanda. He stopped in at the Reist farm, seeming his old friendly self. "I came in to tell you good news," he told Amanda.

"Now what?" asked Millie, who was in the room with Mrs. Reist and Amanda.

"I've been appointed to a place in the bank at Lancaster."

"Good! I'm so glad, Martin!" cried the girl with genuine interest and joy. "It's what you wanted, isn't it?"

"Yes. But I would never have landed it so soon if it hadn't been for Mr. Souders, Isabel's father. He's influential in the city and he helped me along. Now it's up to me to make good."

"You'll do that, I'm sure you will!" came the spontaneous reply.

Martin looked at the bright, friendly face of Amanda. "Why," he thought, "how pleased she is! She's a great little pal." For a moment the renewed friendliness of childhood days was awakened in him.

"Say, Amanda," he said, "we haven't had a good tramp for ages. I've been so busy with school"--he flushed, thinking of the city girl to whom he had been giving so much of his time--"and--well, I've been at it pretty hard for a while. Now I'll just keep on with my correspondence work but I'll have a little more time. Shall we take a tramp Sunday afternoon?"

"If you want to," the girl responded, her heart pounding with pleasure.

Amanda dressed her prettiest for that winter tramp. She remembered Queen Esther, who had put on royal apparel to win the favor of the king. The country girl, always making the most of her good features and coloring, was simply, yet becomingly dressed when she met Martin in the Reist sitting-room. In her brown suit, little brown hat pulled over her red hair, a brown woolly scarf thrown over her shoulders, she looked like a creature of the woodland she loved.

That walk in the afternoon sunshine which warmed slightly the cold, snowy earth, was a happy one to both. Some of the old comradeship sprang up, mushroom-like, as they climbed the rail fence and entered the woods where they had so often sought wild flowers and birds' nests. Martin spoke frankly of his work and his ambition to advance. Amanda was a good listener, a quality always appreciated by a man. When he had told his hopes and aspirations to her he began to take interest in her affairs. Her school, funny incidents occurring there, her basket work with the children--all were talked about, until Amanda in dazed fashion brushed her hand across her eyes and wondered whether Isabel and her wiles was all an hallucination.

But the subject came round all too soon. They were speaking of the Victrola recently purchased for the Crow Hill school when Martin asked, "Have you ever heard Isabel Souders play?"

"Yes, at Millersville. She often played at recitals."

"She's great! Isn't she great at a piano! She's been good enough to invite me in there. Sometimes she plays for me. The first time she played ragtime but I told her I hate that stuff. She said she's versatile, can please any taste. So now she entertains me with those lovely, dreamy things that almost talk to you. She's taught me to play cards, too. I haven't said anything about it at home, they wouldn't understand. Mother and Father still consider cards wicked. I dare say it wouldn't be just the thing for Mennonites to play cards, but I fail to see any harm in it."

"No--but your mother would be hurt if she knew it."

"She won't know it. I wouldn't do anything wrong, but Mother doesn't understand about such things. The only place I play is at Isabel's home. It's an education to be taken into a fine city home like theirs and treated as an equal."

"An equal! Why, Martin Landis, you are an equal! If a good, honest country boy isn't as good as a butterfly city girl I'd like to know who is! Aren't your people and mine as good as any others in the whole world? Even if the men do eat in their shirt sleeves and the women can't tell an oyster fork from a salad one." The fine face of the girl was flushed and eager as she went on, "Of course, these days young people should learn all the little niceties of correct table manners so they can eat anywhere and not be embarrassed. But I'll never despise any middle-aged or old people just because they eat with a knife or pour coffee into a saucer or commit any other similar transgression. It's a matter of man-made style, after all. When our grannies were young the proper way to do was to pour coffee into the saucers. Why, we have a number of little glass plates made just for the purpose of holding the cup after the coffee had been poured into the saucer. The cup-plates saved the cloth from stains of the drippings on the cup. I heard a prominent lecturer say we should not be so quick to condemn people who do not eat as we think they should. He said, apropos of eating with a knife or, according to present usage, with a fork, that it's just a little matter of the difference between pitching it in or shoveling it in."

Martin laughed. "There's nothing of the snob about you, is there? I believe you see the inside of people without much looking on the exterior."

"I hope so," she said. "Shall we turn back now? I'm cold."

She was cold, but it was an inward reaction from the joy of being with Martin again. His words about Isabel and his glad recounting of the hours he spent with her chilled the girl. She felt that he was becoming more deeply entangled in the web Isabel spun for him. To the country girl's observant, analytical mind it seemed almost impossible that a girl of Isabel's type could truly love a plain man like Martin Landis or could ever make him happy if she married him.

"It's just one more conquest for her to boast about," Amanda thought. "Just as the mate of the Jack-in-the-pulpit invites the insects to her honey and then catches them in a hopeless trap, so women like Isabel play with men like Martin. No wonder the root of the Jack-in-the-pulpit is bitter--it's symbolic of the aftermath of the honeyed trap."

Worried, unhappy though she was, Amanda's second year of teaching was, in the opinion of the pupils, highly successful. Some of the wonder-thoughts of her heart she succeeded in imparting to them in that little rural school. As she tugged at the bell rope and sent the ding-dong pealing over the countryside with its call that brought the children from many roads and byways she felt an irresistible thrill pulsating through her. It was as if the big bell called, "Here, come here, come here! We'll teach you knowledge from books, and that rarer thing, wisdom. We'll teach you in this little square room the meaning of the great outside world, how to meet the surging tide of the cities and battle squarely. We'll show you how to carry to commerce and business and professional life the honesty and wholesomeness and sincerity of the country. We'll teach you that sixteen ounces make a pound and show you why you must never forget that, but must keep exalted and unstained the high standards of courage and right."

Some world-old philosophical conception of the insignificance of her own joys and sorrows as compared with the magnitude of the earth and its vast solar system came to her at times.

"My life," she thought, "seems so important to me and yet it is so little a thing to weep about if my days are not as full of joy as I want them to be. I must step out from myself, detach myself and get a proper perspective. After all, my little selfish wants and yearnings are so small a portion of the whole scheme of things.

'For all that laugh, and all that weep
And all that breathe are one
Slight ripple on the boundless deep
That moves, and all is gone.'"

Looking back over the winter months of that second year of teaching Amanda sometimes wondered how she was able to do her work in the schoolroom acceptably. But the strain of being a stoic left its marks upon her.

"My goodness," said Aunt Rebecca one day in February when a blizzard held her snowbound at the Reist farmhouse, "that girl must be doin' too much with this teachin' and basket makin' and who knows what not! She looks pale and sharp-chinned. Ain't you noticed?" she asked Mrs. Reist.

"I thought last week she looked pinched and I asked if she felt bad but she said she felt all right, she was just a little bit tired sometimes. I guess teachin' forty boys and girls ain't any too easy, Becky."

"My goodness, no! I'd rather tend hogs all day! But why don't you make a big crock of boneset tea and make her take a good swallow every day? There's nothin' like that to build abody up. She looks real bad--you don't want her to go in consumption like that Ellie Hess over near my place."

"Oh, mercy no! Becky, how you scare abody! I'll fix her up some boneset tea to-day yet. I got some on the garret that Millie dried last summer."

Amanda protested against the boneset but to please her mother she promised to swallow faithfully the doses of bitter tea. She thought whimsically as she drank it, "First time I knew that boneset tea is good for an aching heart. Boneset tea--it isn't that I want! I'm afraid I'm losing hold of my old faith in the ultimate triumph of sincerity and truth. Seems that men, even men like Martin Landis, don't want the old-fashioned virtues in a woman. They don't look for womanly qualities, but prefer to be amused and entertained and flattered and appealed to through the senses. Brains and heart don't seem to count. I wish I could be a butterfly! But I can never be like Isabel. When she is near I feel like a bump-on-a-log. My tongue is like lead while she chatters and holds the attention of Martin. She compels attention and crowds out everybody else. Oh, yea! as we youngsters used to say when things went wrong when we were little. Perhaps things will come out right some day. I'll just keep on taking that boneset tea!"

CHAPTER XIII

THE TROUBLE MAKER

If "Hell hath no fury like a woman scorned" a man spurned in love sometimes runs a close second.

One day in March Lyman Mertzheimer came home for the week-end. His first thought was to call at the Reist home.

Amanda, outwardly improved--Millie said, "All because of that there boneset tea"--welcomed spring and its promise, but she could not extend to Lyman Mertzheimer the same degree of welcome.

"It's that Lyman again," Millie reported after she had opened the door for the caller. "He looks kinda mad about something. What's he hangin' round here for all the time every time he gets home from school when abody can easy see you don't like him to come?"

"Oh, I don't know. He just drops in. I guess because we were youngsters together."

"Um, mebbe," grunted Millie wisely to herself as Amanda went to see her visitor. "I ain't blind and neither did I come in the world yesterday. That Lyman's wantin' to be Amanda's beau and she don't want him. Guess he'll stand watchin' if he gets turned down. I never did like them Mertzheimers--all so up in the air they can hardly stand still to look at abody."

Lyman was standing at the window, looking out gloomily. He turned as Amanda came into the room.

"I had to come, Amanda--hang it, you keep a fellow on pins and needles! You wouldn't answer my letters--"

"I told you not to write."

"But why? Aren't you going to change your mind? I made up my mind long ago that I'd marry you some day and a Mertzheimer is a good deal like a bulldog when it comes to hanging on."

"Lyman, why hash the thing over so often? I don't care for you. Go find some nice girl who will care for you."

"Um," he said dejectedly, "I want you. I thought you just wanted to be coaxed, but I'm beginning to think you mean it. So you don't care for me--I suppose you'd snatch Martin Landis in a hurry if you could get him! But he's poor as a church mouse! You better tie him to your apron strings--that pretty Souders girl from Lancaster is playing her cards there--"

Amanda sprang to her feet. "Lyman," she sputtered--"you--you better go before I make you sorry you said that."

The luckless lover laughed, a reckless, demoniac peal. "Two can play at that game!" he told her. "You're so high and mighty that a Mertzheimer isn't good enough for you. But you better look out--we've got claws!"

The girl turned and went out of the room. A moment later she heard the front door slammed and knew that Lyman had gone. His covert threat-- what did he mean? What vengeance could he wreak on her? Oh, what a complicated riddle life had grown to be! She remembered Aunt Rebecca's warning that tears would have to balance all the laughter. How she yearned for the old, happy childhood days to come back to her! She clutched frantically at the quickly departing joy and cheerfulness of that far-off past.

"I'm going to keep my sense of humor and my faith in things in spite of anything that comes to me," she promised herself, "even if they do have to give me boneset tea to jerk me up a bit!" She laughed at Millie's faith in the boneset tea. "I hope it also takes the meanness and hate out of my heart. Why, just now I hate Lyman! If he really cared for me I'd feel sorry for him, but he doesn't love me, he just wants to marry me because long ago he decided he would do so some day."

In spite of her determination to be philosophical and cheerful, the memory of Lyman's threat returned to her at times in a baffling way. What could he mean? How could he harm her? His father was a director of the Crow Hill school, but pshaw! One director couldn't put her out of her place in the school!

Lyman Mertzheimer had only a few days to carry out the plan formulated in his angry mind as he walked home after the tilt with Amanda.

"I'll show her," he snorted, "the disagreeable thing! I'll show her what can happen when she turns down a Mertzheimer! The very name Mertzheimer means wealth and high standing! And she puts up her nose and tosses her red head at me and tells me she won't have me! She'll see what a Mertzheimer can do!"

The elder Mertzheimer, school director, was not unlike his son. When the young man came to him with an exaggerated tale of the contemptible way Amanda had treated him, thrown him over as though he were nobody, Mr. Mertzheimer, Senior, sympathized with his aggrieved son and stormed and vowed he'd see if he'd vote for that red-headed snip of a teacher next year. The Reists thought they were somebody, anyhow, and they had no more money than he had, perhaps not so much. What right had she to be ugly to Lyman when he did her the honor to ask her to marry him? The snip! He'd show her!

"But one vote won't keep her out of the school," said Lyman with diplomatic unconcern.

"Leave it to me, boy! I'll talk a few of them over. There was some complaint last year about her not doing things like other school-teachers round here, and her not being a strict enough teacher. She teaches geography with a lot of dirt and water. She has the young ones scurrying round the woods and fields with nets to catch butterflies. And she lugs in a lot of corn husk and shows them how to make a few dinky baskets and thinks she's doing some wonderful thing. For all that she draws her salary and gets away with all that tomfoolery--guess because she can smile and humbug some people--them red-headed women are all like that, boy. She's not the right teacher for Crow Hill school and I'm going to make several people see it. Then let her twiddle her thumbs till she gets a place so near home and as nice as the Crow Hill school!"

Mr. Mertzheimer, whose august dignity had been unpardonably offended, lost no time in seeing the other directors of the Crow Hill school. He mentioned nothing about the real grievance against Amanda, but played upon the slender string of her inefficiency, as talked about by the patrons. He presented the matter so tactfully that several of the men were convinced he spoke from a deep conviction that the interests of the community were involved and that in all fairness to the pupils of that rural school a new, competent teacher should be secured for the ensuing term. One director, being a man with the unfortunate addiction of being easily swayed by the opinions of others, was readily convinced by the plausible arguments of Mr. Mertzheimer that Amanda Reist was utterly unfit for the position she held.

When all the directors had been thus casually imbued with antagonism, or, at least, suspicion, Mr. Mertzheimer went home, chuckling. He felt elated at the clever method he had taken to uphold the dignity of his son and punish the person who had failed to rightly respect that dignity. In a few weeks the County Superintendent of Schools would make his annual visit to Crow Hill, and if "a bug could be put in his ear" and he be influenced to show up the flaws in the school, everything would be fine! "Fine as silk," thought Mr. Mertzheimer. He knew a girl near Landisville who was a senior at Millersville and would be glad to teach a school like Crow Hill. He'd tell her to apply for the position. It would take about five minutes to put out that independent Amanda Reist and vote in the other girl--it just takes some people to plan! He, Mr. Mertzheimer, had planned it! Probably in his limited education he had never read that sententious line regarding what often happens to the best laid plans of mice and men!

The Saturday following Mr. Mertzheimer's perfection of his plans Millie came home from market greatly excited.

"Manda, Manda, come here once!" she called as she set her empty baskets on the kitchen table. "Just listen," she said to the girl, who came running. "I heard something to-day! That old Mertzheimer--he--he--oh, yea, why daren't I swear just this once! I'm that mad! That old Mertzheimer and the young one ought to be tarred and feathered!"

"Why, Millie!" said Amanda, smiling at the unwonted agitation of the hired girl. "What's happened?"

"Well, this mornin' two girls came to my stall and while they was standin' there and I waited on some other lady, they talked. One asked the other if she was goin' to teach next year, and what do you think she said--that a Mr. Mertzheimer had told her to apply for the Crow Hill school, that they wanted a new teacher there for another year! I didn't say nothin' to them or let on that I know the teacher of that school, but I thought a heap. So, you see, that sneakin' man is goin' to put you out if he at all can do it. And just because you won't take up with that pretty boy of his! Them Mertzheimer people think they own whole Crow Hill and can run everybody in it to suit themselves."

"Yes--I see." Amanda's face was troubled. "That's Lyman's work." The injustice of the thing hurt her. "Of course, I can get another school, but I like Crow Hill, I know the children and we get along so well, and it's near home----"

"Well," came Millie's spirited question, "surely you ain't goin' to let Mertzheimers do like they want? I don't believe in this foldin' hands and lookin' meek and leavin' people use you for a shoe mat! Here, come in once till I tell you somethin'," she called as Mrs. Reist, Philip and Uncle Amos came through the yard. She repeated her account of the news the strangers had unwittingly imparted to her at market.

"The skunk," said Philip.

"Skunk?" repeated Uncle Amos. "I wouldn't insult the little black and white furry fellow like that! A skunk'll trot off and mind his own business if you leave him alone, and, anyhow, he'll put up his tail for a danger signal so you know what's comin' if you hang around."

"Well, then," said the boy, "call him a snake, a rattlesnake."

"And that's not quite hittin' the mark, either. A rattlesnake rattles before he strikes. I say mean people are more like the copperhead, that hides in the grass and leaves that are like its own color, and when you ain't expectin' it and without any warnin', he'll up and strike you with his poison fangs. What are you goin' to do about it, Amanda?"

"Do? I'll do nothing. What can I do?"

"You might go round and see the directors and ask them to vote for you," suggested Millie. "I wouldn't let them people get the best of me --just for spite now I wouldn't!"

"I won't ask for one vote!" Amanda was decided in that. "The men on the board have had a chance to see how the school is run, and if it doesn't please them, or if they are going to have one man rule them and tell them how to vote--let them go! I'll hand in my application, that's all I'll do."

"What for need you be so stiff-headed?" asked Millie sadly. "It'll spite us all if they put you out and you go off somewheres to teach. Ach, abody wonders sometimes why some people got to be so mean in this world."

"It is always that way," said Mrs. Reist gently. "There are weeds everywhere, even in this Garden Spot. Why, I found a stalk of deadly nightshade in my rosebed last summer."

"Wheat and chaff, I guess," was Uncle Amos's comment.

"But, Amanda," asked Millie, "ain't there some person over the directors, boss over them?"

"Just the County Superintendent, and he's not really boss over them. He comes round to the schools every year and the directors come with him and, of course, if he blames a teacher they hear it, and if he praises one they hear it."

"Um--so--I see," said Millie.

CHAPTER XIV

THE COUNTY SUPERINTENDENT'S VISIT

The annual visit of the County Superintendent of Schools always carries with it some degree of anxiety for the teacher. Sometimes the visit comes unexpectedly, but generally the news is sent round in some manner, and last minute polish and coachings are given for the hour of trial. The teacher, naturally eager to make a creditable showing, never knows what vagaries of stupidity will seize her brightest pupils and cause them to stand helpless and stranded as she questions them in the presence of the distinguished visitor and critic.

The Superintendent came to the Crow Hill school on a blustery March day of the sort that blows off hats and tries the tempers of the sweetest natured people. Amanda thought she never before lived through hours so long as those in which she waited for the visitors. But at length came the children's subdued, excited announcement, "Here they come!" as the grind of wheels sounded outside the windows. A few minutes later the hour was come--the County Superintendent and the directors, Mr. Mertzheimer in the lead, stepped into the little room, shook hands with the teacher, then seated themselves and waited for Amanda to go on with her regular lessons and prove her efficiency.

Amanda, stirred by the underhand workings of Mr. Mertzheimer, was on her mettle. She'd just show that man she could teach! Two years' experience in handling rural school classes came to her support. With precision, yet unhurried, she conducted classes in geography, grammar, reading, arithmetic, some in beginners' grades and others in the advanced classes.

She saved her trump card for the last, her nature class, in which the children told from the colored pictures that formed a frieze above the blackboard, the names of fifty native birds and gave a short sketch of their habits, song or peculiarities.

After that the pupils sang for the visitors. During that time the eyes of the Superintendent traveled about the room, from the pressed and mounted leaves and flowers on the walls to the corn-husk and grass baskets on a table in the rear of the room.

When the children's part was ended came the time they loved best, that portion of the visit looked forward to each year, the address of the County Superintendent. He was a tall man, keen-eyed and kindly, and as he stood before the little school the eyes of every child were upon him--he'd be sure to say something funny before he sat down--he always did!

"Well, boys and girls, here we are again! And, as the old Pennsylvania Dutch preacher said, 'I'm glad that I can say that I'm glad that I'm here.' "He rattled off the words in rapid Pennsylvania Dutch, at which the children laughed and some whispered, "Why, he can talk the Dutch, too!" Then they listened in rapt attention as the speaker went on:

"Last year my hour in this schoolroom was one of the high-lights of my visits to the rural schools of the county. So I expected big things from you this year, and it gives me great pleasure to tell you that I am not disappointed. I might go farther and tell you the truth--I am more than pleased with the showing of this school. I listened attentively while all the classes were in session, and your answers showed intelligent thinking and reasoning. You had a surprise for me in that bird class. I like that! It's a great idea to learn from colored pictures the names of our birds, for by so doing you will be able to identify them readily when you meet them in the fields and woods. No lover of birds need fear that one of you will rob a bird's nest or use a sling-shot on a feathered neighbor. You show by your stories about the birds that a proper regard and appreciation for them has been fostered in you by your teacher. You all know that it has long been acknowledged that 'An honest confession is good for the soul,' so I'm going to be frank and tell you that as Miss Reist pointed to the birds there were thirty out of the fifty that I did not know. I have learned something of great value with you here to-day, and I promise you that I'm going to buy a book and study about them so that when I come to see you next year I'll know every one of your pictures. You make me feel ashamed of my meagre knowledge of our feathered neighbors on whom, indirectly, our very existence depends.

"I made mention last year about your fine work in basketry, and am glad to do so again. I like your teacher's idea of utilizing native material, corn husk, dried grasses and reeds, all from our own Garden Spot, and a few colored strands of raffia from Madagascar, and forming them into baskets. This faculty of using apparently useless material and fashioning from it a useful and beautiful article is one of our Pennsylvania Dutch heritages and one we should cherish and develop.

"I understand there has been some adverse criticism among a few of the less liberal patrons of the community in regard to the basket work and nature study Miss Reist is teaching. Oh, I suppose we must expect that! Progress is always hampered by sluggish stupidity and contrariness. We who can see into the future and read the demands of the times must surely note that the children must be taught more than the knowledge contained between the covers of our school books. The teacher who can instil into the hearts of her pupils a feeling of kinship with the wild creatures of the fields and woods, who can waken in the children an appreciation of the beauty and symmetry of the flowers, even the weeds, and at the same time not fail in her duty as a teacher of arithmetic, history, and so forth, is a real teacher who has the proper conception of her high calling and is conscientiously striving to carry that conception into action.

"Directors, let me make this public statement to you, that in Miss Reist you have a teacher well worthy of your heartiest cooperation. The danger with us who have been out of school these thirty years or more is that we expect to see the antiquated methods of our own school days in operation to-day. We would have the schools stand still while the whole world moves.

"I feel it is only just to commend a teacher's work when it deserves commendation, as I consider it my duty to point out the flaws and name any causes for regret I may discover in her teaching. In this school I have found one big cause for regret---"

The hard eyes of Mr. Mertzheimer flashed. All through the glowing praise of the County Superintendent the schemer had sat with head cast down and face flushed in mortification and anger. Now his head was erect. Good! That praise was just a bluff! That red-head would get a good hard knock now! Good enough for her! Now she'd wish she had not turned down the son of the leading director of Crow Hill school! Perhaps now she'd be glad to accept the attentions of Lyman. Marriage would be a welcome solution to her troubles when she lost her position in the school so near home. The Superintendent was not unmindful of that "flea in his ear," after all.

"I have found one cause for regret," the speaker repeated slowly, "one big cause."

His deep, feeling voice stopped and he faced the school while the hearts of pupils and teacher beat with apprehension.

"And that regret is," he said very slowly so that not one word of his could be lost, "that I have not a dozen teachers just like Miss Reist to scatter around the county!"

Amanda's lips trembled. The relief and happiness occasioned by the words of the speaker almost brought her to tears. The children, appreciating the compliment to their teacher, clapped hands until the little room resounded with deafening noise.

"That's good," said the distinguished visitor, smiling, as the applause died down. "You stick to your teacher like that and follow her lead and I am sure you will develop into men and women of whom Lancaster County will be proud."

After a few more remarks, a joke or two, he went back to his seat with the directors. Mr. Mertzheimer avoided meeting his eyes. The father of Lyman Mertzheimer, who had been so loud in his denunciation of the tomfoolery baskets and dried weeds, suddenly developed an intense interest in a tray of butterflies and milkweed.

In a few minutes it was time for dismissal. One of the older girls played a simple march on the little organ and the scholars marched from the room. With happy faces they said good-bye, eager to run home and tell all about the visit of the County Superintendent and the things he said.

As the visitors rose to go the County Superintendent stepped away from the others and went to Amanda.

"You have been very kind," she told him, joy showing in her animated face.

"Honor to whom honor is due, Miss Reist," he said, with that winning smile of approval so many teachers worked to win. "I have here a little thing I want you to read after we leave. It is a copy of a letter you might like to keep, though I feel certain the writer of it would feel embarrassed if told of your perusal of it. I want to add that I should have felt the same and made similar remarks to-day if I had not read that letter, but probably I should not have expressed my opinion quite so forcibly. Keep the letter. I intend to keep the original. It renews faith in human nature in general. It makes me feel anew how good a thing it is to have a friend. Good-bye, Miss Reist. I have enjoyed my visit to Crow Hill school, I assure you."

Amanda looked at him, wondering. What under the sun could he mean? Why should she read a letter written to him? She smiled, shook the hand he offered, but was still at a loss to understand his words. The directors came up to say good-bye. Mr. Mertzheimer bowed very politely but refrained from meeting her eyes as he said, "Good-afternoon." The other men did not bow but they added to their good-bye, "I'm going to vote for you. We don't want to lose you."

Amanda's heart sang as the two carriages rolled away and she was left alone in the schoolroom. She had seen the device of the wicked come to naught, she gloried in the fact that the mean and unfair was once more overbalanced by the just and kind. After the tribute from the County Superintendent and the promises from all the directors but Mr. Mertzheimer she felt assured that she would not be ignominiously put out of the school she loved. Then she thought of the letter and opened it hastily, her eyes traveling fast over the long sheet.

"Dear Mister,

Maybe it ain't polite to write to you when you don't know me but I got a favor to ask you and I don't know no other way to do it. Amanda Reist is teacher of the Crow Hill school and she is a good one, everybody says so but a few old cranks that don't know nothing. There's one of the directors on the school board has got a son that ain't worth a hollow bean and he wants Amanda should take him for her beau. She's got too much sense for that, our Amanda can get a better man than Lyman Mertzheimer I guess. But now since she won't have nothing to do with him he's got his pop to get her out her school. The old man has asked another girl to ask for the job and he's talked a lot about Amanda till some of the other directors side with him. He's rich and a big boss and things got to go his way. Most everybody says Amanda's a good teacher, the children run to meet her and they learn good with her. I heard her say you was coming to visit the school soon and that the directors mostly come with you and I just found out where you live and am writing this to tell you how it is. Perhaps if you like her school and would do it to tell them directors so it would help her. It sometimes helps a lot when a big person takes the side of the person being tramped on. Amanda is too high strung to ask any of the directors to stick to her. She says they can see what kind of work she does and if they want to let one man run the school board and run her out she'll go out. But she likes that school and it's near her home and we'd all feel bad if she got put out and went off somewheres far to teach. I'm just the hired girl at her house but I think a lot of her. I will say thanks very much for what you can do.

And oblige,

AMELIA *Hess.*

P. S. I forgot to say Amanda don't know I have wrote this. I guess she wouldn't leave me send it if she did."

Tears of happiness rolled down the girl's face as she ended the reading of the letter. "The dear thing! The loyal old body she is! So that was why she borrowed my dictionary and shut herself up in her room one whole evening! Just a hired girl she says--could any blood relative do a kinder deed? Oh, I don't wonder he said it renews faith in human nature! I guess for every Mertzheimer there's a Millie. I'll surely keep this letter but I won't let her know I have any idea about what she did. I'm so glad he gave it to me. It takes the bitter taste from my mouth and makes life pleasant again. Now I'll run home with the news of the Superintendent's visit and the nice things he said."

She did run, indeed, especially when she reached the yard of her home. By the time the gate clicked she was near the kitchen door. Millie was rolling out pies, Mrs. Reist was paring apples.

"Mother," the girl twined an arm about the neck of the white-capped woman and kissed her fervently on the cheek, "I'm so excited! Oh, Millie," she treated the astonished woman to the same expression of love.

"What now?" said Millie. "Now you got that flour all over your nice dress. What ails you, anyhow?"

"Oh, just joy. The Superintendent was here and he puffed me way up to the skies and the directors, all but Mr. Mertzheimer, promised to vote for me. I didn't ask them too, either."

"I'm so glad," said Mrs. Reist.

"Ach, now ain't that nice! I'm glad," said Millie, her face bright with joy. "So he puffed you up in front of them men? That was powerful nice for him to do, but just what you earned, I guess. I bet that settled the Mertzheimer hash once! That County man knows his business. He ain't goin' through the world blind. What all did he say?"

"Oh, he was lovely. He liked the baskets and the classes and the singing and--everything! And Mr Mertzheimer looked madder than a setting hen when you take her off the nest. He hung his head like a whipped dog."

"Na-ha!" exulted Millie. "That's one time that he didn't have his own way once! I bet he gets out of the school board if he can't run it."

Her prediction came true. Mr. Mertzheimer's dignity would not tolerate such trampling under foot. If that red-headed teacher was going to keep the school he'd get out and let the whole thing go to smash! He got out, but to his surprise, nothing went to smash. An intelligent farmer, more amenable to good judgment, was elected to succeed him and the Crow Hill school affairs went smoothly. In due time Amanda Reist was elected by unanimous vote to teach for the ensuing year and the Mertzheimers, thwarted, nursed their wrath, and sat down to think of other avenues of attack.

CHAPTER XV

"MARTIN'S GIRL"

If the securing of the coveted school, the assurance of the good will and support of the patrons and directors, and the love of the dear home folks was a combination of blessings ample enough to bring perfect happiness, then Amanda Reist should have been in that state during the long summer months of her vacation. But, after the perverseness of human nature, there was one thing lacking, only one--her knight, Martin Landis.

During the long, bright summer days Amanda worked on the farm, helped Millie faithfully, but she was never so busily occupied with manual labor that she did not take time now and then to sit idly under some tree and dream, adding new and wonderful turrets to her golden castles in Spain.

She remembered with a whimsical, wistful smile the pathetic Romance of the Swan's Nest and the musing of Little Ellie--

"I will have a lover,
Riding on a steed of steeds;
He shall love me without guile,
And to him I will discover
The swan's nest among the reeds.
"And the steed shall be red-roan,
And the lover shall be noble"--

and so on, into a rhapsody of the valor of her lover, such as only a romantic child could picture. But, alas! As the dream comes to the grand climax and Little Ellie, "Her smile not yet ended," goes to see what more eggs were with the two in the swan's nest, she finds,

"Lo, the wild swan had deserted,
And a rat had gnawed the reeds!"

Was it usually like that? Amanda wondered. Were reality and dreams never coincident? Was the romance of youth just a pretty bubble whose rainbow tints would soon be pierced and vanish into vapor? Castles in Spain--were they so ethereal that never by any chance could they--at least some semblance to them--be duplicated in reality?

"I'll hold on to my castles in Spain!" she cried to her heart. "I'll keep on hoping, I won't let go," she said, as though, like Jacob of old, she were wrestling for a blessing.

Many afternoons she brought her sewing to the front porch and sat there as Martin passed by on his way home from the day's work at Lancaster. His cordial, "Hello" was friendly enough but it afforded scant joy to the girl who knew that all his leisure hours were spent with the attractive Isabel Souders.

Martin was friendly enough, but that was handing her a stone when she wanted bread.

One June morning she was working in the yard as he went by on his way to the bank. A great bunch of his mother's pink spice roses was in his arm. He was earlier, too, than usual. Probably he was taking the flowers to Isabel.

"Hello," he called to the girl. "You're almost a stranger, Amanda."

He was not close enough to see the tremble of her lips as she called back, "Not quite, I hope."

"Well, Mother said this morning that she has not seen you for several weeks. You used to come down to play with the babies but now your visits are few and far between. Mother said she misses you, Amanda. Why don't you run down to see her when you have time?"

"All right, Martin, I will. It is some time since I've had a good visit with your mother. I'll be down soon."

"Do, she'll be glad," he said and went down the road to the trolley.

"Almost a stranger," mused the girl after he was gone. Then she thought of the old maid who had answered a query thus, "Why ain't I married? Goodness knows, it ain't my fault!" Amanda's saving sense of humor came to her rescue and banished the tears.

"Guess I'll run over to see Mrs. Landis a while this afternoon. It is a long time since I've been there. I do enjoy being with her. She's such a cheerful person. The work and noise of nine children doesn't bother her a bit. I don't believe she knows what nerves are."

That afternoon Amanda walked down the country road, past the Crow Hill schoolhouse, to the Landis farm. As she came to the barn-yard she heard Emma, the youngest Landis child, crying and an older boy chiding, "Ah, you big baby! Crying about a pinched finger! Can't you act like a soldier?"

"But girls--don't be soldiers," said the hurt child, sobbing in childish pain.

Amanda appeared on the scene and went to the grassy slope of the big bank barn. There she drew the little girl to her and began to comfort her. "Here, let Amanda kiss the finger."

"It hurts, it hurts awful, Manda," sniffed the child.

"I know it hurts. A pinched finger hurts a whole lot. You just cry a while and by that time it will stop hurting." She began to croon to the child the words of an old rhyme she had picked up somewhere long ago:

"Hurt your finger, little lassie?
Just you cry a while!

For some day your heart will hurt
And then you'll have to smile.

Time enough to be a stoic
In the coming years;
Blessed are the days when pain
Is washed away by tears."

By the time the verse was ended the child's attention had been diverted from the finger to the song and the smiles came back to the little face.

"Now," said Amanda, "we'll bathe it in the water at the trough and it will be entirely well."

"And it won't turn into a pig's foot?"

"Mercy, no!"

"Charlie said it would if I didn't stop cryin'."

"But you stopped crying, you know, before it could do that. Charlie'll pump water and we'll wash all nice and clean and go in to Mother."

Water from the watering trough in the barn-yard soon effaced the traces of tears and a happy trio entered the big yard near the house. An older boy and Katie Landis came running to meet them.

"Oh, Amanda," said Katie, "did you come once! Just at a good time, too! We're gettin' company for supper and Mom was wishin' you'd come so she could ask you about settin' the table. We're goin' to eat in the room to-night,'stead of the kitchen like we do other times. And we're goin' to have all the good dishes and things out and a bouquet in the middle of the table when we eat! Ain't that grand? But Pop, he told Mom this morning that if it's as hot to-night as it was this dinner he won't wear no coat to eat, not even if the Queen of Sheba comes to our place for a meal! But I guess he only said that for fun, because, ain't, the Queen of Sheba was the one in the Bible that came to visit Solomon?"

"Yes."

"Well, she ain't comin' to us, anyhow. It's that Isabel from Lancaster, Martin's girl, that's comin'."

"Oh!" Amanda halted on her way across the lawn. "What time is she coming?" she asked in panicky way, as though she would flee before the visitor arrived.

"Ach, not for long yet! We don't eat till after five. Martin brings her on the trolley with him when he comes home from the bank."

"Then I'll go in to see your mother a while." A great uneasiness clutched at the girl's heart. Why had she come on that day?

But Mrs. Landis was glad to see her. "Well, Amanda," she called through the kitchen screen, "you're just the person I said I wished would come. Come right in.

"Come in the room a while where it's cool," she invited as Amanda and several of the children entered the kitchen. "I'm hot through and through! I just got a short cake mixed and in the stove. Now I got nothin' special to do till it's done. I make the old kind yet, the biscuit dough. Does your mom, too?"

"Yes."

"Ach, it's better, too, than this sweet kind some people make. I split it and put a lot of strawberries on it and we eat it with cream."

"Um, Mom," said little Charlie, "you make my mouth water still when you talk about good things like that. I wish it was supper-time a'ready."

"And you lookin' like that!" laughed the mother, pointing to his bare brown legs and feet and his suit that bore evidence of accidental meetings with grass and ground.

"Did they tell you, Amanda," she went on placidly, as she rocked and fanned herself with a huge palm-leaf fan, "that we're gettin' company for supper?"

"Yes--Isabel."

"Yes. Martin, he goes in to see her at Lancaster real often and he's all the time talkin' about her and wantin' we should meet her. She has him to supper--ach, they call it dinner--but it's what they eat in the evening. I just said to his pop we'll ask her out here to see us once and find out what for girl she is. From what Martin says she's a little tony and got money and lots of fine things. You know Martin is the kind can suit himself to most any kind of people. He can make after every place he goes, even if they do put on style. So mebbe she thinks Martin's from tony people, too. But when she comes here she can see that we're just plain country people. I don't put no airs on, but I did say I'd like to have things nice so that she can't laugh at us, for I'd pity Martin if she did that. Mebbe you know how to set the things on the table a little more like they do now. It's so long since I ate any place tony. I said we'd eat in the room, too, and not in the kitchen. We always eat in the kitchen for it's big and handy and nice and cool with all the doors and windows open. But I'll carry things in the room to-night. It will please Martin if we have things nice for his girl."

"Um-huh, Martin's got a girl!" sang Charlie gleefully.

"Yes," spoke up Johnny, a little older and wiser than Charlie. "I know he's got a girl. He's got a big book in his room and I seen him once look in it and pick up something out of it and look at it like it was something worth a whole lot. I sneaked in after he went off and what d'you think it was? Nothing at all but one of them pink lady-slippers we find in the woods near the schoolhouse! He pressed it in that book and acted like it was something precious, so I guess his girl give it to him."

Amanda remembered the pink lady-slipper. She had seen Isabel give it to Martin that spring day when the city girl's glowing face had smiled over the pink azaleas, straight into the eyes of the country boy.

"Charlie," chided Mrs. Landis, "don't you be pokin' round in Martin's room. And don't you tell him what you saw. He'd be awful put out. He don't like to be teased. Ach, my," she shook her head and smiled to Amanda, "with so many children it makes sometimes when they all get talkin' and cuttin' up or scrappin'."

"But it's a lively, merry place. I always like to come here."

"Do you, now? Well, I like to have you. I often say to Martin that you're like a streak of sunshine comin' on a winter day, always so happy and full of fun, it does abody good to have you around. Ach"--in answer to a whisper from the six-year-old baby, "yes, well, go take a few cookies. Only put the lid on the crock tight again so the cookies will keep fresh. Now I guess I better look after my short cake once. Mister likes everything baked brown. Then I guess we'll set the table if you don't mind tellin' me a little how."

"I'll be glad to."

While Mrs. Landis went up-stairs to get her very best table-cloth Amanda looked about the room with its plain country furnishings, its hominess and yet utter lack of real artistry in decoration. Her heart rebelled. What business had a girl like Isabel Souders to enter a family like the Landis's? She'd like to bet that the city girl would disdain the dining-room with its haircloth sofa along one wall and its organ in one corner, its quaint, silk-draped mantel where two vases of Pampas grass hobnobbed with an antique pink and white teapot and two pewter plates; its lack of buffet or fashionable china closet, its old, low-backed, cane-seated walnut chairs round a table, long of necessity to hold plates for so large a family.

"Here it is, the finest one I got. That's one I got yet when I went housekeepin'. I don't use it often, it's a little long for the kitchen table." Mrs. Landis proudly exhibited her old linen table-cloth. "Now then, take hold."

In a few minutes the cloth was spread upon the table and the best dishes brought from a closet built into the kitchen wall.

"How many plates?" asked Amanda.

"Why, let's count once. Eleven of us and Isabel makes twelve and--won't you stay, too, Amanda?"

"Oh, no! I'd make thirteen," she said, laughing.

"Ach, I don't believe in that unlucky business. You can just as well stay and have a good time with us. You know Isabel."

"Yes, I know her. But really, I can't stay. I must get home early. Some other time I'll stay."

"All right, then, but I'd like it if you could be here."

"I'll put twelve plates on the table."

"What I don't know about is the napkins, Amanda. We used to roll them up and put them in the tumblers and then some people folded them in triangles and laid them on the plates, but I don't know if that's right now. Mine are just folded square."

"That's right. I'll place them to the side, so. And the forks go here and the knives and spoons to this side."

"Well, don't it beat all? They lay the spoons on the table now? What for is the spoon-holder?"

"Gone out of style."

"Well, that's funny. I guess when our Mary gets a little older once, she'll want to fix things up, too. I don't care if she does, so long as she don't want to do dumb things and put on a lot of airs that ain't fittin' to plain people like us. But it'll be a big wonder to me if one of the children won't say something about the spoons bein' on the table-cloth. That's new to them. Then I need three glass dishes for jelly so none will have to reach so far for it. And a big platter for fried ham, a pitcher for the gravy, a dish for smashed potatoes, one for sweet potatoes, a glass one for cabbage slaw and I guess I ought to put desserts out for the slaw, Amanda. I hate when gravy and everything gets mixed on the plate. Then I'm going to have some new peas and sour red beets and the short cake. I guess that's enough."

"It sounds like real Lancaster County food," said the girl. "Your company should enjoy her supper."

"Ach, I guess she will. Now I must call in some of the children and get them started dressin' once."

She stood at the screen door of the kitchen and rang a small hand bell. Its tintinnabulation sounded through the yard and reached the ears of the children who were playing there. The three boys next in age to Martin were helping their father in the fields, but the other children came running at the sound of the bell.

"Time to get dressed," announced Mrs. Landis. "You all stay round here now so I can call you easy as one gets done washin'. Johnny, you take Charlie and the two of you get washed and put on the clothes I laid on your bed. Then you stay on the porch so you don't get dirty again till supper and the company comes. Be sure to wash your feet and legs right before you put on your stockings."

"Aw, stockings!" growled Charlie. "Why can't we stay barefooty?"

"For company?"

"Ach," he said sulkily as he walked to the stairs, "I don't like the kind of company you got to put stockings on for! Not on week-days, anyhow!"

His mother laughed. "Emma," she addressed one of the girls, "when the boys come back you and Mary and Katie must get washed and dressed for the company. Mary, you dare wear your blue hair-ribbons today and the girls can put their pink ones on and their white dresses."

"Oh," the little girls cried happily. Dressing up for company held more pleasure for them than it did for the boys.

"I laugh still," said Mrs. Landis, "when people say what a lot of work so many children make. In many ways, like sewing and cookin' for them they do, but in other ways they are a big help to me and to each other. If I had just one now I'd have to dress it, but with so many they help the littler ones and all I got to do is tell them what to do. It don't hurt them to work a little. Mary is big enough now to put a big apron on and help me with gettin' meals ready. And the boys are good about helpin' me, too. Why, Martin, now, he used to help me like a girl when the babies were little and I had a lot to do. Mister said the other day we dare be glad our boys ain't give us no trouble so far. But this girl of Martin's, now, she kinda worries me. I said to Mister if only he'd pick out a girl like you."

To her surprise the face of the girl blanched. Mrs. Landis thought in dismay, "Now what for dumb block am I, not to guess that mebbe Amanda likes our Martin! Ach, my! but it spites me that he's gone on that city girl! Well," she went on, talking in an effort at reparation and in seeming ignorance of the secret upon which she had stumbled, "mebbe he ain't goin' to marry her after all. These boys sometimes run after such bright, merry butterfly girls and then they get tired of them and pick out a nice sensible one to marry. Abody must just keep on hopin' that everything will turn out right. Anyhow, I don't let myself worry much about it."

"Do you ever worry, Mrs. Landis? I can't remember ever seeing you worried and borrowing trouble."

"No, what's the use? I found out long ago that worry don't get you nowhere except in hot water, so what's the use of it?"

"That's a good way to look at things if you can do it," the girl agreed. "I think I'll go home now. You don't need me. You'll get along nicely, I'm sure."

"Ach, yes, I guess so. But now you must come soon again, Amanda. This company business kinda spoiled your visit to-day."

Amanda was in the rear of the house and did not see the vision of loveliness which passed the Reist farmhouse about five o'clock that afternoon. One of Martin's brothers met the two at the trolley and drove them to the Landis farm. Isabel Souders was that day, indeed, attractive. She wore a corn-colored organdie dress and leghorn hat, her natural beauty was enhanced by a becoming coiffure, her eyes danced, her lips curved in their most bewitching bow.

The visitor was effusive in her meeting with Martin's mother. "Dear Mrs. Landis," she gushed, "it is so lovely of you to have me here! Last summer while I boarded at Reists' I was so sorry not to meet you! Of course I met Martin and some of the younger children but the mother is always the most adorable one of the family! Oh, come here, dear, you darling," she cooed to little Emma, who had tiptoed into the room. But Emma held to her mother's apron and refused to move.

"Ach, Emma," Katie, a little older, chided her. "You'll run a mile to Amanda Reist if you see her. Don't act so simple! Talk to the lady; she's our company."

"Ach, she's bashful all of a sudden," said Mrs. Landis, smiling. "Now, Miss Souders, you take your hat off and just make yourself at home while I finish gettin' the supper ready. You dare look through them albums in the front room or set on the front porch. Just make yourself at home now."

"Thank you, how lovely!" came the sweet reply.

A little while later when Martin left her and went to his room to prepare for the evening meal the children, too, scurried away one by one and left Isabel alone.

She took swift inventory of the furnishings of the front room.

"Dear," she thought, "what atrocious taste! How can Martin live here? How can he belong to a family like this?"

But later she was all smiles again as Martin joined her and Mrs. Landis brought her husband into the room to meet the guest. Mr. Landis had, in spite of protests and murmurings, been persuaded to hearken to the advice of his wife and wear a coat. Likewise the older boys had followed Martin's example and donned the hot woolen articles of dress they considered superfluous in the house during the summer days.

Isabel chattered gaily to the men of the Landis household until Mrs. Landis stood in the doorway and announced, "Come now, folks, supper's done."

After the twelve were seated about the big table, Mr. Landis said grace and then Mrs. Landis rose to pour the coffee, several of the boys started to pass the platters and dishes around the table and the evening meal on the farm was in full swing.

"Oh," piped out little Charlie as he lifted his plate for a slice of ham, "somebody's went and threw all the spoons on the table-cloth! Here's two by my plate. And Emma's got some by her place, too!"

"Sh!" warned Mary, but Mrs. Landis laughed heartily. "Easy seeing," she confessed, "that we ain't used to puttin' on style. Charlie, that's the latest way of puttin' spoons on. Amanda Reist did it for me."

"Amanda Reist," said Mr. Landis. "Why didn't she stay for supper if she was here when you set the table?"

"I asked her to but she couldn't."

"Oh," the guest said, "I think Amanda is the sweetest girl. I just love her!"

"Me, too," added Mary. "She's my teacher."

"Mine too," said Katie. "I like her."

The Landis children were taught politeness according to the standards of their parents, but they had never been told that they should be seen and not heard. Meal-time at the Landis farm was not a quiet time. The children were encouraged to repeat any interesting happening of the day and there was much laughter and genial conversation and frank expressions about the taste of the food.

"Um, ain't that short cake good!" said Charlie, smacking his lips.

"Delicious, lovely!" agreed the guest.

"Here, have another piece," urged Mrs. Landis. "I always make enough for two times around."

"Mom takes care of us, all right," testified Mr. Landis.

"Lovely, I'm sure," Isabel said with a bright smile.

And so the dinner hour sped and at length all rose and Martin, tagged by two of the younger boys, showed Isabel the garden and yard, while Mrs. Landis with the aid of Mary and one of the boys cleared off and washed the dishes. Then the entire family gathered on the big porch and the time passed so quickly in the soft June night that the guest declared it had seemed like a mere minute.

"This is the most lovely, adorable family," she told them. "I've had a wonderful time. How I hate to go back to the noisy city! How I envy you this lovely porch on such nights!"

Later, when Martin returned from seeing the visitor back to Lancaster, his parents were sitting alone on the porch.

"Well, Mother, Dad, what do you think of her?" he asked in his boyish eagerness to have their opinion of the girl he thought he was beginning to care for. "Isn't she nice?"

"Seems like a very nice girl," said his mother with measured enthusiasm.

"Oh, Mother," was the boy's impatient answer, "of course you wouldn't think any girl was good enough for your boy! I can see that. If an angel from heaven came down after me you'd find flaws in her."

"Easy, Mart," cautioned the father. "Better put on the brakes a bit. Your mom and I think about the same, I guess, that the girl's a likely enough lady and she surely is easy to look at, but she ain't what we'd pick out for you if we had the say. It's like some of these here fancy ridin' horses people buy. They're all right for ridin' but no good for hitchin' to a plow. You don't just want a wife that you can play around with and dress pretty and amuse yourself with. You need a wife that'll work with you and be a partner and not fail you when trouble comes. Think that over, Mart."

"Gosh, you talk as though I had asked her to marry me. We are just good friends. I enjoy visiting her and hearing her play."

"Yes, Martin, I know, but life ain't all piano playin' after you get married, is it, Mom?"

Mrs. Landis laughed. "No, it's often other kinds of music! But I'm not sorry I'm married." "Me neither," confirmed her husband. "And that, Mart, is what you want to watch for when you pick a wife. Pick one so that after you been livin' together thirty years you can both say you're not sorry you married. That's the test!"

"Oh, some test!" the boy said drearily. "I--I guess you're right, both of you. I guess it isn't a thing to rush into. But you don't know Isabel. She's really a lovely, sweet girl."

"Of course she is," said his mother. "You just hold on to her and go see her as often as you like. Perhaps when you've been at the bank a while longer and can afford to get married you'll find she's the very one you want. Any one you pick we'll like."

"Yes, of course, yes," said Mr. Landis. Wise parents! They knew that direct opposition to the choice of the son would frustrate their hopes for him. Let him go on seeing the butterfly and perhaps the sooner he'd outgrow her charms, they thought.

But later, as Mr. Landis unlaced his shoes and his wife took off her white Mennonite cap and combed her hair for the night, that mild man sputtered and stormed. All the gentle acquiescence was fallen from him. "That empty-headed doll has got our Mart just wrapped round her finger! All she can say is 'Delicious, lovely, darling!'"

Mrs. Landis laughed at his imitation of the affected Isabel.

"Good guns, Mom, if any of our boys tie up with a doll like that it'll break our hearts. Why couldn't Mart pick a sensible girl that can cook and ain't too tony nor lazy to do it? A girl like Amanda Reist, now, would be more suited to him. Poor Mart, he's bamboozled if he gets this one! But if we told him that he'd be so mad he'd run to-morrow and marry her. We got to be a little careful, I guess."

"Ach, yes, he'll get over it. He's a whole lot like you and I don't believe he'd marry a girl like that."

"Well, let's hope he shows as good taste when he picks a wife as I did, ain't, Mom?"

CHAPTER XVI

AUNT REBECCA'S WILL

That summer Aunt Rebecca became ill. Millie volunteered to take care of her.

"She ain't got no child to do for her," said the hired girl, "and abody feels forlorn when you're sick. I'll go tend her if you want."

"Oh, Millie, I'd be so glad if you'd go! Strangers might be ugly to her, for she's a little hard to get along with. And I can't do it to take care of her."

"You--well, I guess you ain't strong enough to do work like that. If she gets real sick she'll have to be lifted around and she ain't too light, neither. If you and Amanda can shift here I'll just pack my telescope and go right over to Landisville."

So Millie packed and strapped her old gray telescope and went to wait on the sick woman.

She found Aunt Rebecca in bed, very ill, with a kind neighbor ministering to her.

"My goodness, Millie," she greeted the newcomer, "I never was so glad to see anybody like I am you! You pay this lady for her trouble. My money is in the washstand drawer. Lock the drawer open and get it out"

After the neighbor had been paid and departed Millie and the sick woman were left alone. "Millie," said Aunt Rebecca, "you stay with me till I go. Ach, you needn't tell me I'll get well. I know I'm done for. I don't want a lot o' strangers pokin' round in my things and takin' care of me. I'm crabbit and they don't have no patience."

"Ach, you'll be around again in no time," said Millie cheerfully. "Don't you worry. I'll run everything just like it ought to be. I'll tend you so good you'll be up and about before you know it."

"I'm not so easy fooled. I won't get out of this room till I'm carried out, I know. My goodness, abody thinks back over a lot o' things when you get right sick once! I made a will, Millie, and a pretty good one," the sick woman laughed as if in enjoyment of a pleasant secret. Her nurse attributed the laughter to delirium. But Aunt Rebecca went on, astonishing the other woman more and deepening the conviction that the strange talk was due to flightiness.

"Yes, I made a will! Some people'll say I was crazy, but you tell them for me I'm as sane as any one. My goodness, can't abody do what abody wants with your own money? Didn't I slave and scratch and skimp like everything all my life! And you bet I'm goin' to give that there money just where I want!"

"Ach, people always fuss about wills. It gives them something to talk about," said Millie, thinking argument useless.

"Yes, it won't worry me. I won't hear it. I have it all fixed where and how I want to be buried, and all about the funeral. I want to have a nice funeral, eat in the meeting-house, and have enough to eat, too. I was to a funeral once and everything got all before all the people had eaten. I was close livin', but I ain't goin' to be close dead."

"Now you go to sleep," ordered Millie. "You can tell me the rest some other time."

That evening as Millie sat on a low rocker by the bedside, the dim flare of an oil lamp flickering on the faces of the two women, Aunt Rebecca told more of the things she was so eager to detail while strength lasted.

"Jonas always thought that if I lived longest half of what I have should go back to the Miller people, his side of the family. But I tell you, Millie, none of them ever come to see me except one or two who come just for the money. They was wishin' long a'ready I'd die and they'd get it. But Jonas didn't put that in the will. He left me everything and he did say once I could do with it what I want. So I made a will and I'm givin' them Millers five thousand dollars in all and the rest--well, you'll find out what I done with the rest after I'm gone. I never had much good out my money and I'm havin' a lot of pleasure lyin' here and thinkin' what some people will do with what I leave them in my will. I had a lot of good that way a'ready since I'm sick. People will have something to talk about once when I die."

And so the sick woman rambled on, while Millie thought the fever caused the strange words and paid little attention to their import. But, several weeks later, when the querulous old woman closed her eyes in her long, last sleep, Millie, who had nursed her so faithfully, remembered each detail of the funeral as Aunt Rebecca had told her and saw to it that every one was carried out.

According to her wishes, Aunt Rebecca was robed in white for burial. The cashmere dress was fashioned, of course, after the garb she had worn so many years, and was complete with apron, pointed cape, all in white. Her hair was parted and folded under a white cap as it had been in her lifetime. She looked peaceful and happy as she lay in the parlor of her little home in Landisville. A smile seemed to have fixed itself about her lips as though the pleasant thoughts her will had occasioned lingered with her to the very last.

She had stipulated that short services be held at the house, then the body taken to the church and a public service held and after interment in the old Mennonite graveyard at Landisville, a public dinner to be served in the basement of the meeting-house, as is frequently the custom in that community.

The service of the burial of the dead is considered by the plain sects as a sacred obligation to attend whenever possible. Relatives, friends, and members of the deceased's religious sect, drive many miles to pay their last respects to departed ones. The innate hospitality of the Pennsylvania Dutch calls for the serving of a light lunch after the funeral. Relatives, friends, who have come from a distance or live close by, and all others who wish to partake of it, are welcomed. Therefore most meeting-houses of the plain sects have their basements fitted with long tables and benches, a generous supply of china and cutlery, a stove big enough for making many quarts of coffee. And after the burial willing hands prepare the food and many take advantage of the proffered hospitality and file to the long tables, where bread, cheese, cold meat, coffee and sometimes beets and pie, await them. This was an important portion of what Aunt Rebecca called a "nice funeral," and it was given to her.

Later in the day, while the nearest relatives were still together in the little house at Landisville, the lawyer arrived and read the will.

The Millers, who were so eager for their legacies, were impatient with all the legal phrasing, "Being of sound mind" and so forth. They sat up more attentively when the lawyer read, "do hereby bequeath."

First came the wish that all real estate be sold, that personal property be given to her sister, the sum of five hundred dollars be given to the Mennonite Church at Landisville for the upkeep of the burial ground. Then the announcement of the sum of five thousand dollars to be equally divided among the heirs of Jonas Miller, deceased, the sum of five thousand dollars to her brother Amos Rohrer, a like amount to her sister, Mrs. Reist, the sum of ten thousand dollars to Martin Landis, husband of Elizabeth Anders, and the remainder, if any, to be divided equally between said brother Amos and sister Mary.

"Martin Landis!" exploded one of the Miller women, "who under the sun is he? To get ten thousand dollars of Rebecca's money!"

"I'll tell you," spoke up Uncle Amos, "he's an old beau of hers."

"Well, who ever heard of such a thing! And here we are, her own blood, you might say, close relations of poor Jonas, and we get only five thousand to be divided into about twenty shares! It's an outrage! Such a will ought to be broken!"

"I guess not," came Uncle Amos's firm reply. "It was all Rebecca's money and hers to do with what suited her. She's made me think a whole lot more of her by this here will. I'm glad to know she didn't forget her old beau. She was a little prickly on the outside sometimes, but I guess her heart was soft after all. It's all right, it's all right, that will is! It ain't for us to fuss about. She could have give the whole lot of it to some cat home or spent it while she lived. It was *hers*! If that's all, lawyer, I guess we'll go. Mary and I are satisfied and the rest got to be. I bet Rebecca got a lot o' good thinkin' how Martin Landis would get the surprise of his life when she was in her grave."

In a short time the news spread over the rural community that Rebecca Miller willed Martin Landis ten thousand dollars! Some said facetiously that it might be a posthumous thank-offering for what she missed when she refused to marry him. Others, keen for romance, repeated a sentimental story about a broken heart and a lifelong sorrow because of her foolish inability to see what was best for her and how at the close of her life she conceived the beautiful thought of leaving him the money so that he might know she had never forgotten him and so that he might remember his old sweetheart. But in whatever form the incident was presented it never failed to evoke interest. "Ten thousand dollars from an old girl! What luck!" exclaimed many.

If persons not directly concerned in the ten thousand dollar legacy were surprised what word can adequately describe the emotion of Martin Landis when Amanda's verbal report of it was duly confirmed by a legal notice from the lawyer!

"Good guns, Mom!" the man said in astonishment. "I can't make it out! I can't get head nor tail out the thing. What ailed Becky, anyhow? To do a thing like that! I feel kinda mean takin' so much money. It ought to go to Amos and Mary. They got five thousand apiece and somebody said the farms will bring more than Becky thought and by the time they are sold and everything divided Amos and Mary will get about eleven thousand each. It's right for them to get it, but it don't seem right for me to have it."

But Millie soon paid a visit to the Landis home and repeated many of the things Aunt Rebecca had told her those last evenings by the light of the little oil lamp. "She said, Mr. Landis, that one day she was lookin' at the big Bible and come across an old valentine you sent her when you and she was young. It said on it, 'If I had the world I'd give you half of it.' And that set her thinkin' what a nice surprise she could fix up if she'd will you some of her money. And she said, too, that Jonas was a good man but it worried her that she broke off with a poor man to marry a rich one when she liked the poor one best. I guess all that made her so queer and crabbit. She never let on when she was well that she wished she'd married you but when she come to die she didn't care much if it was found out. You just take that there money and enjoy it; that's what Rebecca wanted you should do."

"Yes, I guess she wanted me to have it," the man said thoughtfully. "But it beats me why she did it. Why, I'd almost forgot that I ever kept company with her and was promised to marry her. It's so long ago."

"Men do forget," said Millie. "I guess it's the women that remember. But the money's for you, that's her will, and she said I should be sure to see that the will is carried out and that the money goes where she said."

"Yes--we can use it. We'll be glad for it. I wish I could say thanks to Becky for it. It don't seem right by Amos and Mary, though."

"Ach, they don't need it. They got lots a'ready. The only ones that begrudge it are the relations of Jonas. None of them come to shake up a pillow for poor Rebecca or bring her an orange or get her a drink of water, but they come when the will was read. I just like to see such people get fooled! They wanted a lot and got a little and you didn't expect nothin' and look what you got! There's some nice surprises in the world, for all, ain't!"

CHAPTER XVII

MARTIN'S DARK HOUR

That summer Martin Landis was well pleased with the world in general. He enjoyed his work at the bank, where his cordiality and adeptness, his alert, receptive mind, were laying for him a strong foundation for a successful career.

He called often at the home of Isabel Souders, listened to her playing, made one in an occasional game of cards, escorted her to musicals and dramas. He played and talked and laughed with her, but he soon discovered that he could not interest her in any serious matter. At the mention of his work, beyond the merest superficialities, she lifted her hands and said in laughing tones, "Please, Martin, don't talk shop! Father never does. I'm like Mother, I don't want to hear the petty details of money-making--all that interests me is the money itself. Dad says I'm spoiled--I suppose I am."

At such times the troublesome memory of his father's words came to him, "You need a wife that will work with you and be a partner and not fail you when trouble comes." Try as he would the young man could not obliterate those haunting words from his brain. Sometimes he felt almost convinced in his own heart that he loved Isabel Souders--she was so appealing and charming and, while she rebuffed his confidences about his work, nevertheless showed so deep an interest in him generally, that he was temporarily blinded by it and excused her lack of real interest on the world-old ground that pretty women are not supposed to bother about prosaic affairs of the male wage-earners of the race.

There were moments when her beauty so thrilled him that he felt moved to tell her he loved her and wanted to marry her, but somewhere in the subconscious mind of him must have dwelt the succinct words of the poster, "When in doubt, *don't!*" So the moments of fascination passed and the words of love were left unsaid.

"Some day," he thought, "I'll know, I'll be sure. It will probably come to me like a flash of lightning whether I love her or not. I shouldn't be so undecided. I think if it were the real thing I feel for her there would be not the shadow of a doubt in my heart concerning it. A man should feel that the woman he wants to marry is the only one in the universe for him. Somehow, I can't feel that about her. But there's no hurry about marrying. We'll just go on being capital friends. Meanwhile I can be saving money so that if the time comes when I marry I'll be able to support a wife. Things look pretty rosy for me at present. Since Father is fixed with that legacy and the boys are old enough to take my place on the farm

I have time to study and advance. I'm in luck all around; guess I got a horseshoe round my neck!"

But the emblem of good luck must have soon lost its potency. The bank force was surprised one day by an unexpected examination of the books.

"What's the trouble?" asked Martin of another worker in the bank.

"I don't know. Ask old Buehlor. He acts as though he knew."

Martin approached the gray-haired president, who was stamping about his place like an angry dog on leash. "Anything the matter, sir? Can I help in any way?"

"Why, yes, there seems to be," he snapped. "Come in, Landis." He opened the door of his private office and Martin followed him inside. He gave one long look into the face of the young man--"I'm going to tell you. Perhaps you can make things easier for us to adjust in case there's anything wrong. An investigation has been ordered. One of our heaviest depositors seems to have some inside information that some one is spending the bank's money for personal use."

"Good guns! In this bank? A thief?" Horror was printed on the face of Martin.

The man opposite searched that face. "Yes--I might as well tell you--I feel like a brute to do so--if it's false it's a damnable trick, for such a thing is a fiendish calumny for an honest man to bear--you're the man under suspicion."

Martin sat up, his eyes wide in horror, then his chest collapsed and his neck felt limber. "Oh, my God," he whispered, as though in appeal to the Infinite Father of Mercy and Justice, "what a thing to say about me! What a lie!"

"It's a lie?" asked the older man tersely.

"Absolutely! I've never stolen anything since the days I wore short pants and climbed the neighbors' trees for apples. Who says it?"

"Well, I can't divulge that now. Perhaps later."

Martin groaned. To be branded a thief was more than he could bear. His face went whiter.

"See here," said the old man, "I almost shocked you to death, but I had a purpose in it. I couldn't believe that of you and knew I'd be able to read your face. You know, I believe you! It's all some infernal mistake or plot. You're not a clever enough actor to feign such distress and innocence. Go out and get some air and come back to-morrow morning. I'll stand for you in the meantime. I believe in you."

"Thank you, sir," Martin managed to blurt out between dry lips that seemed almost paralyzed. "I'll be back in the morning. Hope you'll find I'm telling the truth."

He walked as a somnambulist down the street. In his misery he thought of Isabel Souders. He would go to her for comfort. She'd understand and believe in him! He yearned like a hurt child for the love and tenderness of some one who could comfort him and sweep the demons of distress from his soul. He wanted to see

Isabel, only Isabel! He felt relieved that no older member of the household was at home at that time, that the colored servant who answered his ring at the bell said Isabel was alone and would see him at once.

"What's wrong?" the girl asked as she entered the room where he waited for her. "You look half dead!"

"I am, Isabel," he said chokingly. "I've had a death-blow. They are accusing me of stealing the bank's money."

"Oh, Martin! Oh, how dreadful! I'll never forgive you!" The girl spoke in tearful voice. "How perfectly dreadful to have such a thing said after Father got you into the bank! Your reputation is ruined for life! You can never live down such a disgrace."

"But I didn't do it!" he cried. "You must know I couldn't have done it!"

"Oh, I suppose you didn't if you say so, but people always are ready to say that where there's smoke there must be some fire! Oh, dear, people know you're a friend of mine and next thing the papers will link our names in the notoriety and--oh, what a dreadful thing to happen! They'll print horrible things about you and may drag me into it, too! Say you spent the money on me, or something like that! Father will be so mortified and sorry he helped you. Oh, dear, I think it's dreadful, dreadful!" She burst into weeping.

As Martin watched her and listened to her utterly selfish words, in spite of the misery in his heart, he was keenly conscious that she was being weighed in the balance and found wanting. The lightning flash had come to him and revealed how impotent she was, how shallow and selfish.

"Well, don't cry about it," he said, half bitterly, yet too crushed to be aught but gentle. "It won't hurt you. I'll see to that. If there's anything to bear I'll bear it alone. My shoulders are broad."

There was more futile exchange of words, words that lacked any comfort or hope for the broken-hearted man. Martin soon left and started for his home.

Home--he couldn't go there and tell his people that he was suspected of a crime. Home--its old sweet meaning would be changed for all of them if one of its flock was blackened.

He flurried past the Reist farmhouse, head down like a criminal so that none should recognize him. With quick steps that almost merged into a run he went up the road. When he reached the little Crow Hill schoolhouse a sudden thought came to him. He climbed the rail fence and entered the woods, plodded up the hill to the spot where Amanda's moccasins grew each spring. There he threw himself on the grassy slope, face down, and gave vent to his despair.

CHAPTER XVIII

THE COMFORTER

Amanda Reist knew the woods so well that she never felt any fear as she wandered about in them. That August morning as she climbed the fence by the schoolyard and sauntered along the narrow paths between the trees she hummed a little song--not because of any particular happiness, but because the sky was blue and the woods were green and she loved to be outdoors.

She climbed the narrow trail, gathering early goldenrod, which she suddenly dropped, and stood still. Before her, a distance of about twenty feet, lay the figure of a man, face down on the ground, his arms flung out, his hair disheveled. A great fear rose in her heart. Was it a tramp, an intoxicated wanderer, was he dead? She shrank from the sight and took a few backward steps, feeling a strong impulse to run, yet held riveted to the spot by some inexplicable, irresistible force.

The figure moved slightly--why, it looked like Martin Landis! But he wouldn't be lying so in the grass at that time of day! The face of the man was suddenly turned to her and a cry came from her lips--it *was* Martin Landis! But what a Martin Landis! Haggard and lined, his face looked like the face of a debilitated old man.

"Martin," she called, anxiously. "Martin!"

He raised his head and leaned on his elbow. "Oh," he groaned, then turned his head away.

She ran to him then and knelt beside him in the grass. "What's wrong, Martin?" she asked, all the love in her heart rushing to meet the need of her "knight." "Tell me what's the matter."

"They say I'm a thief!"

"Who says so?" she demanded, a Xantippe-like flash in her eyes.

"The bank, they're examining the books, swooped down like a lot of vultures and hunting for carrion right now."

"For goodness' sake! Martin! Sit up and tell me about it! Don't cover your face as though you *were* a thief! Of course there's some mistake, there must be! Get up, tell me. Let's sit over on that old log and get it straightened out."

Spurred by her words he raised himself and she mechanically brushed the dry leaves from his coat as they walked to a fallen log and sat down.

"Now tell me," she urged, "the whole story."

Haltingly he told the tale, though the process hurt.

"And you ran away," she exclaimed when he had finished. "You didn't wait to see what the books revealed? You ran right out here?"

"Yes--no, I stopped at Isabel's."

"Oh"--Amanda closed her eyes a moment--it had been Isabel first again! She quickly composed herself to hear what the city girl had done in the man's hour of trial. "Isabel didn't believe it, of course?" she asked quietly.

"No, I suppose she didn't. But she cried and fussed and said my reputation was ruined for life and even if my innocence is proved I can never wholly live down such a reputation. She was worried because the thing may come out in the papers and her name brought into it. She's mighty much upset about Isabel Souders, didn't care a picayune about Martin Landis."

"She'll get over it," Amanda told him, a lighter feeling in her heart. "What we are concerned about now is Martin Landis. You should have stayed and seen it through, faced them and demanded the lie to be traced to its source. Why, Martin, cheer up, this can't harm you!"

"My reputation," he said gloomily.

"Yes, your reputation is what people think you are, but your character is what you really are. A noble character can often change a very questionable reputation. You know you are honest as the day is long--we are all sure of that, all who know you. Martin, nothing can hurt *you!* People can make you unhappy by such lies and cause the road to be a little harder to travel but no one except yourself can ever touch *you!* Your character is impregnable. Brace up! Go back and tell them it's a lie and then prove it!"

"Amanda"--the man's voice quavered. "Amanda, you're an angel! You make me buck up. When you found me I felt as though a load of bricks were thrown on my heart, but I'm beginning to see a glimmer of light. Of course, I can prove I'm innocent!"

"Listen, look!" Amanda whispered. She laid a hand upon his arm while she pointed with the other to a tree near by.

There sat an indigo bunting, that tiny bird of blue so intense that the very skies look pale beside it and among all the blue flowers of our land only the fringed gentian can rival it. With no attempt to hide his gorgeous self he perched in full view on a branch of the tree and began to sing in rapid notes. What the song lacked in sweetness was quite forgotten as they looked at the lovely visitant.

"There's your blue bunting of hope," said Amanda as the bird suddenly became silent as though he were out of breath or too tired to finish the melody.

"He's wonderful," said Martin, a light of hope once more in his eyes.

"Yes, he is wonderful, not only because of his fine color but because he's the one bird that sultry August weather can't still. When all others are silent he sings, halts a while, then sings again. That is why I said he is your blue bunting of hope. Isn't it like that with us? When other feelings are gone hope stays with us, never quite deserts us--hear him!"

True to his reputation the indigo bird burst once more into song, then off he flew, still singing his clear, rapid notes.

"Amanda," the man said as the blue wings carried the bird out of sight, "you've helped me--I can't tell you how much! I'm going back to the bank and face that lie. If I could only find out who started it!"

"I don't know, but I'd like to bet Mr. Mertzheimer is back of it, somehow. The old man is a heavy depositor there, isn't he?"

"Yes, but why under the sun would he say such a thing about me? I never liked Lyman and he had no love for me, but he has no cause to bear me ill will. I haven't anything he wants, I'm sure."

"No?" The girl bit her lip and felt her cheeks burn.

Martin looked at her, amazed. Why was she blushing? Surely, she didn't like Lyman Mertzheimer!

"Oh, Martin," she was thinking, "how blind you are! You do have something Lyman Mertzheimer wants. I can see through it all. He thinks with you disgraced I'll have eyes for him at last. The cheat! The cheat!" she said out loud.

"What?" asked Martin.

"He's a cheat, Lyman is. I hope he gets what's coming to him some day and I get a chance to see it! You see if that precious father of his is not at the bottom of all this worry for you!"

"It may be. I'm going in to Lancaster and find out. If he is, and if I ever get my hands on him---"

"Good-bye Lyman!" said Amanda, laughing. "But you wouldn't want to touch anything as low as he is."

"I'd hate to have the chance; I'd pound him to jelly."

"Oh, no, you wouldn't. You'd just look at him and he'd shrivel till he'd look like a dried crabapple snitz!"

Both laughed at the girl's words. A moment later they rose from the old log and walked down the path. When they had climbed the fence and stood in the hot, sunny road Martin said, "I guess I'll go home and get cleaned up." He rubbed a hand through his tumbled hair.

"And get something to eat," she added. "By that time you'll be ready, like Luther, to face a horde of devils."

"Thanks to you," he said. "I'll never forget this half-hour just gone. Your blue bunting of hope will be singing in my heart whenever things go wrong. You said a few things to me that I couldn't forget if I wanted to--for instance, that nothing, nobody, can hurt *me*, except myself. That's something to keep in mind. I feel equal to fight now, fight for my reputation. Some kind providence must have sent you up the hill to find me."

"Ach," she said depreciatively, "I didn't do a thing but steady you up a bit. I'm glad I happened to come up and see you. Go tell them if they're hunting for a thief they're looking in the wrong direction when they look at Martin Landis! Hurry! So you can get back before they think you've run away. I'll be so anxious to hear how much the Mertzheimers have to do with this. I can see their name written all over it!"

Smiling, almost happy again, the man turned down the road to his home and Amanda went on to the Reist farmhouse. She, too, was smiling as she went. She had read between the lines of the man's story and had seen there the moving finger writing above the name of Isabel Souders, "*Mene, Mene, Tekel, Upharsin.*"

CHAPTER XIX

VINDICATION

When Martin Landis entered the bank early in the afternoon of that same day he presented a different appearance from that of his departure in the morning. His head was held erect, his step determined, as he opened the swinging door of the bank and entered.

"What--Landis, you back?" Mr. Buehlor greeted him, while the quizzical eyes of the old man looked into those of the younger.

"I'm back and I'm back to get this hideous riddle solved and the slate washed clean."

"Come in, come in!" Mr. Buehlor drew him into a little room and closed the door. "Sit down, Landis."

"Well, how much is the bank short?" He looked straight into the eyes of the man who, several hours before, had dealt him such a death-blow.

"So far everything is right, right as rain! There's a mistake or a damnable dirty trick somewhere."

"Let's sift it out, Mr. Buehlor. Will you tell me who had the 'inside information' that I was taking bank's money?"

"I'll tell you! It was a farmer near your home---"

"Mr. Mertzheimer?" offered Martin.

"The same! He asked to have you watched, then changed it and insisted on having the books examined. Said your people are poor--forgive me, Landis, but I have to tell you the whole story."

"Don't mind that. That's a mere scratch after what I got this morning."

"Well, he said your father had a mortgage on his farm up to the time you came to work in the bank, then suddenly it was paid and soon after the house was painted, a new bathroom installed, electric lights put into the house and steam heat, a Victrola and an automobile bought. In fact, your people launched out as though they had found a gold mine, and that in spite of the fact that your crop of tobacco was ruined by hail and the other income from the farm products barely enough to keep things going until another harvest. He naturally thought you must have a hand in supplying the money and with your moderate salary you couldn't do half of that. He talked with several of the bank directors and an investigation was ordered. You'll admit his story sounded plausible. It looked pretty black for you."

"To you, yes! But not to him! Mr. Mertzheimer knows well enough where that money came from. My father had a legacy of ten thousand dollars this spring. You people could have found that out with very little trouble."

"We're a pack of asinine blunderers, Landis!" Mr. Buehlor looked foolish. Then he sighed relievedly. "That clears matters for you. I'm glad. I couldn't conceive of you as anything but honest, Landis. But tell me about that legacy--a pretty nice sum."

"It's a romantic little story. An old sweetheart of my father, one who must have carried under her prickly exterior a bit of tender romance and who liked to do things other people never dreamed of doing, left him ten thousand dollars. She was a queer old body. Had no direct heirs, so she left Father ten thousand dollars for a little remembrance! It was that honest money that paid for the conveniences in our house, the second-hand car Father bought and the Victrola he gave Mother because we are all crazy for music and had nothing to create any melody except an old parlor organ that sounded wheezy after nine babies had played on it."

"Landis, forgive me; we're a set of fools!" The old man extended his hand and looked humbly into the face of Martin. The two gripped hands, each feeling emotion too great for words.

After a moment's silence Mr. Buehlor spoke.

"This goes no farther. Your reputation is as safe as mine. If I have anything to say you'll be eligible for the first vacancy in the line of advancement. As for that Mertzheimer, he can withdraw his account from our bank to-day for all we care. We can do business without him. But it puzzles me--what object did he have? If he knew of the legacy, and he certainly did, he must have known you were O.K. Is he an enemy of yours?"

"Not particularly. I never liked his son but we never had any real tilts."

"You don't happen to want the same girl he wants, or anything like that?"

"No--well now--why, I don't know!" A sudden revelation came to Martin. Perhaps Lyman thought he had a rival in him. That would explain much. "There's a son, as I said, and we know a girl I think he's been crazy about for years. Perhaps he thinks I'm after her, too."

"I see," chuckled the old man. "Well, if the girl's the right sort she won't have to toss a penny to decide which one to choose." He noted the embarrassment of Martin and changed the subject.

But later in the afternoon as Martin walked down the road from the trolley and drew near the Reist farmhouse the old man's words recurred to him. Why, he'd known Amanda Reist all his life! He had never dreamed she could comfort and help a man as she had done that morning in the woods. Amanda was a fine girl, a great pal, a woman with a heart.

Now Isabel--a great disgust rose in him for the sniveling, selfish little thing and her impotence in the face of his trouble. "She's just the kind to play with," he thought, "just a doll, and like the doll, has as much heart as a thing stuffed with sawdust can have. I guess it took this jolt to wake me up and know that Isabel Souders is not the type of girl for me."

When he reached the Reist home he found Amanda and her Uncle Amos on the porch.

"Oh, it's all right!" the girl cried as he came into the yard. "I can read it in your face." Gladness rang in her voice like a bell.

"It's all right," Martin told her.

"Good! I'm glad," said Uncle Amos while Amanda smiled her happiness.

"Was I right?" she asked. "Was it the work of Mertzheimers?"

"It was. They must hate me like poison."

"Ach, he's a copperhead," said Uncle Amos. "He's so pesky low and mean he can't bear to see any one else be honest. You're gettin' up too far to suit him. It's always so that when abody climbs up the ladder a little there's some settin' at the foot ready to joggle it, and the higher abody climbs the more are there to help try to shake you down. I guess there's mean people everywheres, even in this here beautiful Garden Spot. But to my notion you got to just go on doin' right and not mind 'em. They'll get what they earn some day. Nobody has yet sowed weeds and got a crop of potatoes from it."

"But," said the girl, "I can't understand it. The Mertzheimer people come from good families and they have certainly been taught to be different. I can't see where they get their mean streak. With all their money and chance to improve and opportunities for education and culture---"

"Ach, money"--said Uncle Amos--"what good does money do them if they don't have the right mind to use it? My granny used to say still you can tie a silk ribbon round a pig's neck but she'll wallow in the dirt just the same first chance she'll get. I guess some people are like that. Well, Martin, I'm goin' in to tell Millie--the women--it's all right with you. They was so upset about it. And won't Millie talk!" He chuckled at the thought of what that staunch woman would say about Mr. Mertzheimer. "Millie can hit the nail on the head pretty good, pretty good," he said as he ambled into the house.

Martin lingered on the porch with Amanda till the sound of the Landis supper bell called him home.

CHAPTER XX

DINNER AT LANDIS'S

The following afternoon little Katie Landis came running down the road and in at the Reist gate. She greeted Amanda with, "Mom says you got to come to our place for supper."

"To-day?"

"Yes. She's goin' to kill two chickens and have a big time and she wants you to come."

"Anybody coming? Any company?"

"No, just you."

"All right. Tell Mother I said thank you and I'll be glad to come."

"All right, I'll run and tell her. I'm in a hurry, for me and Emma's playin' house and I got to get back to my children before they miss me and set up a howlin'." She looked very serious as she ran off down the lane, Amanda smiling after her.

Later, as the girl went down the road to the Landis home she wondered whose birthday it might be, or what the cause of celebration. The child had been in such great haste--but what matter the significance of the festivity so long as she was asked to enjoy it!

"Here's Amanda!" shouted several of the children gleefully, very boldly dropping the Miss they were obliged to use during school hours.

The guest found Mrs. Landis stirring up a blackberry pone, the three youngest Landis children watching the progress of it.

"Oh, hello, Amanda. I'm glad you got here early. Look at these children, all waitin' for the dish to lick. Don't it beat all how children like raw dough! I used to, but I wouldn't eat it now if you paid me."

"So did I. Millie chased me many a time."

"Well, people's tastes change in more than one way when they get older. I guess it's a good thing. Here, Katie, take that doll off of that chair so Amanda can find a place to sit down. You got every chair in the house littered up with things. Ach, Amanda, I scold still about their things laying round but I guess folks that ain't got children would sometimes be glad if they could see toys and things round the place. They get big soon enough and the dolls are put away. My, this will be an awful lonely house when the children all grow up! I'd rather see it this way, with their things scattered all around. But the boys are worse than the girls. What Charlie don't have in his pants pocket ain't in the 'cyclopedia. Martin was that way, too. He had an old box in the wood-shed and it was stuffed with all the twine and wire and nails he could find. But now, Amanda, ain't it good he got that all made right at the bank so they know he ain't a thief?

My, that was an awful sin for Mr. Mertzheimer to make our Mart out a thief! I just wonder how he could be so mean and ugly. I guess you wonder why I asked you up to-night. It ain't nothin' special, just a little good time because Martin got proved honest again. I just said to Mister this morning that I'm so glad for Martin I feel like makin' something extra for supper and ask you up for you ain't been here for a meal for long."

"It's grand to ask me to it."

"Ach, we don't mind you. You're just like one of the family, abody might say. We won't fix like for company, eat in the room or anything like that."

"Well, I hope not. I'm no company. Let's eat in the kitchen and have everything just as you do when the family's alone."

"Yes," agreed Mrs. Landis. "That will be more homelike."

Mary helped to set the table in the big kitchen.

"Shall I lay the spoons on the table-cloth like we did when Isabel was here?" she asked her mother.

"Better put them in the spoon-holder," Amanda told her. "I'm no company."

"I'm glad you ain't. I don't like tony company like that girl was. She put on too much when she talked. And she had the funniest cheeks! Once she wiped her face when it was hot and pink came off on her handkerchief."

Amanda laughed and kept smiling as she helped the child set the table for supper. Later she offered her services to Mrs. Landis. Martin, coming in from the dusty road, found her before the stove, one of his mother's gingham aprons tied around her waist, and turning sweet potatoes in a big iron pan.

"Why, hello!" he said, pleasure written in his face. "Katie ran to meet me and said I couldn't guess who was here for supper. Has Mother got you working? Um," he sniffed, "smells awful much like chicken!"

"Ach," his mother told him, "you just hold your nose shut a while! You and your pop can smell chicken off a mile. But you dare ring the supper bell, Martin, before you go up-stairs to wash, so your pop and the boys can come in now and get ready, too."

Soon the savory, smoking dishes were all placed on the big table in the kitchen and the family with their guest gathered for the meal.

"Ain't I dare keep my coat off, Mom?" asked Mr. Landis, his face flushed from a long hot day in the fields.

"Why, yes, if Amanda don't care."

"Why should I? Look at my cool dress! Take your coat off, Martin. I never could see why men should roast while we keep comfortable."

As Martin stripped the serge coat off he thought of that other dinner when coats were kept on and dinner eaten in "the room" because of the presence of one who might take offense if she were expected to share the plain, every-day ways of the family. What a fool he had been! Their best efforts at style and convention must have looked very amateurish and incomplete to her--what a fool he had been!

"Ah, that looks good!" Mr. Landis said after he had said grace and everybody waited for the food to be passed. "Now we'll just hand the platter around and let everybody help themselves, not so, Mom?"

"Yes, that's all right. Start the potatoes once, Martin. Now you must eat, Amanda. Just make yourself right at home."

"Martin, you must eat hearty, too,", said the father. "Your mom made this supper for you."

"For me? What's the idea? Feeding the prodigal? Fatted calf and all that, Mother?" the boy asked, smiling,

"Calf--nothing!" exclaimed little Charlie. "It's them two roosters Mom said long a'ready she's goin' to kill once and cook and here they are!"

Charlie wondered why everybody laughed at that but he soon forgot about it as his mother handed him a plate piled high with food.

Amanda scarcely knew what she was eating that day. Each mouthful had the taste of nectar and ambrosia to her. If she could *belong* to a family like that! She adored her own people and felt certain that no one could wish for a finer family than the one in which she had been placed, but it seemed, by comparison with the Landis one, a very small, quiet family. She wished she could be a part of both, make the twelfth in that charming circle in which she sat that day.

After supper Mrs. Landis turned to Amanda--"Now you stay a while and hear our new pieces on the Victrola."

"I'll help you with the dishes," she offered.

"Ach, no, it ain't necessary. Mary and I will get them done up in no time. You just go in the room and enjoy yourself."

With little Katie leading the way and Martin following Amanda went to the sitting-room and sat down while Martin opened the Victrola.

"What do you like?" he asked. "Something lively? Or do you like soft music better?"

"I like both. What are your new pieces?"

"McCormack singing 'Mother Machree---'"

"Oh, I like that! Play that!"

As the soft, haunting melody of "Mother Machree" sounded in the room Mrs. Landis came to the door of the sitting-room, dish towel in hand.

"Ach," she said after the last verse, "I got that record most wore out a'ready. Ain't it the prettiest song? When I hear that I think still that if only one of my nine children feels that way about me I'm more than paid for any bother I had with them."

"Then, Mother," said Martin, "you should feel more than nine times paid, for we all feel that way about you."

"Listen, now!" The mother's eyes were misty as she looked at her first-born. "Ach, play it again. I only hope poor Becky knows how much good her money's doin' us!"

Later Martin walked with Amanda up the moonlit road to her home. "I've had a lovely time, Martin," she told him. "You do have the nicest, lively family! I wish we had a tableful like that!"

"You wouldn't wish it at dish-washing time, I bet! But they are a lively bunch. I wonder sometimes how Mother escapes *nerves*. If she feels irritable or tired she seldom shows it. I believe six of us can ask her questions at once and she knows how to answer each in its turn. But Mother never does much useless worrying. That keeps her youthful and calm. She has often said to us, 'What's the use of worrying? Worrying never gets you anywhere except into hot water--so what's the use of it?' That's a pet philosophy of hers."

"I remember that. I've heard her say it. Your mother's wonderful!"

"She thinks the same about you, Amanda, for she said so the other day."

"Me?" The girl turned her face from him so that the moonlight might not reveal her joy.

"You," he said happily, laughing in boyish contentment. "We think Amanda Reist is all right."

The girl was glad they had reached the gate of her home. She fumbled with the latch and escaped an answer to the man's words. Then they spoke commonplace good-nights and parted.

That night as she brushed her hair she stood a long time before the mirror. "Amanda Reist," she said to the image in the glass, "you better take care--next thing you know you'll be falling in love!" She leaned closer to the glass. "Oh, I'll have to keep that shine from my eyes! It's there just because Martin walked home with me and was kind. I don't look as though I need any boneset tea *now!*"

CHAPTER XXI

BERRYING

The next morning Amanda helped her mother with the Saturday baking while Millie and Uncle Amos tended market.

"This hot weather the pies get soft till Sunday if we bake them a'ready on Friday," Mrs. Reist said to Millie, "so Amanda and I can do the bakin' while you go to market. I guess we'll have a lot of company again this Sunday, with church near here."

"All right, let 'em come," said the hired girl composedly. "I don't care if you don't. It's a good thing we all like company pretty good, for I think sometimes people take this place for a regular boarding-house, the way they drop in at any time, just as like when we're ready to set down for a meal as at any other hour. Philip said last week, when that Sallie Snyder dropped in just at dinner, that he's goin' to paint a sign, 'Mad Dog,' and hang it on the gate. But I think we might as well put one up, 'Meals served at all hours,' but ach, that's Lancaster County for you!"

Mrs. Reist liked to do her baking early in the day. So it happened that when Martin Landis stopped in to see Amanda before he went to his work in the city he saw on the kitchen table a long row of pies ready for the oven and Amanda deftly rolling the edge of another.

"Whew!" he whistled. "Mrs. Reist, is that your work or Amanda's so early in the morning?"

"Amanda's! My granny used to say still that no girl was ready to get married till she could roll out a thin pie dough. I guess my girl is almost ready, for she got hers nice and thin this morning. Ach," she thought in dismay as she saw the girl's face flush, "now why did I say that? I didn't think how it would sound. But Amanda needn't mind Martin!"

Merry little twinkles played around Martin's gray eyes as he answered, "I see. Looks as if Amanda's ready for a husband--if she's going to feed him on pies!"

"On pies--Martin Landis!" scorned the girl. "I'd have a dyspeptic on my hands after a few days of pie diet."

"Well, you'd make a pretty good nurse, I believe."

"Nurse--not me! The only thing I know how to nurse is hurt birds and lame bunnies and such things. You just lay them in a box and feed them, and if they get well you clap your hands, and if they die you put some leaves and flowers on them and bury them out in the woods--remember how we used to do that?"

"Do I? I should say I do! The time we had the fence hackey that Lyman Mertzheimer hurt with a stone--"

"Oh, and I nursed him and fed him, and when I let him go he bit my finger! I remember that! I was so cross at him I cried."

"Wretch that he was," said Martin. "But if we begin talking about those days I won't get to work. I stopped in to ask you to go berrying with us this afternoon. I get out of the bank early. We can go up to the woods back of the schoolhouse. The youngsters are anxious to go, and Mother won't let them go alone, since that copperhead was killed near here. I promised to take them, and we'd all like to have you come."

"I'd love to go. I'll be all ready. I haven't gone for blackberries all season."

"That's true, we've been missing lots of fun." He looked at her as though he were seeing her after a long absence. Somehow, he had missed something worth while from his life during the time his head had been turned by Isabel, and he had passed Amanda with a smile and a greeting and had no hours of companionship with her. Why, he didn't remember that her eyes were so bright, that her red hair waved so becomingly, that--

"I'll bring a kettle," she said. "I'm going to pick till I fill it, too, just as we did when we were youngsters."

"All right. We'll meet you at the schoolhouse."

The spur of mountains near Crow Hill was a favorite berrying range for the people of that section of Lancaster County. In July and August huckleberries, elders and blackberries grew there in fragrant luxuriance.

When Amanda, in an old dress of cool green, a wide-brimmed hat on her head, came in sight of the schoolhouse, she saw the Landis party approaching it from the other direction. She swung her tin pail in greeting.

"Oh, there's Amanda!" the children shouted and ran to meet her, tin pails clanging and dust flying.

Martin, too, wore old clothes that would be none the worse for meeting with briars or crushed berries. A wide straw hat perched on his head made Amanda think, "He looks like a grown-up edition of Whittier's Barefoot Boy."

"Here we are, all ready," said the leader, as they started off to the crude rail fence. Martin would have helped Amanda over the fence, but she ran from him, put up one foot, and was over it in a trice.

"Still a nimble-toes," he said, laughing. "Mary, can you do as well?"

"Pooh, yes! Who can't climb a fence?" The little girl was over it in a minute. The smaller children lay flat on the ground and squirmed through under the lower rail, while one of the boys climbed up, balanced himself on the top rail, then leaped into the grass.

"I see some berries!" cried Katie, and began to pick them.

"We'll go in farther," said Martin. "The bushes near the road have been almost stripped. Come on, keep on the path and watch out for snakes."

There was a well-defined, narrow trail through the timbered land. Though the weeds had been trodden down along each side of it there were dense portions where snakes might have found an ideal home. After a long walk the little party was in the heart of the woods and blackberry bushes, dark with clusters, waited for their hands. Berries soon rattled in the tin pails, though at first many a handful was eaten and lips were stained red by the sweet juice. They wandered from bush to bush, picking busily, with many exclamations--"Oh, look what a big bunch!" "My pail's almost full!" Little Katie and Charlie soon grew tired of the picking and wandered around the path in search of treasures. They found them--three pretty blue feathers, dropped, no doubt, by some screaming blue jay, a handful of green acorns in their little cups, a few pebbles that appealed to them, one lone, belated anemone, blooming months after its season.

The pails were almost filled and the party was moving up the woods to another patch of berries when little Mary turned to Amanda and said, "Ach, Amanda, tell us that story about the Bear Charm Song."

"Yes, do!" seconded Charlie. "The one you told us once in school last winter."

Amanda smiled, and as the little party walked along close together through the woods, she began:

"Once the Indians lived where we are living now---"

"Oh, did they?" interrupted Charlie. "Real Indians, with bows and arrows and all?"

"Yes, real Indians, bows and arrows and all! They owned all the land before the white man came and drove them off. But now the Indians are far away from here and they are different from the ones we read about in the history books. The Indians now are more like the poor birds people put in cages---" Her eyes gleamed and her face grew eloquent with expression as she thought of the gross injustice meted out to some of the red men in this land of the free.

"Go on, Manda, go on with the story," cried the children. Only Martin had seen the look in her eyes, that mother-look of compassion.

"Very well, I'll go on."

"And, Charlie," said Mary, "you keep quiet now and don't break in when Manda talks."

"Well," the story-teller resumed, "the Indians who lived out in the woods, far from towns or cities, had to find all their own food. They caught fish, shot animals and birds, planted corn and gathered berries. Some of them they ate at once, but many of them they dried and stored away for winter use. While the older Indians did harder work, the little Indian children ran off to the woods and gathered the berries. But one thing they had to look out for--bears! Great big bears lived in the woods and they are very fond of sweet things. The bears would amble along, peel great handfuls of ripe berries from the bushes with their big clawed paws and eat them. So all good Indian mothers taught their children a Bear Charm Song to sing as they gathered berries. Whenever the bears heard the Bear Charm Song they went to some other part of the woods and left the children to pick their berries unharmed. But once there was a little Indian boy who wouldn't mind his mother. He went to the woods one day to gather berries, but he wouldn't sing the Bear Charm Song, not he! So he picked berries and picked berries, and all of a sudden a great big bear stood by him. Then the little Indian boy, who wouldn't mind his mother, began to sing the Bear Charm Song. But it was too late. The great big bear put his big paws around the little boy and squeezed him, squeezed him, tighter and tighter and tighter--till the little boy who wouldn't mind his mother was changed into a tiny black bat. Then he flew back to his mother, but she didn't know him, and so she chased him and said, 'Go away! Little black bird of the night, go away!' And that is where the bats first came from."

"Ain't that a good story?" said Charlie as Amanda ended. "Tell us another."

"Not now. Perhaps after a while," she promised. "Here's another patch of berries. Shall we pick here?"

"Yes, fill the pails," said Martin, "then we'll be ready for the next number on the program. It seems Amanda's the committee of one to entertain us."

But the next number on the program was furnished by an unexpected participant. The berrying party was busy picking when a crash was heard as if some heavy body were running wild through the leaves and sticks of the woods near by.

"Oh," cried Charlie, "I bet that's a bear! Manda, sing a Bear Charm Song!"

"Oh," echoed Katie in alarm, and ran to the side of Amanda, while Martin lifted his head and stood, alert, looking into the woods in the direction of the noise. The crashing drew nearer, and then the figure of a man came running wildly through the bushes, waving his hands frantically in the air, then pressing them to his face.

"It's Lyman Mertzheimer!" Amanda exclaimed.

"With hornets after him," added Martin.

The children, reassured, ran to the newcomer.

It was Lyman Mertzheimer, his face distorted and swollen, his necktie streaming from one shoulder, where he had torn it in a mad effort to beat off the angry hornets whose nest he had disturbed out of sheer joy in the destruction and an audacious idea that no insect could scare him away or worst him in a fight. He had underestimated the fiery temper of the hornets and their concentrated and persistent methods of defending their home. After he had run wildly through the woods for fifteen minutes and struck out repeatedly the insects left him, just as he reached the berrying party. But the hornets had wreaked their anger upon him; face, hands and neck bore evidence of the battle they had waged.

"First time hornets got me!" he said crossly as he neared the little party. "Oh, you needn't laugh!" he cried in angry tones as Charlie snickered.

"But you look funny--all blotchy."

The stung man allowed his anger to burst out in oaths. "Guess you think it's funny, too," he said to Amanda.

"No. I'm sure it hurts," she said, though she knew he deserved no pity from her.

"We all know that it hurts," said Martin. But there was scant sympathy in his voice.

"Smear mud on," suggested Mary. "Once I got stung by a bumblebee when he went in a hollyhock and I held the flower shut so he couldn't get out, and he stung me through the flower. Mom put mud on and it helped."

"Mud!" stormed Lyman, stepping about in the bush and twisting his head in pain. "There isn't any mud in Lancaster County now. The whole place is dry as punk!"

"If you had some of the mud you slung at me recently it would come in handy now," Martin could not refrain from saying.

Another oath greeted his words. Then the stung young man started off down the road to find relief from his smarts, ignoring the fling.

"Well," said Amanda, "well, of all things! For him to tackle a hornets' nest! Just for the fun of it!"

"But he got his come-uppance for once! Got it from the hornets," said Martin. "Serves him right."

"But that hurts," said Mary sympathetically. "Hornets hurt awful bad!"

"Yes," said Martin as they turned homeward. "But he's getting paid for all the mean tricks he's played on other people."

"Mebbe God made the hornets sting him if he's a bad man," said Charlie.

"We all get what we give out," agreed Martin. "Lyman Mertzheimer will feel those hornet stings for a few days. While I've always been taught not to rejoice at the misfortunes of others I'm not sorry I saw him. I'll call our account square now. You pitied him, didn't you?" he asked Amanda suddenly. "I saw it in your eyes. So did Mary and Katie."

"Of course I pitied him," she confessed. "I'd feel sorry for anything or anybody who suffers. I know it serves him right, that he's earned worse than that, and yet I would have relieved him if I could have done so. Nature meant that we should be decent, I suppose."

The man was thoughtful for a moment. "Yes, I suppose so. It is a woman's nature."

"Would you have us different?"

"No--no--we wouldn't have you different. Many of the best men would be mere brutes if women's pity and tenderness and forgiveness were taken out of their lives--we wouldn't have you different."

CHAPTER XXII

ON THE MOUNTAIN TOP

The following Sunday at noon Martin passed the Reist farmhouse as he drove his mother and several of the children to Mennonite church at Landisville. After the service he passed that way again and noticed several cars stopping at Reists'. Evidently they were entertaining a number of visitors for Sunday dinner after the service, as is the custom in rural Lancaster County. The big porch was filled with people who rocked or leaned idly against the pillars, while in the big kitchen Millie, Amanda and Mrs. Reist worked near the hot stove and prepared an appetizing dinner for them.

Amanda did not shirk her portion of the necessary work, but rebellion was in her heart as she noted her mother's flushed, tired face.

"Mother, if you'd only feel that Millie and I could get the dinner without you! It's a shame to have you in this kitchen on a day like this!"

"Ach, I'm not so hot. I'm not better than you or Millie," the mother insisted, and stuck to her post, while Amanda murmured, "This Sunday visiting--how I hate it! We've outgrown the need of it now, especially with automobiles."

But at length the meal was placed upon the table, the guests gathered from porches and lawn and an hour later the dishes were washed and everything at peace once more in the kitchen. Then Amanda walked out to the garden at the rear of the house.

"Ooh," she sighed in relief, "I'm glad that's over! Visiting on such a day should be made a misdemeanor!" She pulled idly on a zinnia that lifted its globular red head in the hot August sun.

"Hey, Sis," came Phil's voice to her, "he wants you on the 'phone!"

"Who's he?" she asked as the boy ran out to her in the garden.

They turned to the house, talking as they went.

"Well, Sis, you know who *he* is! He's coming round here all the time lately."

A gentle shove from the girl rewarded the boy for his teasing, but he was not easily daunted. "Don't you remember," he said, "how that old Mrs. Haldeman who kept tine candy store near the market house in Lancaster used to call her husband *he*? She never called him Mister or Mr. Haldeman, just *he*, and you could feel she would have written it in italics if she could."

"Well, that was all right, there was only one *he* in the world so far as she was concerned. But do you remember, Phil, the time Mother took us in her store to buy candy and we talked to her canary and the old woman said, 'Ach, yes, I think still how good birds got it! I often wish I was a canary, but then he would have to be one too!' We disgraced Mother by giggling fit to kill ourselves. But the old woman just smiled at us and gave us each a pink and white striped peppermint stick. Now run along, Phil, don't be eavesdropping," she said as they reached the hall and she sat down to answer the telephone.

"That you, Amanda?" came over the wire.

"Yes."

"Got a houseful of company? It seemed like that when we drove past. Overflow meeting on the porch!"

"Oh, yes, as usual."

"What I wanted to know is--are there any young people among the visitors, that makes it a matter of courtesy for you to stay at home all afternoon?"

"No, they are all older people to-day, and a few little children."

"Good! Then how would you like to have a little picnic, just we two? I want to get away from Victrola music and children's questions and four walls, and I thought you might have a similar longing."

"Mental telepathy, Martin! That's just what I was thinking as I was out in the garden."

"Then I'll call for you and we'll go up past the sandpit to that hilltop where the breeze blows even on a day like this."

When Martin came for her she was ready, a lunch tucked under one arm, two old pillows in the other. She had given the red hair a few pats, added several hairpins, slipped off her white dress and buttoned up a pale green chambray one with cool white collar and cuffs. She stood ready, attractive, as Martin entered the lawn.

"Say!" he whistled. "You did that in short order! I thought it took girls hours to dress."

"Then you're like Solomon; you can't understand the ways of women!" She laughed as she handed him the lunch-box.

Her calm efficiency puzzled him. Lately he was discovering so many undreamed of qualities in this lively friend of his childhood. He was beginning to feel some of the wonder those people must have felt whose children played with pebbles that were one day discovered to be priceless uncut diamonds. Until that day she had found him prostrate in her moccasin woods he had thought of her as just Amanda Reist, a nice, jolly girl with a quick temper if you tried her too hard and a quick tongue to express it, but a good comrade and a pleasant companion if you treated her fairly.

Then his attitude had undergone a change. After that day of his great unhappiness he thought of her as a woman, staunch, courageous, yet gentle and feminine, one who had faith in her old friend, who could comfort a man when he was downcast and help him raise his head again. A wonderful woman she was! One who loved pretty clothes and things modern and yet appreciated the charm of the old-fashioned, and seemed to dovetail perfectly into the plain grooves of her people and his with their quaint old dress and houses and manners. A woman, too, who had an intense love for the great outdoors. Not the shallow, pretentious love that would call forth gushing rhapsodies about moonlight or sunsets or the spectacular alone in nature, but a sincere, deep-rooted love that shone in her eyes as she stooped to see more plainly the tracery of veins in a fallen leaf and moved her to gentle speech to the birds, butterflies and woodland creatures as though they could understand and answer.

As they walked down the country road he looked at her. He had a way of noticing women's clothes and had become an observant judge of their becomingness. In her growing-up days Amanda had been frequently angered by his frank, unsolicited remarks about the colors she wore--this blue was off color for her red hair, or that golden brown was just the thing. Later she grew accustomed to his remarks and rather expected them. They still disconcerted her at times, but she had long ago ceased to grow angry about them.

"That green's the color for you to-day," he said, as they went along. "Do you know, I've often thought I'd like to see you in a black gown and a string of real jade beads around your neck."

"Jade! Was there ever a red head who didn't wish she had a string of jade beads?"

"You'd be great!"

"So would the price," she told him, laughing. "A string of real jade would cost as much as a complete outfit of clothes I wear."

"Then you should have black hair and cheap coral ones would do."

"Why, Martin," she said in surprise, "you *are* studying color combinations, aren't you?"

"Oh, not exactly; I'm not interested in all colors. But say, that reminds me--I saw a girl in Lancaster last winter who had hair like yours and about the same coloring. She wore a brown suit and brown hat and furs--it was great."

"I'd like to have that." Daughter of Eve! She liked it because he did! "But don't speak about furs on a day like this! It's hot--too hot, Martin, for a houseful of company, don't you think so?"

"It is hot to stand and cook for extra people."

"Well, perhaps it's wicked, but I hate this Sunday visiting the people of Lancaster County indulge in! I never did like it!"

"I'm not keen about it myself. Sunday seems to me to be a day to go to church and rest and enjoy your family, sometimes to go off to the woods like this. But a houseful of buzzing visitors swarming through it-- whew! it does spoil the Sabbath."

"I never did like to visit," confessed the girl. "Not unless I went to people I really cared for. When we were little and Mother would take Phil and me to visit relatives or friends I merely liked I'd be there a little while and then I'd tug at Mother's skirt and beg, 'Mom, we want to go home.' I suppose I spoiled many a visit for her. I was self-willed even then."

"You are a stubborn person," he said, with so different a meaning that Amanda flushed.

"I know I am. And I have a nasty temper, too."

"Don't you know," he consoled her, "that a temper controlled makes a strong personality? George Washington had one, the history books say, but he made it serve him."

"And that's no easy achievement." The girl spoke from her own experience. "It's like pulling molars to press your lips together and be quiet when you want to rear and tear and stamp your feet."

"Well, come down to hard facts, and how many of us will have to admit that we have feelings like that at times? There is still a good share of the primitive man left in our natures. We're not saints. Why, even the churches that believe in saints don't canonize mortals until they have been a hundred years dead--they want to be sure they are dead and their mortal weaknesses forgotten."

Amanda laughed. A moment later they turned from the country road and followed a narrower path that was bordered on one side by green fields and on the other by a strip of woods, an irregular arm reaching out from Amanda's moccasin haunt. The road led up-hill at a sharp angle, so that when the traveler reached the top, panting and tired, there stretched before him in delightful panorama a view of Lancaster County that more than compensated for the discomfort and effort of the climb.

Amanda and Martin stood facing that sight. Behind them lay the cool, tree-clad hill, before them the blue August sky looked down on Lancaster County farms, whose houses and red barns seemed dropped like kindergarten toys into the midst of undulating green fields. One could sit or stand under the sheltering shade of the trees along the edge of the woods and yet look up to the sky or out upon the Garden Spot and farther off, to the blue, hazy mountain ridge that touched the sky-line and cut off the view of what lay beyond.

Martin threw the pillows on the ground and they sat down in the cool shade.

"Can anything beat this?" he asked lazily as he ruffled the dry leaves about him with his hands. "You know, Amanda, I could never understand why, with my love for outdoors, I can't be a farmer. When I was a boy I used to consider it the natural thing for me to do as my father did. I did help him, but I never liked the work. You couldn't coax the other boys to the city; they'd rather pitch hay or plant corn. And yet I like nothing better than to be out in the open. During the summer I'm out in the garden after I come home from the city, and that much of working the soil I like, but for a steady job--not for me!"

"It's best to do work one likes," said the girl. "Not every person who likes outdoors was meant to be a farmer. Be glad you like to be out in the open. But I can't conceive of any person not liking it. I could sit and look at the sky for one whole day. It's so encouraging. Sometimes when I walk home from school after a hard day and I look down on the road and think over the problems of handling certain trying children so as to get the best out of them and the latent best in them developed, I look up all of a sudden and the sky is so wonderful that, somehow, my troubles seem trivial. It's just as though the sky were saying, 'Child, you've been looking down so long and worrying about little things that you've forgotten that the sky is blue and the clouds are still sailing over you.' And, Martin, don't you like the stars? I never get tired of looking at them. I never care to gaze at the full moon unless there are clouds sailing over her. She's too big and brazen, too compelling. But the twinkle of the stars and the sudden flashing out of dim ones you didn't see at first always makes me feel like singing. Ever feel that way?"

"Yes, but I couldn't put it all into words like that."

"Ah," he thought, "she has the mind of a poet, the heart of a child, the soul of a woman."

"I read somewhere," she went on, as though certain of his understanding and sharing her mood, "that the Pagans said man was made to stand upright so that he might raise his face to heaven and his eyes to the stars. Somehow, it seems those old Pagans had a finer conception of many vital truths than some of us have in this age."

"That's true. We have them beaten in many ways, but when we come across a thing like that we stop to think and wonder where they got it. I always did like mythology. Pandora and her box, Clytie and her emblem of constancy, and Ulysses--what schoolboy escaped the thrills of Ulysses? I bet you pitied Orpheus!"

"I did! But aren't we serious for a picnic? Next thing we know one of us will be saying thirdly, fourthly, or amen!"

"I don't know--it suits me. You're so sensible, Amanda, it's a pleasure to talk with you. Most girls are so frothy."

"No disparaging remarks about our sex," she said lightly, "or I'll retaliate."

"Go on," he challenged, "I dare you to! What's the worst fault in mere man?"

She raised her hand in protest. "I wash my hands of that! But I will say that if most girls are frothy, as you say, it's because most men seem to like them that way. Confess now, how many shallow, frothy girls grow into old maids? It's generally the butterfly that occasions the merry chase, straw hats out to catch it. You seldom see a straw hat after a bee."

"Oh, Amanda, that's not fair, not like you!" But he thought ruefully of Isabel and her butterfly attractions. "I admit we follow the butterflies but sometimes we wake up and see our folly. True, men don't chase honeybees, but they have a wholesome respect for them and build houses for them. After all, the real men generally appreciate the real women. Sometimes the appreciation comes too late for happiness, but it seldom fails to come. No matter how appearances belie it, it's a fact, nevertheless, that in this crazy world of to-day the sincere, real girl is still appreciated. The frilly Gladys, Gwendolyns and What-nots still have to yield first place to the old-fashioned Rebeccas, Marys and Amandas."

Her heart thumped at the words. She became flustered and said the first thing that came into her head to say, "I like that, calling me old-fashioned! But we won't quarrel about it. Let's eat our lunch; that will keep us from too much talking for a while."

Martin handed her the box. He was silent as she opened it. She noted his preoccupation, his gray eyes looking off to the distant fields.

"Come back to earth!" she ordered. "What are you dreaming about?"

"I was just thinking that you *are* old-fashioned. I'm glad you are."

"Well, I'm not!" she retorted. "Come on, eat. I just threw in some rolls and cold chicken and pickles and a few peaches."

The man turned and gave his attention to the lunch and ate with evident enjoyment, but several times Amanda felt his keen eyes scrutinizing her face. "What ails him?" she thought.

"This is great, this is just the thing!" he told her several times during the time of lunch. "Let's do this often, come up here where the air is pure."

"All right," she agreed readily. "It will do you good to get up in the hills. I don't see how you stand being housed in a city in the summer! It must be like those awful days in the early spring or in the fall when I'm in the schoolroom and rebel because I want to be outdoors. I rebel every minute when the weather is nice, do it subconsciously while I'm teaching the states and capitals or hearing tables or giving out spelling words. Something just keeps saying inside of me, 'I want to be out, want to be out, be out, be out!' It's a wonder I don't say it out loud sometimes."

"If you did you'd hear a mighty echo, I bet! Every kid in the room would say it after you."

"Yes, I'm sure of that. I feel like a slave driver when I make them study on days that were made for the open. But it's the only way, I suppose. We have to learn to knuckle very early."

"Yes, but it's a great old world, just the same, don't you think so?"

"It's the only one I ever tried, so I'm satisfied to stay on it a while longer," she told him.

They laughed at that as only Youth can laugh at remarks that are not clever, only interesting to each other because of the personality of the speaker.

So the afternoon passed and the two descended again to the dusty country road, each feeling refreshed and stimulated by the hours spent together.

CHAPTER XXIII

TESTS

That September Amanda began her third year of teaching at Crow Hill.

"I declare," Millie said, "how quick the time goes! Here's your third year o' teachin' started a'ready. A body gets old fast."

"Yes, I'll soon be an old maid school teacher."

"Now, mebbe not!" The hired girl had lost none of her frankness. "I notice that Mart Landis sneaks round here a good bit this while past."

"Ach, Millie, he's not here often."

"No, o' course not! He just stops in in the afternoon about every other day with a book or something of excuse like that, and about every other day in the morning he's likely to happen to drop in to get the book back, and then in between that he comes and you go out for a walk after flowers or birds or something, and then between times there he comes with something his mom told him to ask or bring or something like that --no, o' course not, he don't come often! Not at all! I guess he's just neighborly, ain't, Amanda?" Millie chuckled at her own wit and Amanda could not long keep a frown upon her face.

"Of course, Millie," she said with an assumed air of indifference, "the Landis people have always been neighborly. Pennsylvania Dutch are great for that."

It was not from Millie alone that Amanda had to take teasing. Philip, always ready for amusement, was at times almost insufferable in the opinion of his sister.

"What's the matter with Mart Landis's home?" the boy asked innocently one day at the supper table.

"Why?" asked Uncle Amos. "I'll bite."

"Well, he seems to be out of it a great deal; he spends half of his time in our house. I think, Uncle Amos, as head of the house here, you should ask him what his intentions are."

"Phil!" Amanda's protest was vehement. "You make me as tired as some other people round here do. As soon as a man walks down the road with a girl the whole matter is settled--they'll surely marry soon! It would be nice if people would attend to their own affairs."

"Makes me tired too," said Philip fervently. "Last week I met that Sarah from up the road and naturally walked to the car with her. You all know what a fright she is--cross-eyed, pigeon-toed, and as brilliant mentally as a dark night in the forest. When I got into the car I heard some one say, 'Did you see Philip Reist with that girl? I wonder if he keeps company with her.' Imagine!"

"Serves you right," Amanda told him with impish delight. "I hope every cross-eyed, pigeon-toed girl in the county meets you and walks with you!"

"Feel better now, Sis?" His grin brought laughter to the crowd and Amanda's peeved feeling was soon gone.

It was true, Martin Landis spent many hours at the Reist farmhouse. He seemed filled with an insatiable desire for the companionship of Amanda. Scarcely a day passed without some glimpse of him at the Reist home.

Just what that companionship meant to the young man he did not stop to analyze at first. He knew he was happy with Amanda, enjoyed her conversation, felt a bond between them in their love for the vast outdoors, but he never went beyond that. Until one day in early November when he was walking down the lonely road after a pleasant evening with Amanda. He paused once to look up at the stars, remembering what the girl had said concerning them, how they comforted and inspired her. A sudden rush of feeling came to him as he leaned on the rail fence and looked up.... "Look here," he told himself, "it's time you take account of yourself. What's all this friendship with your old companion leading to? Do you love Amanda?" The "stars in their courses" seemed to twinkle her name, every leafless tree along the road she loved seemed to murmur it to him--Amanda! It was suddenly the sweetest name in the whole world to him!

"Oh, I know it now!" he said softly to himself under the quiet sky. "I love her! What a woman she is! What a heart she has, what a heart! I want her for my wife; she's the only one I want to have with me 'Till death us do part'--that's a fair test. Why, I've been wondering why I enjoyed each minute with her and just longed to get to see her as often as possible--fool, not to recognize love when it came to me! But I know it now! I'm as sure of it as I am sure those stars, her stars, are shining up there in the sky."

As he stood a moment silently looking into the starry heavens some portion of an old story came to him. "My love is as fair as the stars and well-nigh as remote and inaccessible." Could he win the love of a girl like Amanda Reist? She gave him her friendship freely, would she give her love also? A woman like Amanda could never be satisfied with half-gods, she would love as she did everything else--intensely, entirely! He remembered reading that propinquity often led people into mistakes, that constant companionship was liable to awaken a feeling that might masquerade as love. Well, he'd be fair to her, he'd let separation prove his love.

"That's just what I'll do," he decided. "Next week I'm to go on my vacation and I'll be gone two weeks. I'll not write to her and of course I won't see her. Perhaps 'Absence will make the heart grow fonder' with her. I hope so! It will be a long two weeks for me, but when I come back--" He flung out his arms to the night as though they could bring to him at once the form of the one he loved.

So it happened that after a very commonplace goodbye given to Amanda in the presence of the entire Reist household Martin Landis left Lancaster County a few weeks before Thanksgiving and journeyed to South Carolina to spend a quiet vacation at a mountain resort.

To Amanda Reist, pegging away in the schoolroom during the gray November days, his absence caused depression. He had said nothing about letters but she naturally expected them, friendly little notes to tell her what he was doing and how he was enjoying the glories of the famous mountains of the south. But no letters came from Martin.

"Oh," she bit her lip after a week had gone and he was still silent. "I won't care! He writes home; the children tell me he says the scenery is so wonderful where he is--why can't he send me just one little note? But I'm not going to care. I've been a fool long enough. I should know by this time that it's a case of 'Out of sight, out of mind.' I'm about done with castles in Spain! All my sentimental dreams about my knight, all my rosy visions are, after all, of that substance of which all dreams are made. I suppose if I had been practical and sensible like other girls I could have made myself like Lyman Mertzheimer or some other ordinary country boy and settled down into a contented woman on a farm. Why couldn't I long ago have put away my girlish illusions about knights and castles in Spain? I wonder if, after all, gold eagles are better and more to be desired than the golden roofs of our dream castles? If an automobile like Lyman Mertzheimer drives is not to be preferred to Sir Galahad's pure white steed! I've clung to my romanticism and what has it brought me? It might have been wiser to let go my dreams, sweep the illusions from my eyes and settle down to a sordid, everyday existence as the wife of some man, like Lyman Mertzheimer, who has no eye for the beauties of nature but who has two eyes for me."

Poor Amanda, destruction of her dream castles was perilously imminent! The golden turrets were tottering and the substance of which her dreams were made was becoming less ethereal. If Lyman Mertzheimer came to her then and renewed his suit would she give him a more encouraging answer than those she had given in former times? Amanda's hour of weakness and despair was upon her. It was a propitious moment for the awakening of the forces of her lower nature which lay quiescent in her, as it dwells in us all--very few escape the Jekyll-Hyde combination.

When Martin Landis returned to Lancaster County he had a vagrant idea of what the South Carolina mountains are like. He would have told you that the trees there all murmur the name of Amanda, that the birds sing her name, the waterfalls cry it aloud! During his two weeks of absence from her his conviction was affirmed--he knew without a shadow of doubt that he loved her madly. All of Mrs. Browning's tests he had applied--

> "Unless you can muse in a crowd all day,
> On the absent face that fixed you;
> Unless you can love, as the angels may,
> With the breadth of heaven betwixt you;
> Unless you can dream that his faith is fast,

Through behoving and unbehoving;
Unless you can die when the dream is past--
Oh, never call it loving!"

Amanda was enthroned in his heart, he knew it at last! How blind he had been! He knew now what his mother had meant one day when she told him, "Some of you men are blinder'n bats! Bats do see at night!"

As he rode from Lancaster on the little crowded trolley his thoughts were all of Amanda--would she give him the answer he desired? Could he waken in her heart something stronger than the old feeling of friendship, which was not now enough?

He stepped from the car--now he would be with her soon. He meant to stop in at the Reist farmhouse and ask her the great question. He could wait no longer.

"Hello, Landis," a voice greeted him as he alighted from the car. He turned and faced Lyman Mertzheimer, a smiling, visibly happy Lyman.

"Oh, hello," Martin said, not cordially, for he had no love for the trouble-maker. "I see you're in Lancaster County for your vacation again."

"Yes, home from college for Thanksgiving. I hear you've been away for several weeks."

The college boy fell into step beside Martin, who would have turned and gone in another direction if he had not been so eager to see Amanda.

"Yes, Landis," continued the unwelcome companion. "I'm home for Thanksgiving. It'll be a great day for me this year. By the way, I saw Amanda Reist a number of times since I'm here. Perhaps you'll be interested to know that Amanda's promised to marry me--congratulate me!"

"To marry you! Amanda?" Martin's face blanched and his heart seemed turned to lead.

"Why not?" The other laughed softly. "I'm not as black as I'm painted, you know."

"I--I hope not," Martin managed to say, his body suddenly seeming to be rooted in the ground. His feet dragged as he walked along. Amanda to marry Lvman Mertzheimer! What a crazv world it was all of a sudden. What a slow, poky idiot he had been not to try for the prize before it was snatched from him!

Lyman, rejoicing over the misery so plainly written in the face of Martin, walked boldly down the middle of the road, while Martin's feet lagged so he could not keep pace with the man who had imparted the bewildering news. Martin kept along the side of the road, scuffing along in the grass, thinking bitter thoughts about the arrogant youth who walked in the middle of the road. The honk, honk of a speeding automobile fell heedlessly upon the ears of both, till Martin looked back in sudden alarm. His startled eyes saw a car tearing down the road like a huge demon on wheels, its driver evidently trusting to the common sense of the man in the way to get out of the path of danger in time. But Lyman walked on in serene preoccupation, gloating over the unlucky, unhappy man who was following. With a cry of warning Martin rushed to the side of the other man and pushed him from the path of the car, but when the big machine came to a standstill Martin Landis lay in the dusty road, his eyes closed, a thin red stream of blood trickling down his face.

The driver was concerned. "He's knocked out," he said as he bent over the still form. "I'm a doctor and I'll take him home and fix him up. He's a plucky chap, all right! He kept you from cashing in, probably. Say, young fellow, are you deaf? I honked loud enough to be heard a mile. Only for him you'd be in the dust there and you'd have caught it full. The car just grazed him. It's merely a scalp wound," he said in relief as he examined the prostrate figure. "Know where he lives?"

"Yes, just a little distance beyond the schoolhouse down this road."

"Good. I'll take him home. I can't say how sorry I am it happened. Give me a lift, will you? You sit in the back seat and hold him while I drive."

Lyman did not relish the task assigned to him but the doctor's tones admitted of no refusal. Martin Landis was taken to his home and in his semiconscious condition he did not know that his head with its handkerchief binding leaned against the rascally breast of Lyman Mertzheimer.

CHAPTER XXIV

"YOU SAVED THE WRONG ONE"

The news of the accident soon reached the Reist farmhouse. Amanda telephoned her sympathy to Mrs. Landis and asked if there was anything she could do.

"Oh, Amanda," came the reply, "I do wish you'd come over! You're such a comforting person to have around. Did you hear that it was Lyman Mertzheimer helped to bring him home? Lyman said he and Martin were walkin' along the road and were so busy talkin' that neither heard the car and it knocked Martin down. It beats me what them two could have to talk about so much in earnest that they wouldn't hear the automobile. But perhaps Lyman wanted to make up with Martin for all the mean tricks he done to him a'ready. Anyhow, we're glad it ain't worse. He's got a cut on the head and is pretty much bruised. He'll be stiff for a while but there ain't no bones broke."

"I'm so glad it isn't worse."

"Yes, ain't, abody still has something to be thankful for? Then you'll come on over, Amanda?"

"Yes, I'll be over."

As the girl walked down the road she felt a strange mingling of emotions. She couldn't refuse the plea of Mrs. Landis, but one thing was certain--she wouldn't see Martin! He'd be up-stairs and she could stay down. Perhaps she could help with the work in the kitchen-- anything but see Martin!

Mrs. Landis was excited as she drew her visitor into the warm kitchen, but the excitement was mingled with wrath. "What d'you think, Amanda," she exclaimed, "our Mart---"

"Yes, our Mart---" piped out one of the smaller children, but an older one chided him, "Now you hush, and let Mom tell about it."

"That Lyman Mertzheimer," said Mrs. Landis indignantly, "abody can't trust at all! He let me believe that he and Martin was walkin' along friendly like and that's how Mart got hurt. But here after Lyman left and the doctor had Mart all fixed up and was goin' he told me that Martin was in the side of the road and wouldn't got hurt at all if he hadn't run to the middle to pull Lyman back. He saved that mean fellow's life and gets no thanks for it from him! After all Lyman's dirty tricks this takes the cake!"

Amanda's eyes sparkled. "He--I think Martin's wonderful!" she said, her lips trembling.

"Yes," the mother agreed as she wiped her eyes with one corner of her gingham apron. "I'd rather my boy laid up in bed hurt like he is than have him like Lyman."

"Oh, Mom," little Emma came running into the room, "I looked in at Mart and he's awake. Mebbe he wants somebody to talk to him like I did when I had the measles. Dare I go set with him a little if I keep quiet?"

"Why," said Mrs. Landis, "that would be a nice job for Amanda. You go up," she addressed the girl, "and stay a little with him. He'll appreciate your comin' to see him."

Amanda's heart galloped. Her whole being was a mass of contradictions. One second she longed to fly up the steps to where the plumed knight of her girlish dreams lay, the next she wanted to flee down the country road away from him.

She stood a moment, undecided, but Mrs. Landis had taken her compliance for granted and was already busy with some of her work in the kitchen. At length Amanda turned to the stairs, followed by several eager, excited children.

"Here," called the mother, "Charlie, Emma, you just leave Amanda go up alone. It ain't good for Mart to have so much company at once. I'll leave you go up to-night." They turned reluctantly and the girl started up the stairs alone, some power seeming to urge her on against her will.

Martin Landis returned to consciousness through a shroud of enveloping shadows. What had happened? Why was a strange man winding bandages round his head? He raised an arm--it felt heavy. Then his mother's voice fell soothingly upon his ears, "You're all right, Martin."

"Yes, you're all right," repeated the doctor, "but that other fellow should have the bumps you got."

"That other fellow"--Martin thought hazily, then he remembered. The whole incident came back to him, etched upon his memory. How he had started from the car, eager to get to Amanda, then Lyman had come with his news of her engagement and the hope in his heart became stark. Where was her blue bunting with its eternal song? Ah, he had killed it with his indifference and caution and foolish blindness! He knew he stumbled along the road, grief and misery playing upon his heart strings. Then came the frantic honk of the car and Lyman in its path. Good enough for him, was the first thought of the Adam in Martin. The next second he had obeyed some powerful impulse and rushed to the help of the heedless Lyman. Then blackness and oblivion had come upon him. Blessed oblivion, he thought, as the details of the occurrence returned to him. He groaned.

"Hurt you?" asked the doctor kindly.

"No. I'm all right." He smiled between his bandages. "I think I can rest comfortably now, thank you."

He was grateful they left him alone then, he wanted to think. Countless thoughts were racing through his tortured brain. How could Amanda marry Lyman Mertzheimer? Did she love him? Would he make her happy? Why had he, Martin, been so blind? What did life hold for him if Amanda went out of it? The thoughts were maddening and after a while a merciful Providence turned them away from him and he fell to dreaming tenderly of the girl, the Amanda of his boyhood, the gay, laughing comrade of his walks in the woods. Tender, understanding Amanda of his hours of unhappiness--Amanda--the vision of her danced before his eyes and lingered by his side--Amanda---

"Martin"--the voice of her broke in upon his dreaming! She stood in the doorway and he wondered if that, too, was a part of his dream.

"Martin," she said again, a little timidly. Then she came into the room, a familiar little figure in her brown suit and little brown hat pulled over her red hair.

"Oh, hello," he answered, "come in if you care to."

"I *am* in." She laughed nervously, a strange way for her to be laughing, but the man did not take heed of it. Had she come to laugh at him for being a fool? he thought.

"Sit down," he invited coolly. She sat on the chair by his bed, her coat buttoned and unbuttoned by her restless fingers as she stole glances at the bandaged head of the man.

"It's good of you to come," he began. At that she turned and began to speak rapidly.

"Martin, I must tell you! You must let me tell you! I know what you did, how you saved Lyman. I think it was wonderful of you, just wonderful!"

"Ach." He turned his flushed face toward her then. "There's noticing wonderful about that."

"I think there is," she insisted, scarcely knowing what to say. She remembered his old aversion to being lionized.

"Tell me why you did it," she asked suddenly. She had to say something!

The man lay silent for a moment, then a rush of emotion, struggling for expression, swayed him and he spoke, while his eyes were turned resolutely from her.

"I'll tell you, Amanda! I've been a fool not to recognize the fact long ago that I love you."

"Oh!" There was a quick cry from the girl. But the man went on, impelled by the pain of losing her.

"I see now that I have always loved you, even while I was infatuated by the other girl. You were still you, right there when I needed you, ready to give your comfort and help. I must have loved you in the days we ran barefooted down the hills and looked for flowers or birds. I've been asleep, blind--call it what you will! Perhaps I could have taught you to love me if I had read my own heart in time. I took so much for granted, that you'd always be right there for me--now I've found out the truth too late. Lyman told me--I hope he'll make you happy. Perhaps you better go now. I'm tired."

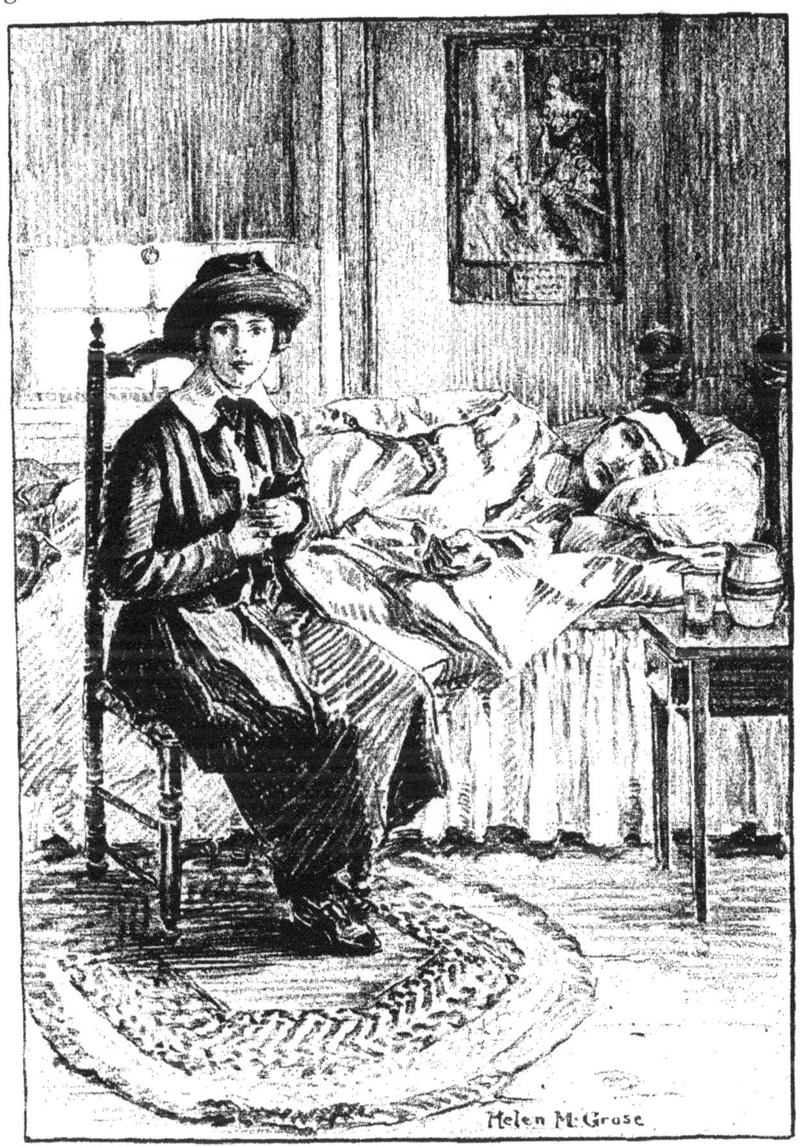

"WHAT DID LYMAN TELL YOU? I MUST KNOW"

But the request fell on deaf ears.

"Lyman told you--just what did he tell you?" she asked.

"Oh," the man groaned. "There's a limit to human endurance. I wish you'd go, dear, and leave me alone for a while."

"What did Lyman tell you?" she asked again. "I must know."

"What's the use of threshing it over? It brings neither of us happiness. Of course he told me about the engagement, that you are going to marry him."

"Oh!" Another little cry, not of joy this time, of anger, rather. There was silence then for a space, while the man turned his face to the wall and the girl tried to still the beating of her heart and control herself sufficiently to be able to speak.

"Then, Martin," she whispered, "you saved Lyman for me, because you thought I loved him?"

He lifted a protesting hand as if pleading for silence.

She went on haltingly, "Why, Martin, you saved the wrong one!"

He raised his head from the pillow then; a strangling sound came from his lips.

The girl's face burned with blushes but her eyes looked fearlessly into his as she said again, "You saved the wrong one. Why, Martin--Martin-- if you wanted to save the man I love--you--you should have saved yourself!"

He read the truth in her eyes; his arms reached out for her then and her lips moved to his as steel to a magnet.

When he spoke she marveled at the tenderness in his voice; she never dreamed, even in her brightest romantic dreams, that a man's voice could hold so much tenderness. "Amanda, I began to read my own heart that day you found me in the woods and helped and comforted me."

"Oh, Martin," she pressed her lips upon his bandaged head, her eyes were glowing with that "light that never was on land or sea"--"Oh, Martin, I've loved *you* ever since that day you saved my life by throwing me into the bean-patch and then kissed my burnt hand."

"Not your hand this time, sweetheart," he whispered, "your lips!"

"I'm glad," Amanda said after they had told each other the old, old story, "I'm so glad I kept my castles in Spain. When you went away and didn't write I almost wrecked them purposely. I thought they'd go tumbling into ashes but somehow I braced them up again. Now they're more beautiful than ever. I pity the people who own no castles in Spain, who have no dreams that won't come true exactly as they dreamed. I'll hold on to my dreams even if I know they can never come true exactly as I dream them. I wouldn't give up my castles in Spain. I'll have them till I die. But, Martin, that automobile might have killed you!"

"Nonsense. I'm just scratched a bit. I'll be out of this in no time."

"That rascal of a Lyman--you thought I could marry him?"

"I couldn't believe it, yet he said so. Some liar, isn't he?"

"Yes, but not quite so black as you thought. He is going to marry a girl named Amanda, one from his college town, and they are going to live in California."

"Good riddance!"

"Yes. The engagement was announced last week while you were away. He knew you had probably not heard of it and saw a chance to make you jealous."

"I'd like to wring his neck," said Martin, grinning. "But since it turned out like this for me I'll forgive him. I don't care how many Amandas he marries if he leaves me mine."

At that point little Charlie, tiptoeing to the open door of Martin's room, saw something which caused him to widen his eyes, clap a hand over his mouth to smother an exclamation, and turn quickly down the stairs.

"Jiminy pats, Mom!" he cried excitedly as he entered the kitchen, "our Mart's holdin' Amanda's hand and she's kissin' him on the face! I seen it and heard it! Jiminy pats!"

The small boy wondered what ailed his mother, why she was not properly shocked. Why did she gather him into her arms and whisper something that sounded exactly like, "Thank God!"

"It's all right," she told him. "You mustn't tell; that's their secret."

"Oh, is it all right? Then I won't tell. Mart says I can keep a secret good."

But Martin and Amanda decided to take the mother into the happy secret. "Look at my face," the girl said. "I can't hide my happiness. We might as well tell it."

"Mother!" Martin's voice rang through the house. At the sound a happy, white-capped woman wiped her eyes again on the corner of her gingham apron and mounted the stairs to give her blessing to her boy and the girl who had crowned him with her woman's love.

The announcement of the troth was received with gladness at the Reist farmhouse. Mrs. Reist was happy in her daughter's joy and lived again in memory that hour when the same miracle had been wrought for her.

"Say," asked Philip, "I hope you two don't think you're springing a surprise? A person blind in one eye and not seeing out of the other could see which way the wind was blowing."

"Oh, Phil!" Amanda replied, but there was only love in her voice.

"It must be nice to be so happy like you are," said Millie.

"Yes, it must be," Uncle Amos nodded his head in affirmation. He looked at the hired girl, who did not appear to notice him. "I just wish I was twenty years younger," he added.

A week later Amanda and Martin were sitting in one of the big rooms of the Reist farmhouse. Through the open door came the sound of Millie and Mrs. Reist in conversation, with an occasional deeper note in Uncle Amos's slow, contented voice.

"Do you know," said Martin, "I was never much of a hand to remember poetry, but there's one verse I read at school that keeps coming to me since I know you are going to marry me. That verse about

'A perfect woman, nobly planned
To warn, to comfort, and command.'"

"Oh, no, Martin! You put me on a pedestal, and that's a tottering bit of architecture."

"Not on a pedestal," he contradicted, "but right by my side, walking together, that's the way we want to go."

"That's the only way. It's the way my parents went and the way yours are still going." She rose and brought to him a little book. "Read Riley's 'Song of the Road,'" she told him.

He opened the book and read the musical verses:

"'O I will walk with you, my lad, whichever way you fare,
You'll have me, too, the side o' you, with heart as light as air.
No care for where the road you take's a-leadin'--anywhere,--
It can but be a joyful ja'nt the whilst *you* journey there.
The road you take's the path o' love, an' that's the bridth o' two--
An' I will walk with you, my lad--O I will walk with you.'

"Why," he exclaimed, "that's beautiful! Riley knew how to put into words the things we all feel but can't express. Let's read the rest."

Her voice blended with his and out in the adjoining room Millie heard and listened. Silently the hired girl walked to the open door. She watched the two heads bending over the little book. Her heart ached for the happy childhood and the romance she had missed. The closing words of the poem came distinctly to her;

"'Sure, I will walk with you, my lad,
As love ordains me to,--
To Heaven's door, and through, my lad,
O I will walk with you.'"

"Say," she startled the lovers by her remark, "if that ain't the prettiest piece I ever heard!"

"Think so?" said Martin kindly. "I agree with you."

"Yes, it sounds nice but the meanin' is what abody likes."

The hired girl went back to her place in the other room. But Amanda turned to the man beside her and said, "Romance in the heart of Millie! Who would guess it?"

"There's romance everywhere," Martin told her. "Millie's heart wouldn't be the fine big thing it is if she didn't keep a space there for love and romance."

CHAPTER XXV

THE HEART OF MILLIE

The Reist farmhouse, always a busy place, was soon rivaling the proverbial beehive. Mrs. Reist, to whom sentiment was ever a vital, holy thing, to be treasured and clung to throughout the years, had long ago, in Amanda's childhood, begun the preparation for the time of the girl's marriage. After the fashion of olden times the mother had begun the filling of a Hope Chest for her girl. Just as she instilled into the youthful mind the homely old-fashioned virtues of honesty, truthfulness and reverence for holy things which made Amanda, as she stood on the threshold of a new life, so richly dowered in spiritual and moral acquisitions, so had the mother laid away in the big wooden chest fine linens, useful and beautiful and symbolic of the worth of the bride whose home they were destined to enrich.

But in addition to the precious contents of the Hope Chest many things were needed for the dowry of the daughter of a prosperous Lancaster County family. So the evenings and Saturdays of that year became busy ones for Amanda. Millie helped with much of the plainer sewing and Mrs. Reist's exquisite tiny stitches enhanced many of the garments.

"Poor Aunt Rebecca," Amanda said one day, "how we miss her now!"

"Yes, ain't?" agreed Millie. "For all her scoldin' she was a good help still. If she was livin' yet she'd fuss about all the sewin' you're doin' to get married but she'd pitch right in and help do it."

Philip offered to pull basting threads, but his generosity was not appreciated. "Go on," Millie told him, "you'd be more bother than you're worth! Next you'd be pullin' out the sewin'!" He was frequently chased from the room because of his inappropriate remarks concerning the trousseau or his declaration that Amanda was spending all the family wealth by her reckless substitution of silk for muslin.

"You keep quiet," Millie often reproved him. "I guess Amanda dare have what she wants if your mom says so. If she wants them things she calls cammysoles made out of silk let her have 'em. She's gettin' married only once."

"How do you know?" he asked teasingly. "Say, Millie, I thought a camisole is a dish you make rice pudding in."

"Ach, that shows you don't know everything yet, even if you do go to Lancaster to school!" And he was driven from the room in laughing defeat.

It is usually conceded that to the prospective bride belongs the privilege of naming the day of her marriage, but it seemed to Amanda that Millie and Philip had as much to do with it as she. Each one had a favorite month. Phil's suggestion finally decided the month. "Sis, you're so keen about flowers, why don't you make it a spring wedding? About cherry blossom time would be the thing."

"So it would. We could have it in the orchard."

"On a nice rainy day in May," he said.

"Pessimist! It doesn't rain every day in May!"

There followed happy, excited times when the matter of a house was discussed. Those were wonderful hours in which the two hunted a nest that would be near enough to the city for Martin's daily commuting and yet have so much of the country about it as to boast of green grass and space for flowers. It was found at length, a little new bungalow outside the city limits in a residential section where gardens and trees beautified the entire street.

"Do you know," Mrs. Reist said to Uncle Amos one day, "there's another little house for sale in that street. If it wasn't for breakin' up the home for you and Millie I'd buy it and Philip and I could move in there. It would be nice and handy for him. I'm gettin' tired of such a big house. There I could do the work myself. There'd be room for you to come with us, but I wouldn't need Millie. I don't like to send her off to some other people. We had her so long a'ready, and she's a good, faithful worker. Ach, I guess I'll have to give up thinkin' about doin' anything like that."

"Well, well, now let me think once." Uncle Amos scratched his head. Then an inscrutable smile touched his lips. "Well, now," he said after a moment's meditation, "now I don't see why it can't be arranged some way. There's more'n one way sometimes to do things. I don't know--I don't know--but I think I can see a way we could manage that-- providin'--ach, we'll just wait once, mebbe it'll come out right."

Mrs. Reist looked at her brother. What did he mean? He stammered and smiled like a foolish schoolboy. Poor Amos, she thought, how hard he had worked all his life and how little pleasure he had seemed to get out of his days! He was growing old, too, and would soon be unable to do the work on a big farm.

But Uncle Amos seemed spry enough several days later when he and Millie entered the big market wagon to go to Lancaster with the farm products. They left the Reist farmhouse early in the morning, a cold, gray winter day.

"Say, Millie," he said soon after they began the drive, "I want to talk with you."

"Well," she answered dryly, "what's to keep you from doin' so? Here I am. Go on."

"Ach, Millie, now don't get obstreperous! Manda's mom would like to sell the farm and move to Lancaster to a little house. Then she wouldn't need me nor you."

"What? Are you sure, Amos?"

"Sure! She told me herself. That would leave us out a home. For I don't want to live in no city and set down evenings and look at houses or trolley cars. You can hire out to some other people, of course."

"Oh, yea! Amos. What in the world--I don't want to live no place else."

"Well, now, wait once, Millie. I got a plan all fixed up, something I wished long a'ready I could do, only I hated to bust up the farm for my sister. Millie--ach, don't you know what I mean? Let's me and you get married!"

Millie drew her heavy blanket shawl closer around her and pulled her black woolen cap farther over her forehead, then she turned and looked at Amos, but his face was in shadow; the feeble oil lamp of the market wagon sent scant light inside.

"Now, Amos, you say that just because you take pity for me and want to fix a home for me, ain't?"

"Ach, yammer, no!" came the vehement reply. "I liked you long a'ready, Millie, and used to think still, 'There's a girl I'd like to marry!'"

"Why, Amos," came the happy answer, "and I liked you, too, long a'ready! I used to think still to myself, 'I don't guess I'll ever get married but if I do I'd like a man like Amos.'"

Then Uncle Amos suddenly demonstrated his skill at driving one-handed and something more than the blanket-shawl was around Millie's shoulders.

"Ach, my," she said after a while, "to think of it--me, a hired girl, to get a nice, good man like you for husband!"

"And me, a fat dopple of a farmer to get a girl like you! I'll be good to you, Millie, honest! You just see once if I won't! You needn't work so hard no more. I'll buy the farm off my sister and we'll sell some of the land and stop this goin' to market. It's too hard work. We can take it easier; we're both gettin' old, ain't, Millie?" He leaned over and kissed her again.

"You know," he said blissfully, "I used to think still this here kissin' business is all soft mush, but--why--I think it's all right. Don't you?"

"Ach," she laughed as she pushed his face away gently. "They say still there ain't no fools like old ones. I guess we're some."

"All right, we don't care, long as we like it. Here," he spoke to the horse, "giddap with you! Abody'd think you was restin' 'stead of goin' to market. We'll be late for sure this morning." His mittened hands flapped the reins and the horse quickened his steps.

"Ha, ha," the man laughed, "I know what ails old Bill! The kissin' scared him. He never heard none before in this market wagon. No wonder he stands still. Here's another for good measure."

"Ach, Amos, I think that's often enough now! Anyhow for this morning once."

"Ha, ha," he laughed. "Millie, you're all right! That's what you are!"

That evening at supper Philip asked suddenly, "What ails you two, Uncle Amos, you and Millie? I see you grin every time you look at each other."

"Well, nothin' ails me except a bad case of love that's been stickin' in me this long while and now it's broke out. Millie's caught it too."

"Well, I declare!" Amanda was quick to detect his meaning. "You two darlings! I'm so glad!"

"Ach," the hired girl said, blushing rosy, "don't go make so much fuss about it. Ain't we old enough to get married?"

"I'm glad, Millie," Mrs. Reist told her. "Amos just needs a wife like you. He worried me long a'ready, goin' on all alone. Now I know he'll have some one to look out for him."

"Finis! You're done for!" Phil said. "Lay down your arms and surrender. But say, that makes it bully for Mother and me. We can move to Lancaster now. May we run out to the farm and visit you, Millie?"

"Me? Don't ask me. It's Amos's."

"Millie, you goose," the man said happily, "when you marry me everything I have will be yours, too."

"Well, did I ever! I don't believe I'll know how to think about it that way. This nice big house won't seem like part mine."

"It'll be *ours*" Uncle Amos said, smiling at the word.

And so it happened that the preparation of another wedding outfit was begun in the Reist farmhouse.

"I don't need fancy things like Amanda," declared the hired girl. "I wear the old style o' clothes yet. And for top things, why, I made up my mind I'm goin' to wear myself plain and be a Mennonite."

"Plain," said Mrs. Reist. "Won't Amos be glad! He likes you no matter what clothes you wear, but it's so much nicer when you can both go to the same church. He'll be glad if you turn a Mennonite."

"Well, I'm goin' to be one. So I won't want much for my weddin' in clothes, just some plain suits and bonnets and shawl. But I got no chest ready like Amanda has. I never thought I'd need a Hope Chest. When I was little I got knocked around, but as soon as I could earn money I saved a little all the time and now I got a pretty good bit laid in the bank. I can take that and get me some things I need."

Mrs. Reist laid her hands on the shoulders of the faithful hired girl. "Never mind, Millie, you'll have your chest! We'll go to Lancaster and buy what you want. Amos got his share of our mother's things when we divided them and he has a big chest on the garret all filled with homespun linen and quilts and things that you can use. That will all be yours."

"Mine? I can't hardly believe it. You couldn't be nicer to me if you was my own mom. And I ain't forgettin' it neither! I said to Amos we won't get married till after Amanda and when you and Phil are all fixed in your new house. Then we'll go to the preacher and get it done. We don't want no fuss, just so we get married, that's all we want. It needn't be done fancy."

CHAPTER XXVI

"ONE HEART MADE O' TWO"

Amanda married Martin that May, when the cherry blossoms transformed the orchard into a sea of white.

To the rear of the farmhouse stood a plot of ground planted with cherry trees. Low grass under the trees and little paths worn into it led like aisles up and down. There, near the centre of the plot, Amanda and Martin chose the place for the ceremony. The march to and from that spot would lead through a white-arched aisle sweet with the breath of thousands of cherry blossoms.

Amanda selected for her wedding a dress of white silk. "I do want a wedding dress I can pack away in an old box on the attic and keep for fifty years and take out and look at when it's yellow and old," she said, romance still burning in her heart.

"Uh," said practical Millie. "Why, there ain't no attic in that house you're goin' to! Them bungalows ain't the kind I like. I like a real house."

"Well, there's no garret like ours, but there is a little raftered room with a slanting ceiling and little windows and I intend to put trunks and boxes in it and take my spinning-wheel that Granny gave me and put it there."

"A spinning-wheel! What under the sun will you do with that?"

"Look at it," was the strange reply, at which Millie shook her head and went off to her work.

"Are you going to carry flowers, and have a real wedding?" Philip asked his sister the day before the wedding.

"I don't need any, with the whole outdoors a mass of bloom. If the pink moccasins were blooming I'd carry some."

"Pink--with your red hair!" The boy exercised his brotherly prerogative of frankness.

"Yes, pink! Whose wedding is this? I'd carry pink moccasins and wear my red hair if they--if the two curdled! But I'll have to find some other wild flowers."

He laughed. "Then I'll help you pick them."

"Martin and I are going for them, thanks."

"Oh, don't mention it! I wouldn't spoil that party!" He began whistling his old greeting whistle. He had forgotten it for several years but some chord of memory flashed it back to him at that moment.

At the sound of the old melody Amanda stepped closer to the boy. "Phil," she said tenderly, "you make me awful mad sometimes but I like you a lot. I hope you'll be as happy as I am some day."

"Ah," he blinked, half ashamed of any outward show of emotion. "You're all right, Sis. When I find a girl like you I'll do the wedding ring stunt, too. Now, since we've thrown bouquets at each other let's get to work. What may I do if I'm debarred from the flower hunt?"

"Go ask Millie."

"Gee, Sis, have a heart! She's been love struck, too. Regular epidemic at Reists'!" But he went off to offer his services to the hired girl.

As Amanda dressed in her white silk gown she wished she were beautiful. "Every girl ought to have beauty once in her life," she thought. "Even for just one hour on her wedding day it would be a boon. But then, love is supposed to be blind, so perhaps Martin will think I am beautiful to-day."

She was not beautiful, but her eyes shone soft and her face was expressive of the joy in her heart as she stood ready for the ceremony which was the consummation of her love for the knight of her girlhood's dreams.

It would be impossible to find a more beautiful setting for a wedding than the Reist cherry orchard that May day. There were rows of trees, with their fresh young green and their canopies of lacy bloom through which the warm May sunshine trickled like gold. As Amanda and Martin stood before the waiting clergyman and in the presence of relatives, friends and neighbors, faint breezes stirred the branches and fugitive little petals loosened from the hearts of the blossoms and fell upon the happy people gathered under the white glory of the orchard.

Several robins with nests already built on broad crotches of the cherry trees hovered about, their black eyes peering questioningly down at the unwonted visitors to the place. Once during the marriage service a Baltimore oriole flashed into a tree near by, his golden plumage made more intense against the white blossoms. With proud assurance he demonstrated his appreciation of the orchard and perched fearlessly on an outer bough while he whistled his insistent, imperious, "Here, here, come here!"

As the words, "Until death do us part"--the old, inadequate mortal expression for love that is deathless--sounded in that white-arched temple Amanda thought of Riley's "Song of the Road" and its

> "To Heaven's door, and *through*, my lad,
> O I will walk with you."

After the ceremony the strains of a Wedding March fell upon the ears of the people gathered in the orchard.

Amanda's lips parted in pleasure. "That's Phil's work!" she cried and ran behind the clump of bushes from where the music seemed to come. Philip was stooping to grind the motor of Landis's Victrola.

"Phil, you dear!"

"Aren't I though!" he said frivolously. "I had the heck of a time getting this thing here while you were dressing and keeping it hidden. I had to bribe little Charlie twice to keep him from telling you. He was so sure you'd want to know all about it."

"It's just the last touch we needed to make this perfect."

"Leave it to your devoted brother. Now go back and receive the best wishes or congratulations or whatever it is they give the bride."

Later there was supper out under the trees. A supper at which Millie, trim in her new gray Mennonite garb and white cap, was able to show her affection for the bride, but at which the bride was so riotously happy that she scarcely knew what she was eating.

Of course there was a real bride's cake with white icing. Amanda had to cut it and hand out pieces for the young people to dream upon.

After a while the bride slipped away, took off her white dress and put on a dark suit. Then she and Martin dodged rice and were whirled away in a big automobile.

The other members of the household had much to occupy their hands for the next hour, setting things to rights, as Millie said, the while their hearts and thoughts were speeding after the two who had smiled and looked as though no other mortals had ever known such love.

When the place was once more in order and the Landis family, the last guests, had gone off in the darkness, the children flinging back loud good-nights, Mrs. Reist, Philip, Millie and Uncle Amos sat alone on the porch and talked things over.

"It was some wedding, Mother," was the opinion of the boy.

"Yes." "Prettiest thing I ever seen," said the hired girl.

"Yes, so it was," Uncle Amos agreed. "But say, Millie, it's dandy and moonlight. What d'you say to a little walk down the road? Or are you too tired?"

"Ach, I'm not tired." And the two went off in the soft spring night for a stroll along the lane, Millie in her gray Mennonite dress, Uncle Amos in his plain suit of the faith. The two on the porch saw her homely face transfigured by a smile as she looked up into the countenance of the man who had brought romance into her life, then they saw Uncle Amos draw the hand of Millie through his arm and in that fashion they walked along in the moonlight, the man, contented and happy, holding the hand of the woman warmly in his grasp. To them, no less than to the youthful lovers, was given the promise of happiness and in their hearts was ringing Amanda's and Martin's pledge:

> "Sure, I will walk with you, my lad,
> As love ordains me to,--
> To Heaven's door, and *through,* my lad,
> O I will walk with you."

Lector House believes that a society develops through a two-fold approach of continuous learning and adaptation, which is derived from the study of classic literary works spread across the historic timeline of literature records. Therefore, we aim at reviving, repairing and redeveloping all those inaccessible or damaged but historically as well as culturally important literature across subjects so that the future generations may have an opportunity to study and learn from past works to embark upon a journey of creating a better future.

This book is a result of an effort made by Lector House towards making a contribution to the preservation and repair of original ancient works which might hold historical significance to the approach of continuous learning across subjects.

HAPPY READING & LEARNING!

LECTOR HOUSE LLP
E-MAIL: lectorpublishing@gmail.com

Lightning Source UK Ltd.
Milton Keynes UK
UKHW040603110220
358531UK00003B/357